Lotte R. James tra... director, but spent ... day jobs crunching ... stories of love and ad... finally writing those stories, and when she's not scribbling on tiny pieces of paper can usually be found wandering the countryside for inspiration or nestling with coffee and a book.

Also by Lotte R. James

A Liaison with Her Leading Lady

Ladies of Scandal

A Lady on the Edge of Ruin
A Governess to Redeem Him

Gentlemen of Mystery miniseries

The Housekeeper of Thornhallow Hall
The Marquess of Yew Park House
The Gentleman of Holly Street

Discover more at millsandboon.co.uk.

THE EARL AND THE MARRIAGE DEAL

Lotte R. James

MILLS & BOON

First published in Great Britain 2025
by Mills & Boon, an imprint of HarperCollins*Publishers* Ltd,
1 London Bridge Street, London, SE1 9GF

www.harpercollins.co.uk

HarperCollins*Publishers*, Macken House, 39/40 Mayor Street Upper,
Dublin 1, D01 C9W8, Ireland

The Earl and the Marriage Deal © 2025 Victorine Brown-Cattelain

ISBN: 978-0-263-34548-3

12/25

MIX
Paper | Supporting
responsible forestry
FSC™ C007454

This book contains FSC™ certified paper
and other controlled sources to ensure responsible forest management.

For more information visit www.harpercollins.co.uk/green.

Printed and Bound in the UK using 100% Renewable Electricity
at CPI Group (UK) Ltd, Croydon, CR0 4YY

To all the Hypatias. I hope you find your Gadmin Hall, and all that comes with it.

To friends old and new,
though this one is especially for Alec & David.
Thank you for Truffél, and many lovely times.

And always, to my mother, Brigitte.

Chapter One

Those doubting that we find ourselves at the dawn of a new age should turn their gazes to the newest member of our most distinguished House of Lords. Whilst this writer acknowledges other members have, over the centuries, had intriguing and unexpected origins, one cannot deny that an Essex smith is rather a novelty. The newly minted Earl of Gadmin, only recently plucked from his forge and informed of his illustrious heritage and duties thanks to a most clever special remainder, appeared undeniably overwhelmed at his introduction. However, this writer's hope prevails that in time, such a common man will prove to be as industrious and hard-working as his prior profession implies. He will certainly need employ such talents to not only restore the title hitherto tarnished by its previous holders, including the last, the new Earl's great-great-uncle and his passion for swine; however equally one would wager, to

survive his first Season, and perhaps even con-
vince one of our great Society's misses to become
a countess. This writer wishes him the very best
of luck in these endeavours, and truly hopes that
with time, he will prove to be, along with our il-
lustrious Majesty herself, a beacon of a new age
worthy of Gloriana.

Jack the Cat, Londoner's Chronicle, January 1839

London, late April 1839

'Don't suppose you'll marry me?' Thorn grumbled, gesturing at the feminine form half ensconced in the hedges' shadows across from the tiny, perfect, *infinitesimally* annoying little…*square* he supposed he should call it, considering this bloody section of the gardens was about as large as a village, complete with its own little trickling fountain.

It was a rhetorical sort of rant, or grumble, or whatever polite society might wish to call it—if in fact they indulged in such things—which was undeniably impolite, even for an uncouth country ruffian such as himself. Though truthfully, they might've been glad to witness some impropriety, some *uncouthness*, for it seemed that was the only reason he'd been invited to so many events these past three months. So he could entertain them all with his uncouth country ruffian ways, novelty that he was. Sadly, they'd found him mostly wanting in that regard, merely unrefined, not entirely in tune with all *moeurs*, precedence, *etiquette* and so on, rather than boorishly rough and laughable. The novelty of him had worn off, and along with it, the invitations. If there were others, who might want him for something other than amusement, he hadn't had occasion to meet them yet. And so tonight was one of his last chances.

He'd had hope, for some idiotic reason. However, word had spread, it appeared, that though he had a title to bestow on some lucky woman in want of one, it was not a solid wager, nor in any manner a smart invest-ment. He was not a solid wager nor a smart investment. His sole estate, in debt as much as one could be, and populated with pigs, was not worth the title of count-ess. Thorn couldn't blame them really. Any of them, be they fathers, daughters, mothers, aunts, chaperones, brothers or so on. He couldn't blame them for prefer-ring any other option—any other title, some others as equally indebted—to one which came with a set of rustic disgrace rather than reputation or long bygone glory at the very least.

A smith and some pigs. No, I cannot blame them.

Though it did sadden him. It saddened him person-ally, that his inadequacy as an earl was so potent they could smell it twenty miles off, not that he blamed them nor resented them in any manner for knowing what he did in his own heart; he was not one of them, nor could ever be, no matter what the law said. It saddened him more generally, albeit still personally, for marriage to some portion of money was the only way for him to save his inheritance. His inheritance from a man he'd never known, but whom he somehow still felt a duty to. His great-great-uncle, of whom he'd never heard until some solicitor's man came knocking on his door one grim winter's eve. He recalled wondering even, if his father had known there was nobility in their ancestry, or if he too might've felt as stunned and disbelieving at such news. Still, no matter that he had not known the man whose title he now bore, whose inheritance was now his, Thorn felt a duty towards his ancestor, his benefactor some might even say, though he couldn't quite bring himself to see the good fortune in his, well, change in fortune. A duty not to fail. A duty to do all he could to save the title, the estate, the name, from further disrepute, ridicule, and disaster. Though if there was anything in this world he felt less equipped to do, any task he felt less suited to, he could not think of it. He felt doomed to fail, unworthy of such high hopes as those of that annoying little writer who'd taken some unfathomable interest in him, and whose words had been salt in a very fresh wound.

Only those who wager against me shall not be disappointed, I fear, Mr Cat.

Sighing, he pushed that all away, and glanced again at his silent and shadowed interlocutor. He hadn't meant to scare the poor mite, ranting at her as she obviously sought refuge and escape considering she had no *beau* nor friend accompanying her, only he'd expelled as much of his frustrations out on the hedges, and roses, and topiaries, and *little tiny perfect lanterns and decorations* that had littered his path from the ballroom, and he needed…

Another pair of eyes. Of ears. Someone to bloody talk to.

Only that was the problem in and of itself—mostly— and he was so fed up, yes, he'd arrived at the point of accosting women in the dark night to ask what precisely was wrong with him, even though he bloody well knew, but she, unlike stodgy, severe old solicitors, might actually have some sort of miracle cure or wisdom to offer.

'You are the new Earl of Gadmin, are you not?' the woman said suddenly, scaring him half to death, as she tore him from his thoughts and grim mood.

Her voice too, was smooth, and deeper, richer, than he'd expected, but then he'd expected one of the debutantes from inside that Hell that resembled confectionary, and now he realised she wasn't wearing the usual light colours, but from what he could tell even in the poor—some might argue, romantic—light, some drab…

'My sister and mother advise me it is maroon,' the woman enlightened him, and wasn't she sharp indeed? 'Typically I find maroon to be a very attractive colour, and I like it very much, however, this is not maroon. It is closer to *mud*. In my opinion, at least.'

'Then why wear it?' he found himself asking, which

wasn't to any point whatsoever, yet he found his frustration melting away with every passing second.

Perhaps I might enjoy myself for five minutes this evening after all.

'It is what was chosen, and my lack of appreciation of it, in the end is not so great as to provoke greater conflict by asking for something else.'

'Very wise,' he nodded.

'How much money do you actually require?'

'Pardon?'

'To save your estate, or should I say, the only remaining thing of value in the earldom. Everyone who need know in the kingdom is aware of your circumstances, my lord,' she added after a moment—if he had to guess, spotting his dumbfounded look of shock. 'They might've been even without Jack the Cat's introductory piece. Though I found it rather complimentary.'

'Yes, it might've been worse. He did express hope I might overcome, and become a symbol of a new age. Though I fear it is likely I will disappoint. As I have the *beau monde* thus far, apparently.'

'You are not quite as savage as they'd hoped. You have conducted yourself admirably well, which has disappointed them greatly.'

'So you hear, or…?'

'If you are asking if I have been watching you, then yes. We attended quite a few of the same events. You, searching for a wife, my sister, for a husband.'

'Don't suppose your sister would marry me? It sounds as if we would make the perfect match.'

'She has her sights set on a duke, I fear. A marquess at the very least.' The woman's tone suggested that wasn't the only reason her sister and he would be a good match, and truth be told, he rather liked this one. Thus far. Without having even seen her.

'Should I recognise you? Have we been introduced? Having attended many of the same events,' he clarified. 'I hope we haven't danced, and I have since forgotten.'

'No, you should not, and we have not, on both counts of dancing and introduction. And before you apologise for having not taken notice of me across this crush or that, I should warn you that I care very, very little for such inane sentiment.'

'Noted.'

'So, as regards my original question. How much money do you require? While you are upholding a tradition of the nobility in marrying for a fortune, you are a novelty in that you are so…'

'*Un*-genteel?'

'Isn't that a diplomatic turn of phrase.'

'What would you have said instead?' he grinned, truly, undeniably, enjoying himself now. To the point of forgetting even where he was, or that he was stuffy, and uncomfortable in these ridiculous clothes that made him feel even more an imposter but five minutes ago.

'Poor, allegedly rough, and uneducated.'

'You disagree with the latter at least?'

'You know already I disagree with both of the latter. The most I can say is that your broader tones betray your rural origins slightly, but otherwise your manners and words suggest some education.'

'Fer I don't talk as dem peasants do? Fer I don't talk as a smithy should, he who was plucked from destitution though t'would have been bedder to leave the earldom crumble than bestow it up some dirty cur?'

'See now, if you'd spoken thusly, you might not be in your current predicament. Or perhaps you might be. One can never truly tell what will amuse them enough to become ensnared. However, your eyes give you away to those who'd pay any attention.'

'My eyes?'

'Yes. They sparkle.' He blinked twice, sure he'd misheard, then shook his head, wondering what he'd stepped into. 'To return to my earlier point about you being a novelty, it had nothing to do with any of that. Merely that you are departing from tradition in not advising the most incorrigible gossips just how much of a fortune you are seeking. No one seems to know, it's most bothersome. So how much, to save it?'

'At least fifteen hundred pounds, I expect.'

'Well then, I fear we would be ill-suited,' she said, almost sadly, and he understood, for he doubted very much that they would be ill-suited at all. 'I've only a thousand.'

A thousand could work.

He'd only made *very* rough calculations, based off of

what information he could get from the solicitors and strange men of business who had plucked him from blissful anonymity and thrust him into alleged fortunate infamy, working from there to find an heiress.

'*'Tis the only way, young man,*' one of those same old solicitors had advised him over half-rimmed glasses in an office that looked fit to burst with paper, parchment, rolls, books, ledgers, and everything in between. '*Marry rich, for no amount of work will save you now. There are many ready to purchase a title by such means.*'

Initially, Thorn had huffed and puffed and dismissed every bit of it as *all that was wrong with nobility in this country*; however, three days later, after looking at all he could, his own meagre savings—he had some success and was no spendthrift, however there were savings and *fortunes*—he'd crawled back to the same office, and asked if the old man had any suggestions.

An hour later he'd left with a list of venues and names to search for, and then of course, the invitations had begun to flood in, and he'd truly thought he might manage it.

Perhaps I did, for in the end, I arrived here; perhaps here is where I was always meant to be.

'I could make do with a thousand,' he said seriously, throwing all caution to the wind. 'However, you know my faults, what are yours that you and your acceptable portion remain untouched?'

'I know nothing of your faults, one out of two of

those statements is correct, and I posit society would consider my faults to be that I am rather plain, and past thirty, therefore in my dotage. Now, as to why I remain unmarried at thirty with such an acceptable portion, well, it is very simple. The amount was designed to ensure that I had no access to suitors of any *greatness*, shall we say, so that whenever those of more desperate circumstances come sniffing, my father can play the benevolent protector, and send them packing.'

'Your father wishes you to remain unmarried? Why provide a dowry at all?'

'For appearances, of course. And as regards the former, someone must care for him, and my mother, and anyone else who may be in need in the future. My sister is the pretty one, and she is to marry.'

'The one who will have a duke, or a marquess, at the very least. The reason you are here tonight.' He barely saw it, but caught a nod, and the flash of lantern and moonlight on bright red curls. *Hm.* 'What would your father say then, if I came courting?'

Thorn didn't see the grimace though he certainly felt it.

'You are an earl,' the woman said eventually. 'It has been mostly second sons ready to debase themselves for a thousand pounds until now, so I don't rightly know. I can only suspect it would be a fight.'

'If I came courting. Then again, you are thirty. Would I be correct in wagering that your father wouldn't risk public dishonour by refusing the dowry were you to marry without his consent?'

'The banns would still need be read.'

'Or a licence obtained. I have now resided in London for well over a month.'

'Though I've heard many need not even pass that test to obtain one.'

'Hm.'

'Hm.'

They fell into silence for a moment, and Thorn thought about it, *truly*.

Thought about marrying this woman he couldn't even see, but whose voice was delightful, and who was obviously clever and grounded. He had been prepared to marry for less, if only to marry for more financially.

A thousand could work.

He wondered what any of it said about him, and whether he cared. If it was worth the risk. His heritage, himself, even the damned pigs somewhere in Kent.

I feel my last chance is the one I've been waiting for.

'You'd be content marrying a stranger you've spoken to for perhaps ten minutes—and I am being generous—tying yourself to a man you don't know for a lifetime, a man who mere months ago was a lowly blacksmith, with all the education you probably received before you were twelve? A man who will now make his living as a pig farmer, and whose only wealth is a house that for all intents and purposes is derelict?'

'Your eyes sparkle, and you've incredibly rare sharpness and truth. Being shackled to you would signify freedom from my family.'

'They are that bad?'

'I suppose as with all things, it is about perspective. However, if you are asking whether my freedom is enough of a price to marry you as it stands, then yes.' Thorn nodded, accepting, and admittedly curious, but knowing now was not the right time to ask pertinent, yet unnecessary questions. 'Will you strike me if I displease you?'

'God, *never*.'

'Do you want children? I've no desire for them, though I understand the tradition would have you passing on the title to your sons yet-to-come.'

'I intend to save the estate, do my now duty, then pass it along to the next poor sod in whatever twisted line the experts can decipher. I've no desire for children, in fact I had none for a wife.'

'Only a dowry.'

Thorn nodded, feeling the weight of the moment settling on his shoulders.

'Will you control me, dictate my days?'

'As long as you do not spend frivolously, or engage in public affairs, I'll keep my opinions on your occupations to myself. Can you make the same promise?'

'I can. You won't regret tying yourself to a woman when you could perhaps still find love, as well as fortune?'

'I can still find love. This is a business transaction, after all. A contract. We shall remain…'

'Ourselves.'

'Indeed.'

'Very well then.'

'You'll marry me?'

'Yes, I think I would like that.'

'I'm Thorn, by the way.'

'Hypatia. Hypatia Quincy.'

What a name.

One that suits the woman I've yet to see—though how I know that, I cannot say.

Since the dawn of philosophers—admittedly perhaps, since the dawn of time—the question of the cost of freedom had been asked, debated, answered, asked again, and debated again. Thoroughly, and to no true conclusion.

Some part of Hypatia had been content to accept that *freedom had no price*, and that *so long as one was free of spirit and mind, they were free.* Some nights, she had comforted herself with such assertions, only now, in this moment, she knew that though such assertions were likely unfathomable truth, the tangible truth of her life, was that her freedom had a price.

A very neat and tidy price: one thousand pounds.

A fortune for some; a paltry pittance to others.

To her, the most blessed number in existence right then.

Perhaps she was being somewhat overdramatic—so

many were in worse circumstances, so many whose freedom truly had been wholly stripped away—only it didn't feel thus. It felt as if she could hear the doors to her admittedly comfortable prison unlocking, not quite cracking open yet, but unlocking. She could almost see a path beyond them, a path of hope, and possibility. Of a future, beyond that which she'd believed she'd been condemned to for so long.

One might wonder, what precisely it was that was so terrible about her life, that would make her exult so at this new future, married to a stranger she'd met approximately eleven minutes ago. That would make her so easily eschew and abandon her family and known comforts, for uncertainty, and a pig farm; that would make her call the shackles of marriage *freedom*. And Hypatia would readily tell you, that it was a lack of freedom, a lack of agency, and a lack of existence as herself, that defined the terrible nature of it. Not anything highly unusual for her sex, however something which in some cases could be remedied with the right choices, and so therefore here she was, remedying it.

Once, well, many times actually, she'd pondered running away, only good sense, common sense, and yes, fear had won out. There was a difference between knowing you had some skill and will, and going out into the world with only that and a very small sum, scrimped and saved over the years, to your name. For someone as practical as Hypatia, who knew well enough how quickly the world could swallow up whole and spit out the best intentioned and most capable, there was risk, and then there was *risk*. In her position, she could afford the former, but not the second.

She had also pondered marrying—as she was agreeing to now—a few times. However, she'd never met anyone remotely interested in her or her thousand pounds worthy of the risk—only of her father's predictable refusal—and she might've looked further afield, perhaps for love, except really, she had better things to do. With her skills and education, she might've also found employment, as a governess or a teacher or something of the sort—however that she had never tried, for it would have been too easy for her family to come fetch her, and drag her back. Were they truly so desperate... That she couldn't know for certain, but she wagered they might be, after a time, *indispensable* as she apparently was to them all. As for more permanent choices—such as entering the nunnery or becoming a missionary or so on—well, one had to believe in the Almighty, and the cause, and she did not. Therefore that was that.

So yes, in the end, she'd contented herself with her lot. Hoping that some other opportunity or chance might cross her path in time. Her existence not terrible, not happy, but known, and therefore endurable. A slow erosion, of will, of want, of hope; one which might've very well eroded her to the last grains of herself, made her too well accustomed to *endurable* and *known comforts* to ever leave them, had it not been for this man. This chance, the one she had been waiting for; perhaps the last and only she would ever have. Well timed too, for if her family had her way, her sister would be wed and birthing her own brood within the year—God and everyone willing save Hypatia—and then where would Hypatia be?

Either covered in the dirty linens of babes or tending to Mother and Father.

Or both.

Therefore, Hypatia was now choosing to take a chance on a man she'd met twelve minutes ago, rather than accept that fate, or any such. Choosing to leap into the unknown, rather than facing another untold number of decades catering to her family's every whim, every dictate, every supposed need; a known future which would only get worse as her parents aged ever more, and her sister grew her own family. Hypatia would be expected to serve and care for them all, as she'd always done, and that was not something she was prepared to do.

Some might view it as duty, or honour, to care for one's family thus. And in many cases, it was. In this case however, it was neither of those things, and to boot, love was lacking from the equation too. For in her experience, love, duty, familial obligation, could all be eroded away, like the self, by a lack of agency and freedom. Love, in her opinion, was a choice; one couldn't therefore love, if no choice to do so freely was given. Once perhaps, she had loved them all, her sister Epi most of all, before diverging paths and purposes divided them; once perhaps, she might've given them a second thought in all this, however not now. Not to-night. She had to think about herself, not everyone else for once; they would fare well enough without her. If not, well…she did not wish them ill, but neither could she set herself aside again because they expected her to. So here she was, making the first choice she'd made truly, entirely, and without reserve for herself; the first choice thus she'd perhaps ever made in her life.

If an Essex smith can become an earl, perhaps I can become…someone entirely of my own.

'Should we…shake on it?' Thorn said, startling her from her little self-indulgent moment of reverie and marked solemnity.

She thought of him thus instinctually—Thorn—as that was how he'd just introduced himself, and they were to be married if all went according to this spon-taneous plan, so she supposed some familiarity was al-lowed, and would foster a good partnership.

Pushing any doubts or fears aside that he might re-scind his offer once he fully saw her—not that anyone had before, and besides, she had told him of her plain-ness, and that didn't seem to factor into this transac-tion, *money for freedom*—she rose, and stepped away from her shadowed nook to meet him as he rounded the ridiculous miniature fountain standing between them.

Extending her hand, she watched for any sign of shock, displeasure, or disappointment, but found nothing but a reassuring smile, and continued sparkling in his gaze.

'I suppose we should discuss some details,' he said, wrapping his hand around hers, and she smiled, not just because he continued to prove himself ieminently clever and practical, but because he had a good handshake.

Strong, and sure; warm but not despicably wet as some were wont to be, and overall she noted that her body felt at ease in his presence.

It had from the moment he'd appeared along the path, bursting into her bubble of respite and peace, hence why she'd indulged in conversation as opposed to sinking further into the shadows, and making herself discreetly scarce, which would've been her typical *modus operandi*.

Something which should be said, was that her instinctual lack of wariness of him, had absolutely nothing at all to do with his objective, and striking, handsomeness—nor did her agreeing to these marriage plans. Hypatia might've been called many things by various persons of varying levels of acquaintance, however, *a fool who trusted a pretty face* would've never been one of them.

However, yes, objectively, he was handsome. Square-jawed, with symmetrical but finely honed features. Long, straight, somewhat blunt nose. Thick, mostly straight, but also gently arched brows, over slightly hooded, downturned eyes, of a sparkling cerulean blue, visible even in the gloom of the dusky garden. A wide mouth, with the perfect little dip in the upper lip, which itself was that little bit smaller than the lower—though both the right balance between full and narrow to follow the symmetry of the other features. All that topped off with non-noticeable ears, a mostly tamed mop of semi-curled, semi-straight thick hair, and a thick, solidness of figure that demonstrated the strength required for his previous occupation, though she suspected the broader-than-average shoulders, and towering height he worked to diminish by curving inwards slightly, were inherited from his forebears.

Overall, he had the air and energy of a pastorally perfect and quintessential British son; mixed in with a charming rogue, and potential of a rather endearing pup, the latter mainly due to those downturned eyes which looked entirely capable of mischief and pity-inducement. This was all reinforced somehow, by his fine, but not *exceptional*, evening dress, which both suited him, yet didn't in the least.

In all honesty, this handsomeness didn't hurt—in her decision to marry him—it was rather like choosing one painting or ornament over another for one knew one could bear to look at it for years on end.

However, it was primarily her instinctual ease which, along with desperation, was one of the main reasons she was going along with this seemingly impetuous and foolhardy plan.

'We should,' she agreed, releasing his hand. 'There

will be no time to meet again, I think, and all my correspondence is read.'

He frowned at that, a line appearing perpendicular to his right eyebrow.

'That will present a problem, as we'll need to agree on a time and date, once I've obtained a licence, if I in fact manage to do so.'

'I trust you to.'

Thorn's frown deepened—two lines against either brow tipping inwards to form an almost triangle, and Hypatia understood the gesture, for inwardly, she frowned too.

There is time to think on all that later, along with everything you haven't given yourself time to consider.

The vows have not been spoken; you have not fully cast your bets yet.

'Have you ever written with lemon?' she asked, choosing to abide by her own declarations, though something inside her knew her bets *had* been fully cast the moment she first opened her mouth in Thorn's presence.

'Aye, I did, as a boy,' he chuckled, nodding his head. ''Twas mostly maps; I pretended I was some great spy that would defeat Napoleon.'

Hypatia grinned, once again caught off-guard by the sparkling of his gaze, and the piece he offered somewhat unknowingly, and unpretentiously, of himself.

'You could write, pretending this time to be some matron or other I met tonight, whom I promised to give my stain banishing formulas to,' she suggested after a moment, their smiles not dimming, but reminded of the semi-urgency of the situation. 'Write the time, date, and place we are to be wed in between the lines, and I shall respond accordingly to confirm receipt.'

'You have stain banishing formulas?'

'Developed over many years,' she nodded.

'How eminently useful.'

'I suppose I might've listed that in my favour earlier, as an offset to my lacking five hundred pounds in desired dowry.'

'With the money it might save in garments, I suppose so.'

They stared at each other, smiling softly for a few moments which seemed to stretch longer than that, the sounds of the party trickling towards them on the growing and cooling breeze.

'I shall do as you direct, then, I need only your address.' Hypatia gave it to him, and he nodded, before sharing his own temporary one. 'You will manage to slip away when the time comes?'

'I will manage. You will find us witnesses and any other necessaries?'

'I will. Should I plan for you to return to your home after the ceremony?'

'As much as I would like to say no, if only to avoid further issue, it would be advisable that I return, tell of the news, and collect what little I must.'

'Very well then.'

'May I kiss you?'

Thorn's surprise manifested itself as she realised now it likely always would: by him freezing, eyes blinking wide like some animal caught in a lantern's light in the dark.

'Um…why?' he asked, with slight trepidation.

'Have you some aversion to it?' she asked in turn, and he shook his head slowly, waiting for the rest of what she might say. 'Well, then, I thought, despite our allowing each other certain discreet freedoms, and despite this being a business transaction, perhaps in future we may wish to indulge in some intimate benefits, and so best to know now whether or not that is a possibility, or whether I shall be shackled to someone whose taste I cannot abide.'

'In which case those benefits would be removed from the equation of our transaction?'

'Precisely. Unless you would like the possibility removed now, which I would understand and respect, of course.'

'Of course. Well then, I suppose I can see the wisdom in your request.'

'Excellent.'

Unhesitatingly, Hypatia took a step closer, so they were toe-to-toe, having been standing thus far at much less than the Society-prescribed distance which equated to *proper*.

However, sensing his own awkwardness, and hesitation, Hypatia paused.

'If you do not desire me enough to kiss me, I shan't take offence.'

'It isn't that,' Thorn huffed out, and part of Hypatia relaxed, not that she would've been truly offended. She'd found many persons were democratic to say the least when offered certain intimacies, however, not everyone was thus. 'It's only… You caught me off-guard, and I've never kissed someone on command.'

'I do not command you now, sir.'

'I think the proper form of address is *my lord*,' he commented with a grin, relaxing. 'And I'm afraid, Miss Hypatia Quincy, you're rather mistaken. For you do.'

Before she could entirely decipher his meaning—not that it wasn't patently clear, however, the implication, that she, Hypatia Quincy, could command such another being within a few minutes of meeting them was patently unfathomable—he'd scrunched inwards to lower himself, slid an arm around her waist, and pulled her into himself, as his lips descended unto hers.

Given the certainty, confidence, and admitted rapidity of the movement, some part of Hypatia expected the kiss that followed to be on the more roguish, passionate and sweeping scale—the sort one read about in books when handsome pirate captains ravished lost maidens. However, though there was cheekiness, passion, and quite a lot of *sweeping off her feet*, the kiss which followed was nothing like what she'd expected, in the best way.

It was tender, questing, and simple. A teasing, a

slow sort of *hello, let us get to know each other* kiss. Her hands found their way, and stability, resting on his arms, just below his shoulders, where she could feel every muscle and sinew move and tense beneath the layers of fabric. Breathing into her, he relaxed as she did into the kiss, a simple dance of the lips slowly becoming *more*. Teeth nipping, tongues seeking and finding—for mere seconds before retreating. Fingers brushed along her arm, then below her ear, and her cheek, as the kiss deepened, and liquid heat and pleasure spread through her veins; warm breezes and lazy brooks waking the land after a long winter.

There was comfort in him, in the kiss, that she hadn't expected; that same natural ease, the instinctual moulding of herself within his sphere, the pleasantness of his taste and scent—notes of all the best things in life in both, from the ripest sun-touched berries to the sea winds she'd never smelt but that gulls carried on their wings when they came to visit inland.

Someone moaned, or perhaps they both did, and grips tightened, and—

'Patty!'

Blast and damn and hell.

'Patty!'

Groaning her annoyance, she peeled away from Thorn, his reluctance making itself known—and warming her heart even more than it already was—by his arm remaining around her, as he tried to clear the desire from his eyes.

'My sister,' she explained, and there was that single-lined frown again.

'She calls you *Patty*?' Hypatia nodded, and he released her slowly, pouting his disgust. 'Appalling does not even begin to cover my thoughts on that sin.'

'An opinion I wholeheartedly share, unfortunately I must go before she finds me. Here. Thus. With you.'

A nod, and Thorn slowly released her, though not before placing some of her errant curls back into place—a useless task, really, particularly considering no one would ever consider their disorder a result of such activities as she'd been partaking in—and finally running his thumb along and around her lips, as if to cleanse them of any traces of their kiss, which was disappointing, and yet dangerously seductive. As was the thing he did next, which made her insides jolt, and told her in no uncertain terms, that she'd rather underestimated the rogue, and deliciously dangerous nature of this particular man.

He placed his thumb into his mouth, and savoured the remnants of themselves upon it as though it were a taste of the finest ambrosia.

'Your verdict then, Miss Quincy? Find you my taste as abideable as I do yours?'

'Yes. *My lord.*'

Thorn grinned—or perhaps it was a self-satisfied smirk—either way, it too was dangerous, and thrilling, and made her smile brightly.

'Patty!'

'I must go.'

'Until we meet again, at our wedding, Miss Quincy. Thank you for a most—perhaps *the* most—intriguing and strange evening of my life.'

'Until then, goodnight.'

And with that, though she dearly wanted nothing more than to remain there, perhaps always, for the oddness, beauty, simplicity, and strangeness of those minutes she no longer counted, Hypatia scampered off back into the maze of hedges, heading for her sister's voice.

'Patty, where are you!'

Here, for now, though not for long, if tonight brings all it promised.

Especially an end to being called Patty.

Well, perhaps not especially.

Chapter Two

'What do you mean you're married?!' the less than affable Mr Quincy shouted, his voice booming against the walls to a rather surprising degree. Surprising, given his small stature, which looked incapable of producing such powerful noise, and also his heretofore, if not warm manner, then warily and somewhat obsequiously welcoming manner. But then, Thorn supposed whatever Mr Quincy had expected from seeing an earl appear with his daughter, it wasn't this, and therefore the man could be given some leniency.

Especially considering the fact that Thorn was experiencing rather a strange and surprising day himself. In fact, when Thorn had been told of his astronomical rise in the ranks of Society, of his new, *blessed* future as Earl of Gadmin, he'd been certain that was to go down in personal history as the oddest day of his life. However, he was finding that this one was rapidly giving him cause to rethink that determination. Truth be told, the past few days—ever since that night with

Hypatia in the garden—had quite the air of an incongruous nursery rhyme about them.

Met on a Wednesday,
Affianced on said Wednesday,
Obtained a licence on the Saturday,
Secured the church and witnesses on the Monday,
Advised the bride on the Tuesday,
Received confirmation from her on a Wednesday,
Married on a Friday.

It was amazing, he'd found, how much could be achieved with a title—no matter the infamy or unworthiness of the holder, nor even the lack of fortune to complement said title. Perhaps it was that, if not surprise, then true realisation, and a need to simply *get things done*, which had made it possible to get through the days without thinking too much. Doubting it all too much.

Whether it was the right choice; whether Hypatia would hold to their agreement.

What life would be like once they were married; if there would be more brain-numbing kisses to be shared.

If he could save the estate. If he could be a good earl. Become all he needed to be once—*if*—he did save the estate. Sitting in the House. Making decisions that would affect the whole of the country.

If he would have to become part of Society. Who he would be if he did. If he would lose himself. What would become of Hypatia with all this.

If one day he would wake up, to find it had all been

a cruel joke; if he would be returned from whence he'd come once they all realised he had no business even masquerading as an earl.

If he was doing the right thing, in any aspect; *what the Hell would become of them all.*

Generally, he wasn't much of a doubter, or ponderer—only as much as most everyone else he supposed—and so he'd reminded himself that gaining a title, and living through such strange circumstances as he was, was no reason to become one.

He needed money. Hypatia needed escape.

She was clever, and capable, and one mightily nice kisser.

Life would be what it would be, they would figure it out as it came along.

Once we leave this place.

Which he—and undoubtedly Hypatia—was looking forward to doing imminently.

'I am not entirely certain how one can fail to comprehend the meaning of such a simple statement, Father,' Hypatia said, not ungently, but so simply it might've felt thus, before Thorn could say what he'd been about to, which was tantamount the same. 'We were married this morning at St Bart's in Smithfield, I am now Countess of Gadmin, and I shall be leaving this house forever once I've collected what I must, and you've made all the proper arrangements with my husband. Congratulate me or don't, either way the deed is done, and cannot be undone.'

Mr Quincy, along with his wife—whose hair colour Hypatia had inherited, though luckily not her bitter, displeased doltish fish qualities—and her sister—a blonder creature, who Thorn could see some would call pretty, but whom he found as sickeningly and artificially sweet and spoiled as a rotten pile of icing—all gaped at her disbelievingly.

They made quite a picture there—Quincy framed by the women as he stood before where they sat on the settee, the mother rapidly progressing into *potential faint* territory—the bright Junspring sun streaming in from the windows decorated with too much lace, and walls covered in too many pastels. Thorn had a fleeting thought about knowing precisely where much of Quincy's fortune—earned by fabricating essential components for industrial mills and mining machines—went.

Walls with too many pastels, and garments with too many frills as demonstrated by the ladies before me, though luckily not the one beside me.

Indeed, though it was her wedding day, and some might argue the occasion if any there were to dress more coquettishly than habitually, Hypatia had opted for a plain, serviceable and far from delicate gown, in worn navy cotton. Though perhaps the circumstances surrounding their secretive wedding—she pretending to attend to chores—had been the reason for the lack of ceremonial dress.

Thorn himself had made an effort—though admittedly he'd not gone for *full* ceremony, merely paid more attention to his grooming, and worn his best suit—and he didn't begrudge her in any way the choice of a worn gown. Merely, admittedly, when he'd spotted it, he'd felt an urge to offer her all the best gowns in the land; before he'd remembered he had not the coin, and she seemed not the type to desire such extravagance.

Though perhaps, in time, I might buy her new clothes to her own liking, or make enough so as to spare her coin to do so herself.

'Like *Hell* it cannot be undone,' her father spluttered, and though Thorn hadn't expected jolly celebration to meet their news—particularly after Hypatia's predictions—he had expected slightly more restraint from a man who, for all intents and purposes, was attempting to do as many feared, and infiltrate the highest rungs of Society, with money, and an advantageous marriage for his youngest. 'Why, I should hail a Peeler right now, and have this one taken in for fraud, and theft, money-grabbing opportunist—'

'Do calm yourself, and desist, Father,' Hypatia ordered, in such a tone which could not be disobeyed, resting her hand on Thorn's forearm, to stop his intervention, undeniably obvious for the step he'd taken towards Quincy. Thorn obeyed, as her father did, knowing this was her battle. 'You shall not call the Peelers. We shall settle this like the civilised people we purport to be. You will take Thorn to your study. You will make the arrangements pertaining to my marriage. I will pack my things. And then I will bid you all farewell, wish you well, and leave this house.'

'Actually, if I may, I'd like to make one small amendment to that plan,' Thorn said. Hypatia turned back to him, and he met her eyes briefly, offering a small reassuring smile. She nodded. 'We shall all meet in the study together. Then I shall help my wife pack her things, and we shall bid you farewell, wish you well, and leave this house.'

He felt an odd jolt at saying the word *wife* so casually—he supposed it was just a lack of habit, as was hearing the words *husband* and *Thorn* leave Hypatia's mouth. Somehow, none of those words, nor even the promises and vows they'd spoken to each other in the brightly simple, yet solemn church this morning, had given him any manner of jolt. Any manner of doubt, or fear. The circumstances of his previous life and prior relationship had meant he'd always wondered rather a lot about marriage. Felt, if not fear, then slight trepidation at the thought of it; pondered the finality and seriousness of it. Normal, he supposed, when one was so close as he'd been then, to the possibility becoming reality. He'd wondered, if he was a man up to the task. The duty, the commitment. A man to be a good husband. And he'd had his doubts, and felt that trepidation, and honestly thought, particularly these past months when marriage had become necessity rather than possibility, that when and if the day came, he'd feel some manner of nerves. Some manner of that same trepidation.

However, this morning, he'd felt supremely calm, and, well, *certain*.

Likely because this was all just business, a contract, and he was marrying a woman who, by all accounts, was like-minded and level-headed.

Or perhaps it just all happened so bloody fast I haven't had time to be nervous.

'Do we mean so little then to you?' Mrs Quincy finally chimed in, and Thorn blinked, focusing on her. She looked less as if she were about to faint over the arm of the settee, and more like she might succumb to insincere tears—as did the daughter currently clutching her hand. 'That you would throw your lot in with such a man, and abandon us so callously? Abandon your father and I? Abandon dear Epi, to traverse the rest of the season, and her eventual marriage, all by herself? Abandon us all to face the consequences and *talk* of this most inadvisable match you have made? Did you even think of how this might affect her chances? Ours?'

'I admit, I gave no thought to such nonsense as the judgement and thoughts of others. There have been far more scandalous matches than mine, and if anything, one would think having a countess in the family would only ameliorate Epi's chances. She is clever, and determined, and she has you, Mother. She will fare well enough. As for you and Father, you have plenty of people who can attend to you, or the funds to employ more should the need arise. You are not abandoned. You are being left, as a bird leaves the nest. I thank you, for you have fed me, and clothed me, and taught me, and loved me to the best of your abilities. However, I have been given the chance to make a choice as regards the path my life shall now take, and I have seized it. Wish me well, or don't, I care little. Though I hope we may part with civility, and less histrionics.'

Thorn might've applauded. Commissioned a painter— if he knew where to find one, and how to do so—to immortalise this moment, and the fierceness of the woman at his side.

Yet at the same time, some part of him felt a twinge of sorrow for her, for having lived so long with such a family as she would say such things to—for he knew it wasn't out of meanness, or spite, merely from a place of truth.

I wonder which is worse; to have a family such as hers, or to have had such a great, incomparable father as I did, only to lose him.

'Well, Father? What shall it be? Civility and good-will? Or shall I go fetch the Peelers and tell them you refuse to give what is owed to one of this kingdom's earls?' Hypatia asked in the ever-lengthening silence.

'Let us be done with it, though you are no daughter of mine to behave in such a manner,' Quincy finally sighed, throwing up his hands as behind him, his wife and daughter sniffled and cried and made much of the drama of the situation. *Civility* and *histrionics in the end, I see.* 'I should disavow you completely, for this ingratitude and insult.'

'You are welcome to do so once today's business is concluded, Father.'

Quincy shook his head, and grumbled as he stepped away from the women, and led the way to the study.

Thorn slipped his hand into Hypatia's as they followed, giving not one last look to those left behind, and though she seemed not to note the gesture in any way, he thought he felt her relax, ever so slightly.

And though it meant nothing at all really—he was merely being human, and supportive of this new creature who in the eyes of the law and God, was his responsibility, something else he hadn't entirely fathomed until now—it felt rather momentous indeed.

The arrangements with Mr Quincy completed—as much as they could be, the rest left to the solicitors and men of business to ensure everything was signed, sealed, and delivered to the appropriate financial institutions—Thorn and Hypatia left him in his study, and went up to her room to see her packed, and removed from this house which was increasingly unwelcoming with every minute.

He wasn't entirely surprised to find that there was somewhat of a misnomer in calling it *her* room, for one glance at it told him it was anything but—the oversaturated pastels, patterns, and *things*, suggesting it had suffered the mark of either the mother, the sister, or some decorator with too much freedom, and not enough good sense. The room wasn't uncomfortable, tiny, relegated to the eaves, nor somehow marking of Hypatia's status amongst her family as *other*—she wasn't some little Cinder girl, banished to the fireplace—yet it was remarkably dismissive of who she was. Which was something that Thorn naturally had no true idea of, considering he'd now spent perhaps a sum total of about four hours in her company, yet that even he, in their brief acquaintance, had a better idea of than her family.

Or so it seemed to him then.

It was all the queerer—purporting to know her better than her family—considering he couldn't even purport to know her face well. If forced to describe her, in the event of some ghastly catastrophe for instance, he wouldn't have been able to give a proper description, and it wasn't that he'd not deigned to look at her. Only perhaps, that he'd not allowed himself to *pay attention*.

In the garden, when she'd emerged from the shadows into the lambent light of that ridiculous miniature square they'd found themselves in, he'd briefly noted that she was what *could* be called plain—not that he thought himself an Adonis by any right—but only because she wasn't what one would call *striking*, though her presence was. Her presence commanded attention, respect, heeding, and that night, yes, it had commanded desire.

Perhaps that was why he'd not allowed himself to truly study her in those few moments, having been slightly off-put by the sudden comfort and interest he felt in her regard; why he'd not allowed himself to pay too much attention all day today, even as they were married, lest he lose focus, or allow himself fancies that had no bearing on their current situation.

Or something of the sort.

Whatever the reasons not to pay Hypatia much attention, he lost sight of them then, as he stood there, just inside the threshold, and watched her go about her business, not a single movement wasted.

He could see the plainness others had quantified her with, though he would've termed it simplicity. She was neither tall nor short; her head naturally reaching about his shoulders. Neither thin nor overly abundant, but again, somewhere in between; strength denoting capability, and curves balancing them denoting nothing, though he couldn't deny he had *some* response to them. Her features and limbs were generally unnoteworthy, caught in the in-between of denominators as her figure was. Her hair was noticeable by its colour, and refusal to be tamed; even the curls refusing in some manner to be fully quantified thus as they also refused to be bound into any version of a tamed coiffure.

There was a softness to her face, a roundness to her cheeks and chin, yet a fineness in the edges. Her nose was somewhat crooked at its base, but it offset the longer front tooth on the opposite side, that was unnoticeable except when she smiled. The thickness of her brows might've been unfashionable had her large round eyes—of a soft honey green he hadn't noted until this morning, in the brightness of the church—not offset them, even despite one of them being ever so slightly smaller than the other. There was a crookedness to her mouth, too, a general lack of symmetry, which couldn't be noticed without study, but was felt upon first glance. Yet contrary to many, who placed such value on symmetry, and apparent beauty, Thorn found it was in fact all these little details—*flaws* some might call them— that he'd not allowed himself to catalogue till now, and of which he knew there were many more, that composed the sum of Hypatia, and that was wherein precisely the beauty lay.

Where the charm lay.

'Is there nothing I can do to help?' Thorn asked finally, stirring from his study as Hypatia paused, frowning down into the open chest at the foot of the bed, hands on her hips.

'No, thank you,' she said, somewhat perplexed it seemed, still frowning.

'Have you not enough room?' He glanced in, noting the pile of clothes already put away as he advanced slowly, then peeked at the small collection of items— books and journals mostly—which had been set upon the bed in a neat pile. 'Should I find another bag…?'

'There is plenty of room.'

'And that is the problem.'

Hypatia nodded, and Thorn dared get even closer. After all, she was his wife now.

Wife...why does the word drip so casually from my mind? So easily?

'It isn't that I lack belongings,' she specified, those green-honey eyes meeting his, an openness in them he decided was particularly *Hypatia*. 'I have what I need, and more than many. It's only that looking at it all, gathering it all, I am struck by how little would remain to signify my time on this earth, and half of it wouldn't quite signify it properly. I am tempted to leave whatever I feel isn't mine, however I would then be forced to travel without clothes, and merely a stack of books. And I am aware of the fact we've no money for frivolities such as new garments.'

We.

Thorn hadn't been a *we* in a very long time.

He decided then, that he had missed it, and was reminded how much he liked it. Though he still had *one* friend remaining, years of grief, loss, and betrayal, along with a natural penchant for solitude, had conspired to perhaps harden him to the company of others. But whether it be with his father once, or with Helen, he'd liked approaching life's everyday and grand moments with another. Though he'd not looked on it all quite so fondly once upon a time, nor had he and Helen admittedly ever had such conversations as he was having now with Hypatia about money and frivolities. But then much of that was his own fault; not that he could fully admit it quite then.

The point was, simply, that he liked being a *we*

again, just as he liked Hypatia's sensibility, as much if not more.

'As tempting an image as that would present... I'm afraid I must ask you to make do. Which reminds me...' He sighed, massaging his forehead, as Hypatia quirked her head inquiringly. 'With all the haste, I hadn't the time to warn you, or perhaps I was reluctant to. I must ask you to travel on alone to Gadmin Hall, and remain there a few days by yourself. Well, I am told a cook and a footman remain, so not entirely alone. I must to Essex, to settle my own affairs—I had not the time to do so after I was informed of the change in my circumstances, and can only afford to engage my solicitors for the bare minimum. You'll have the carriage,' he added hastily, referring to the contraption they'd ridden in when coming here from church—one of the title's last remaining assets, which, along with its semi-ancient driver, luckily had been in London with the previously departed earl upon his leaving his mortal coil. Hypatia continued to but stare at him, her impressions on this change of plans unreadable. 'It is not so fine as you are accustomed to, I know, but I have been promised it will make the journey back to Kent, at the very least. The house will be yours, to do with what you will whilst you are there, if you have a fancy to, or perhaps just enjoy your freedom, get to know the place...'

'I will be fine, Thorn, thank you,' she said gently, her hand finding its place on his forearm, and he breathed easier.

'Very well then.'

A nod, and she took her hand back, before he could think to do anything silly, or sentimental, or unwanted, like take it up, and place a kiss upon it as a gentleman might.

Gathering up the pile waiting on the bed into her arms so that it seemed she carried the Leaning Tower of Pisa, she then stepped around him again, and summarily half-dropped, half-arranged it all into the trunk within mere seconds. That done, she shut the lid, locked it tight, and even made to pick it up—though Thorn quickly intervened. He might've called for a servant to assist, however, he had no need, and didn't want to ask for anything further from this house. And so, he picked up her trunk, and followed her back downstairs.

No one but a footman remained in the hall—all but the front door closed—and Thorn ground his teeth. But then, as they made their way over the threshold, the footman cleared his throat, and glanced back meaningfully at the staircase. Tucked in beside it, along the corridor, were what Thorn imagined was the entirety of the staff, who all sniffed and waved, and mouthed *congratulations* to Hypatia. Mouthing *thank you* back at them, she smiled, nodded at the footman, and continued on her way, Thorn following behind.

As he secured the trunk, then handed her into the carriage, he glanced back at the house, if only to cement in his mind an image of the sort of house he never wished to create.

Looking a bit too far ahead there, Thorn. Right now you just need to ensure your house does not crumble, and sports a roof which can shelter this new wife of yours; this new being you've added to your life.

'Drive on, Ian,' he called, leaping up into the carriage himself, before slamming the door shut, and settling next to his wife, for a short time at least.

So the old retainer did, spiriting them away with as much haste as possible, and Hypatia turned to him, and smiled; an undecipherable smile he decided he liked very much.

Chapter Three

As the carriage rocked, rumbled, creaked and jolted, Hypatia was forced to wonder whether or not Thorn's promise—and Ian's when he'd handed her back up into it, after dropping Thorn off at his temporary London home and bidding him safe journey, while he continued on his own way—that the dusty, musty old contraption that smelt of damp and old patchouli, would survive the trip to Kent.

However, the thing did appear to have solid bones, and wasn't entirely uncomfortable—if slightly used, especially as concerned the dips in the cushions, or flaking leather of the squabs—and thus far, it had held true. And given their speed, and the hours travelled, the miles covered, they had only about an hour or so left before they arrived at Gadmin Hall, so she could only hope the men's promises would hold true; though admittedly there were enough stops along the road that were they to encounter any issue, they would not be far from aid or shelter.

Though we do not have much coin for either.

Indeed, she had only what she had squirrelled away over the years—portions from what little pin money she was on occasion allowed, or bits and bobs she kept after running errands—not an insignificant amount altogether as she'd never done much with it, hoping to someday use it to build her own future, but an amount she now considered as hers *and* Thorn's; and which would likely be needed to aid in building *their* future given all she'd heard about the house and farm, and despite her portion.

Some might find it odd, just how quickly she'd come to think of things in terms of *her and Thorn*, *their future*, having only been married this morning, having only met the bridegroom days prior, knowing practically nothing about him, and given that this was a contract which obliged her to nothing more than speaking vows and keeping to them in many ways; however, that was a great part of who Hypatia was. Someone adept at quick and efficient adaptation; someone who found themselves in new situations, faced with new obstacles, and who merely accepted them, and soldiered on. Not entirely without grudging, but with a clear-cut understanding that no amount of dislike would change what was necessary for her to do, and so, on she would go.

In this respect—her marriage—she couldn't say she was in any fraction grudging. In fact, she was rather excited, and hopeful. She'd liked Thorn well enough in the garden, and in every small moment since, she'd not seen or felt anything to counter that liking. Of course, she'd had doubts and questions—from the first; wondered if she was making the right choice, or if she was somehow being a hopeless, romantic dreamer for the first time, being impulsive when really, that wasn't her at all. She'd asked herself quite often after their first encounter, what she was agreeing to; who she was entrusting herself to. Wondered if this all didn't work out, would he let her go, in peace? Would he give her the means to do so, or would she have to survive another way? Would he turn out to be a terrible person, once her dowry was his, and she was trapped? Should she be thinking of her money as *hers*; as a means to escape in that eventuality? Or generally, should she be thinking of *hers* as hers, and *his* as his, rather than *ours*, and *we*, and committing herself to anything more than their initial agreement of money for freedom?

Only she couldn't help but be certain that he was a *good man*. From all she'd heard, seen, and felt—even his wanting to stand up for her with her father this morning—every little detail, every word, had been a clue to build the somewhat picture of a man with a head on his shoulders, who told no lies, and was…*simple*. She had as much conviction of his character as one could ever have, and in the end time would tell. For now, she trusted him, to behave as he had thus far— with honour, decency, and integrity—and that was what trust had always been to her. A conviction that someone would behave as they'd demonstrated they were apt to.

There was an allowance for surprises, naturally. However, betting on a certain pattern was as good a bet as one could lay; or so she had found thus far. So no, in the end, she'd concluded that she wasn't being a hopeful romantic dreamer, but instead pragmatic, seizing a most welcome opportunity. And as regarded her small savings, well, she would keep a portion of it, enough, just in case escape was ever required as she too had a head on her shoulders, or so she liked to think, but the rest… The rest would be theirs. As for *their* future, the farm, the house, any of that, well, she would have to see what awaited her in Kent, however, she posited that success and solvency for the estate and the title would require more than simply Thorn's efforts, and if she could help, she would. In the end, there was nothing wrong with ensuring all that would likely be providing her a life and a future, would do just that.

Toying with the simple silver band beneath her glove—somehow a perfect fit, and decorated inside with ivy, a touching detail she wondered if Thorn had even noticed when he'd purchased it, likely at some pawnbroker's, not that she minded—she glanced outside the dusky window as the road eased slightly. She wondered, for a moment, if like so much else of her character, people would think her odd for so quickly thinking of herself as a wife, but giving no second thought to herself as a *bride*. For not truly feeling anything but calm and settled this morning; excited and hopeful for her marriage, just not for her wedding. While some brides were nervous she knew, she hadn't felt anything such.

Perhaps it was that the marriage had been her choice, and she had no fear of any potential time spent in the marital bed, not being so unknowledgeable as others. Or perhaps it was that it had merely felt so *right*. Simple. Seeing Thorn there, waiting outside the church at the appointed hour, it had settled the only nerves she'd had; that he wouldn't be there. After that, it had all been eminently lovely, and without fuss, just as she might've hoped had she ever truly dreamt of a wedding day for herself. And it wasn't that she hadn't cared about it at all, she took the vows she made seriously even if she didn't believe in God, and therefore made such vows without the fear of Him and His retribution and judgement, only of her own. Really, it was just that to her, the wedding day held no great importance in her heart; the vows, the journey which followed, the years, those were the things of great importance.

As the miles continued to blur past hastily, Hypatia tried to guess how far Thorn had gotten by now, and curiosity besting her, she wondered what awaited him whenever he finally arrived; what his old home was like. Some part of her wished she might've gone with him, to see the sea, to learn more about him, but she knew it was better this way. And it couldn't be discounted in the least, that this parting demonstrated the trust he held in her—sending her to begin their work alone. Inherently accepting, asking for her help. She didn't feel as though he'd abandoned her, or cast her off now that he'd gotten what he wanted, but again, time would tell.

Just as time would tell what kind of life they might have, what they could build. Together, and yes, perhaps eventually, apart. For no matter that their fates were entwined now, this was a business agreement, and no promises beyond a certain level of partnership had been agreed to. They might be husband and wife; time alone again would tell what that might look like two, five, ten, or even twenty years from now.

If we shall be friends, or partners still, or perhaps nothing more than civil strangers.

After all, nothing lasts forever.

In the meantime, Hypatia couldn't but be rather excited again at the prospect of building something together, just as she couldn't help but be excited at the prospect of discovering what would be her new home, soon.

If the surrounding countryside is as lush, and full of dips, hills, meadows and trees as these vistas, I think I shall rather like it.

The sun emerged from behind a rather fluffy bunch of white clouds, dancing shadows upon the colourful landscape beyond, as if to thank her for her compliments, and promise that it would in fact be so.

Now you are in fact being a hopeful romantic.

But as I have never been one, I think, I should rather like to try it.

Dreaming, too. That has always sounded rather pleasant.

'Oh dear,' Hypatia mumbled as the carriage jerked to a stop before the Tudor erection, which was more or less erect. *Mostly thanks to the swathes of ivy that appear to hold it together.* She grimaced slightly, her eyes travelling over what she could see of it, as she waited for Ian to come open the door. 'Well, as promised, derelict it is, so at least it will keep you busy,' she sighed, preparing herself as she heard him leap down, and crunch on the gravel.

The carriage's door opened with a now familiar *thud*, *bump*, *screech* and *creak*, and Hypatia took a deep breath as Ian's bony arm, swathed in his worn coat, appeared in the empty space before her.

This is a challenge, not a disappointment; regardless, you must show neither.

Descending the carriage, she reminded herself that she was no longer Hypatia Quincy, but Lady Hypatia Ackerman, mistress of this house, Countess of Gadmin, and that ladies such as her smiled, and were kind and respectful of those around them—at least so she believed ladies of such standing should be, there were always plenty to disprove the rule.

'Welcome to Gadmin Hall, my lady,' Ian said, as a light, welcoming summer breeze drifted through the courtyard, shuffling the leaves of the surrounding oaks, and the ivy holding the place together with verve and determination.

'Thank you, Ian,' she smiled, her eyes darting across the edifice, cataloguing the state of it a bit clearer—*roof in disrepair, chimneys unmentionable, windows... unmentionable*—just as a ruckus sounded beyond the portico-sheltered great oak and iron door before her. 'It is charming,' she said, frowning slightly at the continued banging and bickering.

Ian didn't move, so neither did she, merely waiting; for what, now that was the question.

Finally, after what seemed an eternity of anticipation, the great door burst open—and when she said burst, she meant it. With a cacophony of sounds—including a mighty '*I said pull, damn you lad!*', and a boom that resounded through the gravel to her feet, sending quite a few previously chirping birds flying—half the door split open and back, Hypatia spying bodies tumbling into darkness with it.

She made a move to go assist, but Ian gently held her back, mindful of her position even when she wasn't, though his eyes were as big as hers as he stared at the half-open door.

'I may be a lady now, Ian, however I shall not be the sort to sit by without lending a hand merely because it may be uncomely.'

He hesitated, but finally nodded, and they rushed

over together to the door—or rather what remained of it.

Beyond the splintered half, hanging from impossibly rusted tight hinges, two bickering bodies were twisting and slipping as they cast off the half they'd taken with them.

'Told you we should've gotten Lawrence to come sort it, but *noooo*, a bit of oil and twill be right as rain you swore!' said the lighter of the two voices, the first to manage a return to upstanding from what Hypatia could tell in the barely illuminated and dusty gloom within.

'And who was to pay for the expense?' boomed the second, huffing and puffing on the floor, as it tried to heave off the half door upon itself. 'D'ye think the master'd be happy comin' home to discover we couldn't even get the door open without payin'? We shoulda been workin' on it since dawn, that's the problem—'

'He might've preferred that to discovering this!'

'Just help me up you fool b'fore he—'

'Are you both unhurt?' Hypatia asked, gently as she could, her amusement growing by the second though she didn't dare smile or laugh until she knew they were both safe.

Stillness and silence immediately followed her words, and had Hypatia been able to see clearer into the dimness, she might've spied, she was sure, two persons attempting to work out how best to next proceed, having been caught out thus.

'Answer her ladyship, or are ye both swine that

should be sent down to the farm?' Ian prompted them harshly, but not meanly.

'Aye, I mean yes, my lady,' called the lighter voice. 'We are both unharmed, merely some scratches and soreness for the morrow.'

'Have you need of assistance?'

'No, no!' cried the other, and with a great heave and bang, they disposed of the door keeping them in place.

'Very well,' Hypatia said, taking a step back and pretending to examine the inside of the portico as she waited.

In surprisingly good condition, though the ivy here too seems to keep it together.

Before long, two figures—still brushing themselves off and attempting to put some order into their appearance—climbed and slipped through the now passage, out into the somewhat crowded portico.

'My lady,' they said, bowing in unison as much as they could, their eyes darting around, no doubt searching for Thorne.

'Henry Brookwood,' Ian introduced, as solemnly as he could, indicating the younger of the two, presumably the footman given the tired and frayed old livery.

He had a pleasant face, with a small pointedness that spoke more of a fae's delicacy than sharp handsomeness, with a litheness and meaningfulness of movement that was rather endearing.

Only his hair had a wildness, a bit longer, with a dashing clutch of it mischievously falling over his right eye.

'And Joseph Langton,' Ian said, of the second man.

Somewhere between Ian and Henry's age, this was the cook presumably, one of those men seemingly caught in middle age—though he might've been eighty—barrel-chested, peppered with lines and silver hair, roughened by time and the land, yet with soft kind eyes, and surprisingly elegant hands that spoke of trade mastery.

He wore the attire of a simple worker—homespun coat, old-fashioned breeches, with a remarkably old yet strong linen shirt and cravat, and buckled shoes that would've been more at home on the feet of a country squire some twenty years ago—but then, what really did Hypatia have to comment on his choice considering she'd no idea of his life, or days, or indeed, what working at Gadmin Hall required.

And what really did she have to comment, when she doubted she looked any bit the part of the countess they expected.

'It is a pleasure to meet you both,' Hypatia smiled gently, and both surveyed her, likely trying to determine whether her pleasantness was affliction or affectation. 'My husband was very disappointed not to be here today, however, business detained him, and he will be joining us in a few days.' They both seemed to breathe easier at that, and Hypatia smiled wider. 'Plenty of time for us all to get acquainted, find a solution for this door, and for me to acquaint myself with Gadmin Hall. I look forward to your assistance.'

'Yes, my lady,' they said again in unison.

'Well now, shall we?'

'Of course, my lady,' Henry said, somewhat literally jumping to the occasion, by shooing Joseph out of the way, and bowing again as ceremoniously as he could, before leading her inside.

Strange though this welcome has been, I think I shall indeed like my new home.

It, like its inhabitants, has...character.

Chapter Four

With immense pleasure, I take it upon myself to announce the blessed union of Thorn William Ackerman, Earl of Gadmin, and Miss Hypatia Quincy, of the most enterprising Quincys previously of Birmingham, now Mayfair. Given that no attachment was previously noted nor rumoured, this writer can only hope that these dizzyingly rapid nuptials, and quickest of departures to the country signifies the match to be one of most passionate and fateful love. One would very much despair otherwise to believe their new favourite earl was so very desperate to see his situation improved; there is quite enough nobility to behave thusly.

Jack the Cat, Londoner's Chronicle, May 1839

Two mornings after Hypatia's arrival at Gadmin Hall—not that Thorn would know—and some one hundred and thirty or so miles away, Thorn was busying himself saying goodbye to his former life, his former home, his former everything, with a haste that was remarkable even to him. It wasn't alacrity, excitement driving him, but a sense of duty, of needing it to be done, lest the melancholy and strange sense of loss take too strong a hold; particularly given that he was a man who'd never had an affinity for any of the above throughout his life.

Only he supposed he was allowed a little of the stuff—be it excitement or melancholy—for it wasn't every day that one was plucked from a pleasant life of work and simplicity, and thrust into a world he'd not even dreamed of, complete with a wife, title, and responsibilities beyond anything he'd ever thought to imagine he might bear the burden of. It wasn't every day that one was obliged to relinquish the trade they'd been taught by their father; to leave behind the final pieces of that father, of that legacy he'd worked so hard to be worthy of, uphold and honour, and abandon much of what they'd been to become another altogether. And Thorn might've allowed himself a little of the stuff—excitement or melancholy—before he'd arrived back here, only he'd not really had the opportunity, considering how quickly everything had happened. In the end, he supposed, perhaps it was better that he was taking these little moments for himself now, as he said *fare thee well* to his previous life, and didn't have to concern himself with anyone including his new wife discovering him indulging in such uncharacteristic emotional indulgences.

Which included too—it must be said—wondering often what his new wife was up to, and how she was adjusting to *her* new life.

Though I know her not, I think Hypatia rather adjustable, so she's probably faring better than I...

A slash of guilt struck him again at having left her as he had, perhaps he might've—

'Think that's everything, Thorn,' Malek, his once apprentice, now successor as local smith to the high and low of this corner of the world, said, offering out a crate full of tools and other assorted trade-related items.

Thorn eyed the box, then the young man, whose eagerness had always appeared so tightly contained within his boxy, short frame and features.

From what little Malek had shared over the years, he was an orphan, who'd stowed away, then worked on a variety of ships and conveyances from his native Morocco all the way to Cape Horn, before arriving in, then wandering southern England for a time, doing odd jobs. Thorn had found him in Ipswich when he was about fourteen or so, seen his sharpness and hard-working nature, and, seeking an apprentice, asked him what he thought of such a profession. Malek had said he rather liked the idea, and wanted something more stable than a life at sea, and so, Thorn had taken him on. Beyond those few details, Thorn knew little of the lad, not for lack of asking in the first few years, but Malek found as much use in sharing and dwelling in the past as Thorn did, and so he'd let it lie about three years into their acquaintance—some five years ago now.

And now, at the end of our acquaintance in all likelihood, is not the time to ask.

'You keep them,' Thorn said, only realising the inanity of having asked Malek to help him collect all he had then. 'You remained an apprentice past the years you should've only because you wished to. Now...this is all yours.'

'But they're your father's.'

'They were. And they were mine, and I am leaving the trade, so now they're yours.'

He didn't say that Malek was probably the closest he'd ever come to having a child, to passing on the legacy which had been passed to him, but perhaps it was in his voice, for Malek stared at him with wide misty eyes, before nodding solemnly.

'Thank you.'

'Just put them to good use.'

Malek nodded, then turned and set the crate down on a work bench.

'Is there nothing you'll take then?'

'No... I don't think there is,' Thorn said on a half-chuckle, half-sigh, looking around the dusky forge. 'I've taken my clothes and papers from the cottage, beyond that... I suppose there's nothing I'll be needing. Even the clothes, I take them only for I've nothing else.'

Much like my wife. What a pair we make—

'So it's true then. You're leaving for good,' said another voice, and both Thorn and Malek turned to the open doors on their left, in the midst of which stood Thorn's former best friend, Frank; as ever the opposite to Thorn, dark where the latter was fair, short and lean where Thorn was tall and thick.

Water, powerful, treacherous, and sly to Thorn's stone; determined, patient, and unyielding.

'I'll um…go do something,' Malek muttered, almost inaudibly and Thorn might've laughed had he not been so busy clenching his teeth.

And fists, and every muscle and possible limb in his body.

He'd thought, somehow, it might have lessened, the wound. But then, it had been quite a while since he'd had to face either Frank, or his former sweetheart, Helen, who'd left him for the *enterprising* and *ambitious* Frank when he'd set off on his ventures of trade and speculation, both finding a poor, simple, life in the country stifling. In the end, they hadn't made it very far in the past couple years; however, that was neither here nor there.

It wasn't that Thorn begrudged either of them their ambitions, their desire for a life beyond the one they'd lived and shared here for so long; it was the betrayal, really, that he had difficulty forgiving. It was the fact that Thorn had had to discover them *in flagrante delicto* before either of them deigned to inform him that the future they'd all imagined living together would never come to pass. That friendships and relationships were broken, and that that was that.

And perhaps what smarted most was that Thorn had been content with his own life, aspirations, and future, until he'd allowed their discarding of him in the name of *more*, to make him feel as though he weren't enough. That he too should want and aspire to more than merely a *good* life, which he hadn't ever really, not even when he'd been bestowed a title, and been raised up in the world. It was that wound which had perhaps festered most of all since everything had shattered two or so years ago. That wound which made forgiveness difficult, and which had meant Thorn's change in circumstance had had one great silver lining: that he would not be forced to spy Frank and Helen as often as he might've dwelling here for the remainder of his days; a prospect he'd not ever relished.

Though, in fairness to his character, he'd not even once thought of his raising to an earldom as sweet revenge; wondered if Helen regretted her choice after hearing the news, so perhaps there was a measure of forgiveness in his heart after all.

'What are you doing here, Frank?' Thorn asked, sighing, hoping it might release some of the tension inside him, which it did, for a few seconds; until Frank dared to step in further.

Thorn glared at him and Frank nodded sadly.

'Heard you were back. I thought… I hate how we left things, Thorn. We were brothers once, and—'

'Your choices led us here, Frank. Yours and Helen's. You were both content for the past years to leave things as they were, and now you wish me to believe there is nothing more driving your need for reparation?'

'If you're implying I'm here because of anything beyond profound regret, *my lord*, then you're sorely mistaken. I've not been content these past years, and I know it is my fault things ended so grievously, however, yes, now that you are leaving, and I've no idea when I might see you again, I thought I might chance repairing our bond to some degree.' Thorn sighed, shaking his head, and turning away to stare at everything and nothing. 'Will you at least accept my congratulations on your marriage? Believe me when I say I wish you and your new wife a wonderful life, and I was glad to see you'd found such joy so quickly?'

For a split second, Thorn considered admitting the truth: that contrary to *Jack the Cat's* fantastical and ill-advised wishes—and why the man continued to be so interested in his life was baffling and disturbing to say the least—it was in fact necessity, *desperation*, and not love which had seen him married. That had he the choice, he likely never would have married; after all, he'd had his reservations before the betrayal, but after, the idea of committing to another who might show they had no loyalty or love until it was too late, held no appeal whatsoever. He considered telling Frank that though in future there might be some measure of joy to be found in his life, for now, he couldn't truly say he had such stuff in his heart.

However, such confessions would be too close to something friends might say, to seek advice or blessings, and as they weren't friends, he wouldn't say anything such; he would merely say whatever might get Frank out of his life for good, so he could be back on his merry way, to his aforementioned wife.

'Thank you,' Thorn said, only half begrudgingly. 'I would offer you congratulations as well, however as I've heard it, you and Helen remain unmarried.'

Though I don't care.

I don't.

All I care is that I find, when once such congratulations would have tasted of bitter ash, now, were I to be obliged to offer them, it would not be so.

'We are waiting until I am further established, which shouldn't be long, God willing,' Frank said, with a spot of bitterness that spoke of a contentious and oft-debated consensus.

I. Don't. Care.

'God willing,' Thorn agreed, feeling an odd sense of closure, and liberation.

Not quite forgiveness yet, but a sense, that like the rest, Frank, Helen, their history, any resentment, his tools, this place, it was all to be left in the past.

So he could say, *God willing you and Helen be married soon*, and mean it.

'Good luck, Thorn,' Frank said, nodding. 'I am sorry

it ended as it did, but I do wish you all the best in your life.'

He turned to leave, and just as he passed the threshold, Thorn spoke, a truth flooding into his heart with the finality of the moment.

'I wish you and Helen the best,' he said, and Frank stopped, but didn't turn. 'I don't think I can truly say I have forgiven you, though I hope someday I might. However, I bear neither of you ill will, and I see now… many things I mightn't had you not made the choices you did.'

Frank seemed to ponder whether or not to respond, until finally, he gave one final nod, and disappeared into the bright day.

Not long after Malek reappeared, and though there wasn't much else for Thorn to do, his business—personal and professional—all tidied and closed so that he could begin anew, they found little bits to do together, be it tea, or tidying some final projects, and even discussing when the tiles on the roof would need repairing. Having thus not wasted, but well-spent the afternoon, Thorn bid Malek a final farewell, gave one last glance to the seaside village below the hill he'd dwelled on his entire life, mounted his horse, and set his course to Kent.

To Gadmin Hall, to his new self, to his new life, and for perhaps the first time since he'd come to learn of his supposed good fortune, he was rather excited and eager to see all his future would bring.

And in truth, I am rather curious and eager to meet my wife again, and know her better.

Chapter Five

'Henry, is there anything I should know about our bailiff Mr Warren?' Hypatia asked, as nonchalantly as possible, as the footman poured her more tea. Despite her having told him she could do it very well herself, and all they had witnessed her doing these past days, it seemed both he and Mr Langton refused to forget she was a countess, the lady of the house, and therefore insisted some ceremony was required. On occasion, at least.

It wasn't that she minded terribly. In fact, it was rather nice in its heartfelt nature, and particularly considering all the three of them had achieved together since her arrival, she found their solicitude supremely touching.

Henry paused, then realising he couldn't remain thus lest her cup literally overflow with the best of what scraps of tea their pantry held, he straightened and returned to the sideboard to busy himself. Hypatia waited, sipping her tea, munching on her toast and eggs, which lacked salt and butter as those too were scarce—in fact the larders and pantries were rather lacking, though not to the point of being unable to make do, which was a blessing—knowing that silence was in most instances the best extractor of secrets.

She waited some more then, her eyes turning to the newly cleaned windows—all intact in here thankfully—and the gorgeous, breezy sunshine-filled day outside.

'Why do you ask, my lady?' Henry finally said, still, from what she could tell, examining the wood-panelled walls and pretending there was more to be done despite her small, and un-extravagant breakfast needs.

'Why match my question with a question, Henry? After all we've been through recently, I thought we'd quite gotten the measure of each other, and established some trust.'

Hypatia turned in her seat, raising her brow, and searing the back of Henry's head with a meaningful glare he surely felt, for he sighed heavily, his shoulders bowing inwards.

'He's a clever man, knows his business well. Knows how to make himself indispensable, and appreciated by those required, and advantageous.'

'Neither category do I apparently fall into, as Mr Warren has been so inevitably detained these past days, unable to even call and meet the new Countess of Gadmin. Not that I find myself truly regretful of such a slight.'

Indeed, she wasn't.

It had given her if not ample, then sufficient opportunity to get an objective measure of the man, his skills, abilities, as well as a summation of the work he'd done for the estate. Henry's words, diplomatic as they were, did however confirm the suspicions she harboured having spent what waking hours she hadn't on getting the house into somewhat of a liveable state and studying up on the rearing of swine, on sorting through the mess that were the account books and ledgers which had been left here—though presumably Warren had the most recent ones in his possession.

Though I suspect they will tell the very same tale—or perhaps an even more fantastical one, for he'll have had time to prepare them for the new master.

Yes, she rather suspected such preparations were what had been occupying Mr Warren since news of her and Thorn's imminent return here had come; what had prevented him from ingratiating himself with whom he likely suspected was the new, silly little countess.

He must've breathed much easier knowing Thorn wouldn't arrive for a few more days...

And perhaps she should wait for her husband before she did what she was about to, however, Thorn had still not returned, and though she didn't *truly* doubt he would at all, he had made her lady of the house, and she would not shirk her responsibilities.

'Henry, would you have Ian prepare two horses please? I am going to visit our farm.'

'Two horses, my lady?'

'Yes, Henry, if you would accompany me, I should be rather grateful of the company.'

And a witness.

Even if she didn't say the latter, she was quite certain Henry heard it, though he made no comment, and simply went off to do as he was bid, while she finished her breakfast, and prepared herself.

No amount of preparation, however, could've sufficed, or so Hypatia discovered as soon as they traversed the small wood behind Gadmin Hall's gardens, and emerged onto the outer limits of the land constituting the pig farm—the previous earl's final project; his last hope to save the earldom from *complete* ruin.

It was her nose which first alerted her to her lack of preparation, and though she couldn't claim to be particularly squeamish—or at least not half as much as most people she knew—she found herself having to raise her arm to cover her nose before her breakfast found itself somewhere other than her stomach. When she'd managed to recompose herself just enough, she shot a glance over her shoulder at Henry, who seemed intently occupied by his horse's mane, shame written in every part of his countenance.

Oh dear.

And as she found the further they advanced, *oh dear* didn't even begin to encapsulate the magnitude of the despicable sights and goings-on; she found not even the worst expletives in her repertoire—of which there were shockingly many—could even begin to encapsulate it.

The *corps de ferme* was, if at all possible, in worse shape than the house had been—roofs holeyer than not, pieces of white Caen stone missing, and those still in place, hardly so. Doors with more patchwork than a quilt hung from rusty hinges, and boarded-up windows. That wasn't even to mention the lack of tending to the patches of land between the wood and U-shaped farm buildings, nor the muddy disgrace of the courtyard—though surely there must be stone *somewhere* beneath it—the state of the pieces of equipment and tools lying about, nor the complete lack of well, *anyone*. Of anything, save for a putrid stench, and the sounds, by Jove, the *sounds*. Wretched, sad, mournful, and gut-wrenching.

In a trice, Hypatia had dismounted, and was stomping towards the nearest of the buildings, slipping and sliding in mud—or so she preferred to believe. With difficulty, but pure rage fuelling her, she tugged and pulled at the door until finally it gave, opening onto a horror she by now expected, yet still wasn't prepared for.

The bastard.

Dozens of pigs had been packed into the long building that had once been something other than a giant, disgusting sty; trapped and shoved together without care nor reason, to rot in their own filth. It was beyond inhuman; it was something which didn't have a name.

Hypatia wanted to cry, and retch, and strike the beast who had done this to the poor creatures, and—

'My lady,' Henry said gently from the doorway, looking as green as she felt, though she suspected he knew some of what had happened here, and they would have a talk later. For now, however, she followed his gaze, moving so she could see what he attempted to show her.

The beast himself.

'Mr Warren, I presume,' she said loudly, clearly, though every bit of her was clenched and ready to flay him alive as she stomped across the courtyard.

He hadn't been expecting her, that much was certain from the widened eyes as he dismounted, though to his credit, the debonair, much too slickly handsome for his own good idiot quickly hid it, smiling brightly as he hailed her.

No bow? How very, very, disappointing, Mr Warren.

'My Lady Gadmin, what a pleasant surprise! I must offer my apologies—'

'There is no penitence of any kind which could ever suffice as regards your sins, Mr Warren,' she said, shaking her head, as they met in the midst of the courtyard, coming toe-to-toe. He was taller than her, bigger than her, and she could tell he still thought his cleverness and good looks might win her over—insincere regret flashing in crystal blue eyes—but she felt mightier than Boudica just then. 'If you believe in a God, I suggest you begin your prayers this very instant, and spend the rest of your days on this earth repenting, but even then, Mr Warren, *even then*, I doubt redemption will ever be yours.'

'My lady, I must ask you to calm yourself, I understand such business as can be seen on a farm can be rather shocking and distressing to persons of refinement, however—'

'Do not even *attempt* to patronise me, Mr Warren,' she warned him, somehow managing to not raise her voice, and yell, and scream—which would surely lose her this battle, and indeed this war. *Calm myself, indeed.* 'The only words I will hear from you are *yes, my lady, I shall be gone, my things cleared out within the hour, and the ledgers from the past year in your hands by that time as well.*'

'You cannot, the earl, your husband—'

'I am the Countess of Gadmin, and you are a despicable wretch who has been thieving, swindling, and torturing innocent animals for the sake of laziness, profit, and greed, and you will be gone. It is your only chance at escape, which you do not deserve, but which I grant you now for the sake of peace. Either way, be certain, proof of your misdeeds will be handed to the magistrate without delay, and some day, *some day*, Mr Warren, your years of fraud, and theft, and whatever else I am bound to uncover—for you are not even *half* as clever at covering your tracks as you believe yourself to be, I've seen illiterate butlers more adept at concocting accounts than you—every single thing you have ever done wrong in your damned life, will catch up with you.

And you had better hope, or pray, or beg the Devil for all I care that it will merely be gaol waiting for you. Be grateful now that I am not my husband, though if ever I was tempted to strike a man until he could move no longer, it would be today, and if you test me, I am quite certain I could find the will, and the strength.'

Breathing hard, she raised a brow, meeting the ice-cold, dagger-filled gaze of Mr Warren, who she was very sure, wanted to throttle her, or strike her, or perhaps feed her to the pigs, and so they were alike in that.

But perhaps he saw the wisdom, the boon which she offered—though it hurt her to offer it—for finally he relented, sucking through his teeth, and nodding viciously as he stepped back.

'Yes, my lady,' he bowed mockingly.

'Henry shall accompany you to fetch the ledgers, and you shall advise him, if he doesn't already know, the names of those you've employed to do your horrid bidding. They too, are dismissed.'

'You'll regret this,' Warren threatened, whispering, still backing away, a smile that spoke of retribution on his face.

'Come near me, mine, or my land, threaten me again, and they won't even find a hair of yours to bury. I know as well as the next person how useful such animals as are plentiful here can be,' Hypatia warned him, with a touch of chilling sweetness that wiped that smile right off his face.

Not once did she lose sight of him as he rode off,

Henry on his heels, and though she knew she had to go begin taking care of those poor animals—and all those she hadn't seen but could hear in the other buildings—she couldn't move.

All she could do was stand there for a long while, getting her breathing and heart back under control, getting her emotions back where they belonged, and returning to her more useful self.

Badly done, Hypatia. Badly done. You should've gone to the magistrate first, or waited for Thorn, not let your emotions cloud your judgement...

What is done is done. So be still, and clean up this mess.

Finally, she turned around, ready and stable enough to do what she must, only to be confronted with a sight she hadn't expected: that of her husband, standing right there, by her horse, looking at her with something so utterly confounding and for which she had no name; something that held her completely frozen in place, her heart so mightily struck as it was.

And feeling somehow utterly relieved that I am no longer alone.

'You're back.'

Chapter Six

Having known what little he did of Hypatia, Thorn hadn't precisely expected to find her sitting prettily at Gadmin Hall, waiting like some manner of potted plant for his return. He wasn't entirely certain what he *had* been expecting; his expectations had floated in the back of his mind whilst he was away, but he'd not brought them to the forefront, nor considered too hard, just *wondered* generally what his wife might be up to, just as he wondered generally at what he might find Gadmin Hall, the legacy and duty entrusted to him, to be.

What he could say in all certainty, however, was that he'd not expected to find her thus, nor indeed had all he found so far in the hour or so since he'd arrived featured in any manner in his casually floating expectations.

He'd expected to find a derelict house—though admittedly perhaps not *so* ruinous, rather more than he'd been advised, leading him to wonder if some message had been misunderstood or if someone had tried to spare him such grimness—and so he had. He had thought to himself as he'd ridden up that it was a nice enough place, with good bones—or so he hoped for already the tally of the rest was adding up in his mind, and he cringed.

He'd not expected a shining turquoise blue door to be the centrepiece of the place, but then, he'd thought he could handle one surprise, and it seemed really like an old door—or doors—had been patched together to form a new one, and really, a coat of paint couldn't but help to make that seem a little more charming than desperate.

He knew only two members of the house staff remained, so he hadn't expected a hero's welcome, but he had expected *someone* to greet him—he would say even after he'd rung the bell; however, that attempt had failed since the rope had broken off in his hand, and the bell itself had no clapper. He'd knocked, thinking perhaps even his wife might come to the door, or a servant she might've engaged in his absence—*with what funds, you dullard*—only no one had, so he'd let himself in, calling out '*Hullo?*', wondering if perhaps he'd gotten the wrong long-neglected mansion after all.

And he'd had to revise that thought quickly enough, for dilapidated though it was in many ways, it was no longer *long neglected*. He'd expected dust, and mould, and unbreathable air; damp and festering—and he meant that as no insult to those who'd chosen to remain with the house, it was a large place to tend to without proper staff nor funds. Instead, he'd found a sharp scent of wax, polish, lemon, and *freshness*; not a speck of dust, and it wasn't just that the place lacked furniture or adornment.

He'd wandered about, still crying out his *hullos* with less verve as his astonishment grew, finding room after room having undoubtedly been touched by some manner of cleaning sprite. It was in the library—bare of anything save for empty bookshelves and a vase full of Michaelmas daisies on the windowsill looking out onto the overgrown gardens—that Langton, the cook, had found him toying with those daisy petals.

'We did what we could this past year but hadn't much heart nor direction, my lord,' Langton had told him once he'd realised Thorn was no intruder, but rather his new employer. *The new earl. A title I fear will take longer to get accustomed to than husband.* 'Her ladyship hasn't stopped since she's come 'ere, up before dawn and if she sleeps I'd be surprised. She's got lists upon lists of things to be done, and Henry and I's been helpin' all we can,' he'd told Thorn, an unmistakable smile of pride in his voice, and Thorn had understood the sentiment; shared the smile. Even if part of him felt very badly indeed that he'd sent his new wife to this place, without…anything. *That I sent her to such a place at all.* 'If I can say so, my lord, she's a clever one the mistress, makin' those funds you gave her carry farther than the meanest miser could. And ye should've seen 'er on the roof, milord!' Langton had chuckled as Thorn's eyes had grown the size of saucers, not that Langton had noticed. ''Er book on patching roofs in one 'and a 'ammer in the other! Henry and I thought we might die of fright, but she weren't to be dissuaded.'

'No, I don't suspect she would,' Thorn said uneasily, somehow finding it not at all surprising to learn his wife had been climbing rooftops to repair them herself. *And what are these funds he speaks of that I apparently sent?* A question for his wife, which prompted his next question to Langton. 'And where is my lovely countess?'

Langton's face had fallen then, making Thorn frown, concern flooding his heart.

'She's gone to the farm, with Henry.'

'A direction for it, if you please.'

Langton had given it, though he might've only said: *go through the woods and follow the stench.*

It had been sickening, distressing, and infuriating, and had he not heard raised voices—including a woman's which could only be Hypatia's—he might've ridden into the farm's courtyard like some berserker of yore. Instead, he'd dismounted, and approached quietly, but rapidly on foot, listening to the conversation—or disagreement at hand—and finally gotten close enough to spy the scene, without being seen.

Hypatia in the middle of the courtyard, flaying whom he knew to be the farm's bailiff as she called him by what he knew to be the man's name, another standing at her back, ready to defend—Henry, he presumed. He heard Warren mention *her husband*, and was about ready to make himself known, as he didn't like at all how the man dared to speak or even look at his wife, but then he heard Hypatia proclaim herself Countess of Gadmin, with such force, magnitude, and strength he knew he couldn't interfere.

This was her battle, that she was fighting valiantly, for him, for his pigs, who he'd gathered had been most ill-treated, for his name, for his lands, for his everything, and so he wouldn't diminish her by interfering, and presuming she needed a man. She'd done…so much already without him, he wondered briefly if she even required him at all; something which might've been a relief, had it not provoked an odd twinge of fear. One which vied for attention for the briefest second with the flash of envy that traversed his heart; Hypatia unmistakably bore the title, the responsibility, the duty, with more ease and grace than he could ever hope to. Quickly, all that washed away however, fascinated, blessed, and proud as he was; so much so that he couldn't move nor even breathe. All he could do was stand there and watch her take down the miscreant, with more grace and fortitude than he'd ever witnessed in one single person before then.

He watched as the bailiff and the footman finally left, and as his wife gathered herself, and then, finally, he found he could move again, so he began to go towards her, because he could see she was upset, and—

'You're back.'

Smiling, feeling… Relieved wasn't quite the word

but then he couldn't find the one to describe how he felt—*at home, welcome, at ease, happy that she appears relieved I have returned*—he closed the few remaining steps dividing them, and searched her flushed face, and eyes full of turmoil.

'I'm so sorry, Thorn, I should've waited for you, or at least gone to fetch the magistrate, only I didn't know when you'd be back, and I just thought to come and find Warren, not confront him, but when I saw those poor creatures, I don't know what came over me, I'm never one to let emotions run away with me thus—'

'You've nothing to apologise for,' he said, slightly confounded, for it felt as if she thought he'd be angry, and she must've, for when he said that, she relaxed further, and he dared to brush his fingers against hers, clasping them gently and loosely. 'What you've done… I've no words, Hypatia. Are you all right?' She searched his own gaze, pondering her response, before finally shaking her head. 'Let's back to the house. A cup of tea will always set one right. We can discuss…everything.'

'The pigs—'

'We will certainly discuss them too. We won't leave them thus much longer, but we need to make a plan, and I suspect, enlist what help we can find.'

'Very well,' she agreed, somewhat begrudgingly, allowing him to fully take her hand and lead her away, though she threw one last despondent glance at the open doors of the building beside her as they passed.

Thorn glanced in too, his fury mounting again,

though he shoved it away, somewhat safe in the knowledge his wife had taken care of those responsible.

And here I thought the house would be our greatest task to undertake, not the rescue of however many pigs are still alive in that terrible place.

'Thorn,' Hypatia said mournfully once he'd brought them back to their mounts, though he inexplicably refused to let go of her hand, so instead he just waited as she grabbed her horse's reins, and then he took his own. 'The tea will be rather disappointing I fear, it'll be the remnants of this morning's.'

He couldn't help but laugh, somewhat startling her, and he shook his head apologetically.

'It will suit perfectly,' he reassured her.

And seemingly content with that, she allowed him to walk her back to Gadmin Hall.

To our...new home.

Hm.

'So that is where we stand,' Hypatia sighed, staring down into her cup of tea whilst Thorn sipped his; not the worst he'd ever had, by far. 'Perhaps thirty acres of land left, the buildings, three horses, a cart, an old carriage which barely survived the journey here, and three staff whom we can trust. Two beds, one dining table, four good chairs, assorted old bits such as the screen currently in my room, some cracked water jugs, a near-empty larder, two sets of linens, and however many pigs have survived that hellscape.'

'You forgot to mention the near-complete tea-set, and bits of crockery,' Thorn said wryly, managing to extract a weak smile from Hypatia. 'I am sorry, I had no idea…it was this bad. Everything the solicitors gave me, the reports, the rest of it… I knew even the old earl inherited debts, and that he'd had to make hard choices to remain some manner of afloat, and then there was his passion for pigs, and his illness. I knew it was grim, however not quite so grim.'

'Warren probably made a friend of whoever came here to tally and evaluate it all. And the rest… Your predecessor did what he could, as you say, and it wouldn't have perhaps been so grim without that vermin stealing and swindling for—as far as I could tell—the three years he's been here. The poor earl, he had no idea, he just…'

'I know,' Thorn said gently, feeling a tug in his own heart for the previous earl, who'd suffered a long illness in mind and body by all accounts, and been apparently fodder for a swindler. 'He will get his comeuppance, I am sure.'

'We would be surer of that, and know he'd never harm another soul if I had kept my wits about me—'

'Hypatia,' Thorn stopped her, softly, but with enough force and seriousness she couldn't but heed him, truly. 'Seeing what had been done, I would not have kept my wits about me either. You did well. What Warren did was… The law will not let it stand. We will see to it. But neither could you be certain he hadn't made a friend of the magistrate. You prevented more harm being done, and so we must trust that the law will find a way. If it doesn't, in time, when we have more funds, we can hire an investigator. Most of what he took is likely gone, the damage done, but I promise, we will not let his misdeeds go unpunished.'

Hesitating for a long moment, Hypatia wrestled with his words, finding some peace or sense of it; best she could. Balance, justice, rightness, in an untidy outcome.

'We'll have rent from any tenants who wish to remain on the land that pathetic excuse for a human didn't sell,' she said finally, half changing the subject, and half not. Still not fully accepting of her own choices, yet moving forward nonetheless. 'Though I've a feeling we've more surprises to come. There was so much which didn't add up in the papers, and I've not had time to untangle it all.'

Thorn suspected as much as well—men such as Warren rarely satisfied themselves with one or two schemes when they had such a victim in their grasp—and from what Hypatia had told him, if he was content selling off land and livestock, pocketing the profits, taking all but shillings of the tenants' rents for himself, he was content getting up to much more repugnant mischief.

But that was neither here nor there right now, though a more responsible man would've disagreed. What was important right now was that Hypatia know...

'I am in awe of all you've done thus far, Hypatia,' he said most seriously, and yet again she looked up at him as though he'd grown hundreds more heads, like a creature of old. 'I have been trying to think of what I was expecting, but I can tell you in all honesty, it wasn't to return here and find you'd taken charge of everything.'

'But you're not angry.'

'Why should I be? If anyone should be angry, it is you. I sent you here... Knowing the place was in disrepair, but even had it been the most glorious estate in the kingdom, I should've been with you. And when I said you were to do what you would with the house... Idiot that I was, I meant make it your own, put up some curtains or...something. Not clamber on roofs to fix them.'

Thorn said this with a smile, but Hypatia coloured deeply, mistaking his words as rebuke.

'You're right, I shouldn't have,' she said, almost shamefully. 'Waited, as I used to, only I thought I could do it, and it felt like an adventure, and I've never—'

'Hypatia,' he said, as gently as he could, placing his hand on hers, forcing her to look at him again. When she did, he saw many things, understood much more of her than he had but moments ago. 'Do not misunderstand me. I am not angry, nor displeased. I am astonished, and impressed. I am likely the only earl to boast a roof-climbing countess. I should be angry,' he noted, with a very clear reassuring smile. 'That you would endanger yourself so. But if it was an adventure, and you wished to do it, and you enjoyed yourself, well, I am glad. Still, the fault is mine, at sending you here to deal with a mess that is not yours. You have in but a few short days, saved me more work than I'd ever know how to do, and as we're on the topic of my shortcomings, Langton said something about you bringing funds?'

'I had some savings,' she told him, taking back her hand, downing her tea, and pretending her admission signified nothing. 'Ten pounds. Now we have three.'

'You shouldn't have. *I* should've thought, given you funds for the journey, and this place, before sending you off. I'm sorry. You shouldn't have had to use your own money.'

'How could I keep it and what should I keep it for when this place needs so much? Though I did keep two pounds. Do not take this ill, however, I need something in the event you decide to be rid of me. Or worse.'

Thorn thought briefly of promising he would never do anything of the sort, yet he knew very well how cheap promises could be, and if it made Hypatia feel safer, more comfortable, he cared not one whit. In fact, he'd much rather she'd have kept her ten pounds, and perhaps taken his fortune too—if he'd had one—just to be certain.

I would pay any price for her freedom to always be hers. I will.

For now, however, he had to keep focused on the task, and important matters at hand.

'I will pay you back.'

'We are married, Thorn. You'll see me taken care of in time, but for now, our resources must go to saving this place so we may live, and those loyal to this house may live. Unless you wish to take it all from here, in which case I understand.'

'I… I don't,' he said quietly, feeling as though someone had come and hit the back of his head—and perhaps heart too—with a mighty rock.

He couldn't quite comprehend all she said, and the simplicity with which she continuously proclaimed it, and perhaps that was his own past coming to play—be it in feeding his general distrust of people's words and promises, or making him question why anyone would want to live such a life of drudgery as this if they had a choice—or perhaps it wasn't.

Trust. Marriage. We. Not alone.

Perhaps it was simply that since the beginning of this ordeal, adventure, fever dream—whatever his new life was to be called—there had always been one certainty in Thorn's mind. That he would be alone. The debts, the crumbling earldom, they were his to right, though they never should've been his to right. It was that same inexplicable sense of duty, to a stranger, to an old man who'd been alone, that had seen him do all he had until now, and he might've done it gladly, except now he saw he did not have to do it alone, and he was…

Grateful. Beyond measure or words, to this woman who sits by me now.

To boot, in the light of the afternoon sun, streaming through the diamond-pane windows, reflecting off the blanket of ivy outside, and the wood inside, Hypatia seemed to him then the most stunning creature he'd ever seen. He was finding her more fascinating, more beautiful by the minute, and something told him he should be wary of that, lest he mistake an offer of aid, partnership, their contract, for something else neither had any need nor desire for, because at the end of all this, they might be married, husband and wife, but they would never be *husband and wife*. Working towards a common goal now—a liveable home and income—did not negate their initial deal; which promised both of their freedoms.

All that notwithstanding, Thorn reasoned that he could very well allow himself to be fascinated by the glint of her freckles, and the lightness of the tips of her eyelashes, and the way the shadows around her throat moved when she breathed, and he—

'I don't want to do this alone, Hypatia, if you are willing to help,' he said finally, clearing his throat, and downing his own tea. 'It is only that I never expected anything but to be alone. When you agreed to marry me, I thought you'd want your own life.'

'We agreed to be business partners,' she said, a slight frown between her brows, and he swore he heard the tiniest little clink inside his mind; a cog setting itself into place, as he understood the mechanism of Hypatia just a little bit better. He breathed a little easier too, knowing they were in agreement still; of the same mind. 'Perhaps some day I shall find a better occupation, something I wish to do with my life, however, for now, if this place should fall, we shall be destitute.

And though I believe you would see me taken care of, if I can help, I will. This is my home now. So we shall make a plan, and be the best pig farmers this country has ever seen.'

'Mayhaps we settle for the county in the first instance,' he grinned, that notion of *we*, of *partnership*, of being less alone, ever more tantalising and foreign with every mention.

'The county today,' Hypatia agreed with a smile. 'The country tomorrow.'

'Very well then, my lady. As you bid it, so it shall be.'

And as they sat there, and began making plans, *together*, Thorn had the queerest sensation that whatever Hypatia were to bid him, he would see it done.

Rather than that being a terrifying prospect as it might be for some, he found it incredibly invigorating and reassuring.

Chapter Seven

'So… Where do we go from here? That is unless today
has been the proverbial feather to break the horse's back
for any of you, and you wish to leave, which would be
understandable,' Thorn said, glancing first at Henry
and Langton, then at her, as if extending that offer to
Hypatia too, which was absurd, because she thought
they'd already discussed that this morning, and she'd
made it clear she wasn't going anywhere.

*What is absurd is how it reassures you, being given
that choice again. Always.*

*How it makes you appreciate and trust him all the
more.*

Even if his asking again was perhaps more to do with
his continued doubts she *would* remain, which she supposed was akin to growing pains, as they got to know
each other; she was certainly truly realising the scope
of all there was left to learn of each other. Which was
entirely normal, yet somehow surprising also, considering that from the first few minutes of their acquain-

tance, she felt as if she'd gotten the measure of the man; her husband.

However, the measure is only a small part of the full knowledge.

Indeed it was, and so far today she'd learned a great deal more of him than she'd known yesterday; as he likely knew more of her, or so she hoped. She felt she also saw Henry and Langton with better clarity, but then spending twelve hours tending to one hundred and three pigs and clearing as much as they could of at the very least one year's worth of neglect, couldn't fail to teach you more of anyone, as any adversity couldn't.

They were far from finished. Today they'd only managed to return the pigs' quarters to something further from squalor; to sort the animals and lodge them with others of similar condition, and hopefully, to reassure them that their worst days on this earth were past.

For all of them, it had taken strength beyond anything they'd required for a while—that much had been clear—to not retch, or cry, or exclaim in horror every second. To mourn or rage every time they turned a corner, opened a new pen, shifted some beasts, and found another mound of endless refuse, or the remnants of a lost swine. The struggle to remain focused on the task and to not be affected by what they found was in all their eyes, and shaking heads, as they moved along, pen by pen, inch by inch, their faces covered with scarves and cloths.

They'd broken only for water on occasion, and to

light lamps once the sun had finally set, allowing themselves food and rest only now—a spot of cheese, bread, and cider, sitting at the worn but comforting oak slab of a table by the kitchen's fire. They'd done what they could today, washed up best they could and discarded what old things Henry had dug up from somewhere— smock-frocks, boots and the like—though what they'd swum through still hung in the air, on their skin, and on their clothes. Hypatia—and she was sure the others shared the sentiment—might've sworn loyalty to any supernatural being in exchange for a proper warm bath; however, she knew that was not in the cards for tonight.

Perhaps tomorrow.

Or I shall find some stream to bathe in, I'm certain we've one of those somewhere, and that would be an adventure.

And there will be laundry to be done; I've only two dresses left unmarred and all our bedlinens will need refreshing very soon...

Another problem for tomorrow; or perhaps tonight, as the question of hiring more staff would need to be posed before long, as regarded the house, and the farm.

'I've worked 'ere ten years,' Langton said, tearing Hypatia from her thoughts, and bringing Thorn's attention away from her, which felt like both a relief and a loss. 'Weren't no one but the old earl who'd give me work, and I'll not leave now. I want t'chance to make things right, as we didn't this past year,' he added, looking to Henry, who sat with his head bowed, eyes fixed on an empty cup of cider.

'Joseph is right,' Henry agreed quietly, meeting Thorn, then Hypatia's gaze. 'We sat by, and did nothing as Warren thieved and mistreated those beasts. We knew he couldn't be trusted, even as the earl lived, but remained silent, too scared to lose our own places. We knew Warren had his friends hereabouts, including the magistrate, and that man who came when the earl died, but still, we might've spoken to the earl before, or sent word to his solicitors so someone might help, but we just…waited, and kept quiet. If only for that, we should not be permitted to leave until we've atoned, but in the end, Gadmin Hall is the only place I've ever felt was home, so if you can forgive us our inaction, we shall remain as long as you'll have us.'

Thorn nodded, then looked to Hypatia, as if to reassure her that in the end, she'd done right, not going to the magistrate at least. She did feel *somewhat* better, though questions swirled of where they should go with all their claims, and what to do with a magistrate such as that in the environs, serving the community.

Questions for later.

She smiled, and dipped her chin instead, acknowledging Thorn's point, and he quirked his head, raising a brow, as if telling her that he would follow her lead again, as concerned Joseph and Henry.

'I've never been a servant,' she said flatly, and Thorn frowned. When she turned to Joseph and Henry they too were frowning, looking most confused. 'I've not lived your lives,' she continued. 'But I can understand not wishing to upset a status quo which sees you fed, clothed, housed, and safe. I was angry, that none of you said anything, that you allowed this to happen, I'll not deny it. However, I see that even had you tried... A man such as Warren has the ability to dig their claws into their victims most profoundly. Had you spoken up, you might've lost all, and still not succeeded in your aim. I understand that is not a risk you were prepared to take, and it is not my place to judge either of you. If Tho—the earl is of the same mind, I for one would be glad if you both stayed.'

'Indeed,' Thorn agreed.

'Thank you,' Langton and Henry said, only slightly off-unison.

'So...now we have two employees,' Thorn said, with a wry smile. 'Hopefully Ian will agree to remain as well, so there's a start.'

'Ian'll stay,' Langton told them. His tone suggesting that like he and Henry, Ian had nowhere else he'd rather go; no one else to give him a chance but the Earls of Gadmin. Old or new.

'We'll need more help in the house,' Hypatia said after a moment, hoping Thorn wouldn't be offended by her taking charge again. However, considering his words this morning—*was it only this morning?*—and his acceptance of her help all day, without argument though with some surprise, she wagered he wouldn't begrudge her stepping in. 'Perhaps a maid or a house-keeper, whichever would be most useful as I don't think we've the funds for both just now.'

'A maid would be less expensive,' Thorn shrugged. 'But that would give you more work in the house, Hypatia.'

Was he leaving the choice up to her? She wasn't sure, but it certainly felt like it. Though she wasn't entirely sure how *that*—being trusted, respected, and heeded—made her feel. Not that she thought about it too profoundly, recognising only that it was a very pleasant change indeed from having to hide her counsel and decisions behind pretty words, or discreet nudges.

'Unless we wish to employ a new bailiff, steward or manager, and I for one think that to be an expense we could do without,' she said carefully, waiting for a shoe to drop which never would, it appeared. 'I think I could be of more use with the farm, and estate, if you wish for the help. We can run it ourselves, once we get the lay of the lands, examine those missing books and ledgers we got back today—though it'll be a task untangling fact from fiction—and decide how best to proceed with what we have.'

'A housekeeper it is then, though whoever she is must be happy to do more than just a housekeeper's duties,' he agreed with a smile. 'Know you of anyone who might fit the bill in the environs?' he asked Langton and Henry.

The two shared a long look, both digesting the queerness of this scene—an earl and a countess sitting at the table, making plans *with* their staff—and thinking of options.

Thorn and Hypatia waited, and after a while, Henry stared at Joseph most insistently, and the other relented.

'There's a cousin o' mine,' he sighed reluctantly. 'Over in Tonbridge, doin' some odd jobs, but things is gettin' 'arder, as she 'as a young marm, girl's three now, and no 'usband. There's maybe others, an advert—'

'Is she a hard worker?' Thorn asked, unfazed by the revelation of the woman's situation, which made him go up in Hypatia's esteem, that little bit more.

'Aye,' Joseph said.

'And she wouldn't be uprooted, or feel a loss coming here?'

'I'm the only family she 'as left.'

'Well then, we shall bring her here if she wishes for the position,' Thorn decreed. 'But be sure she knows—and be sure you both understand—what we are asking is for everyone to do more than would otherwise be expected. Which I know you both and Ian have been for a while now, and we shall do our best to compensate you fairly, however it won't be tomorrow this house, this estate, will be running as smoothly as they should be.' Henry and Joseph nodded. 'One matter decided then. Look at us.'

'We'll need to examine the tenant farms and other lands we still hold,' Hypatia said, having allowed herself a small moment to smile. 'To determine where our primary funds need to be concentrated, and what revenues we will have before we can make many more decisions on expenditure. We need to see what fields can still be used for crop and feed, what if anything remains in any stores… We'll certainly need at least one person to help with the pigs. Someone who can help us build some shelters, and renovate the farm buildings. We will likely have to call a veterinarian, and that will be an expense I suspect. We should keep some funds aside too, for clothes and more hands when it comes time for us to get to market. The original thirty purchased five years ago are listed as '*Glosters*'—I think they are called other such things as well—and from what I saw so they fit the few descriptions of such I've found. The old earl went to great lengths to fetch them all from Gloucestershire himself, selecting each one carefully so they would be all he posited such pigs could be. According to what little I've been able to find, they are excellent animals. Maintaining such a good quality product, in time, I believe we could make a name for ourselves. The earl saw something in these beasts, and perhaps, he was not so eccentric as people said, but rather ahead of his time, or perhaps not, as there are many others seeking to do similar things. Perhaps he merely ran out of time, or money, he did wager most of what he had left to go fetch them, or it was his will or health that failed, but he thought this endeavour could be the thing to restore this place, and I do not think he was so very wrong as others made out… Apologies, I am getting ahead of myself.'

Blushing slightly, she took a sip of cider, glancing over at Thorn, who regarded her again with that confounding and blinding thing in his eyes she didn't recognise.

Henry and Langton were no help, they just looked amused, and surprised, but then perhaps any confusion was aided by all their exhaustion and the late hour.

'There's a couple lads in the village who could 'elp,' Joseph said finally, breaking the odd silence. 'Used to workin' farms, but 'aven't seen work in a few months. Danny and Fred,' he added, looking to Henry.

'Fred would be good for the building,' Henry agreed. 'And Danny's good in the fields. If you've the coin for both, they'd be worth it.'

'Then we'll have them both,' Thorn agreed. 'The countess and I will inspect our lands over the next few days, and tend to the pigs. We'll hire our new people, and go from there. As for the rest… Perhaps we could meet weekly, see where we stand, and what we need?' The two other men looked to each other, confounded again, before shrugging and nodding. 'Excellent. In the meantime, Langton, we'll trust you to keep us all fed as you have, and Henry, the house is yours until further notice.'

'Very well, my lord,' Henry said.

'Thank you,' Langton added, Henry nodding in agreement.

'Well then, I think that's enough of a plan for one night, and we all need some rest before we begin again tomorrow. So thank you, both of you, and I hope… I hope we can all make Gadmin Hall into something we can be proud of.' The others nodded, and Hypatia and Thorn rose, Thorn gesturing the others to sit and finish their meal or conversation, which they did reluctantly. 'Good night, all.'

'Good night, my lord, my lady,' they both said, half bowing awkwardly as they remained seated.

Hypatia smiled, then grabbed a candle and set it in a holder before lighting it, and followed Thorn as he made his way out, though he stopped just outside the doorway.

'I've just realised, I've no idea where I'm to be laying my head tonight,' he chuckled.

'I'll show you to your room.'

'Well, here it is,' Hypatia said, opening the door to Thorn's room, and going to light the two candles she'd left in here—one by his bedside, the other on the mantel—so he could see it for all it was, and wasn't.

He wandered in slowly, his eyes flitting over the moth-eaten curtains, antique four-poster bed set up with the best of what linens and pillows there were, moth and time-eaten rug, and small jug and basin set on a miniscule table.

She'd done her best to make it comfortable, and she was glad to see his bag had been brought up, his clothes set out in the trunk at the foot of the bed, but she wondered if perhaps he was disappointed to find her summation of their diminished state not so off the mark.

'I can light a fire,' she offered, as he wandered to the bed, and brushed his hands over the sprig of rosemary and lavender she'd left on his pillow. 'I've been comfortable without, but there is a draught, especially if the winds pick up tonight.'

'I'll be comfortable, I'm sure,' he said gently, looking over at her. 'If not, I am very capable of lighting a fire myself.'

'I'm just next door. You've what was a dressing room or study through the other door,' she added, nodding towards the one to the right of his bed. 'But there's nothing in it, I fear, not even the spiders and other beasties we found, we did clear them out before you arrived.'

'Company I shall certainly not miss.' Hypatia smiled, and so did he, nodding absent-mindedly before sitting on his bed. She was about ready to go find her own when he spoke again. 'If I did not say it earlier, you astonish me, Hypatia,' he said quietly, before looking over at her, again as if trying to decipher her; a look she knew very well, though it didn't feel so horrid when Thorn looked at her thus, rather than strangers, acquaintances, or even family. 'And I want to give you another chance, as downstairs, before the others, you might not have dared to make another choice. You left a life of forced labour, or forced care, and now I'm asking you to do the same, in a different, but extremely demanding manner. I offered you escape, not to become a pig farmer.'

'Thank you, Thorn. I do…appreciate your offer. But as I said before, I'm not going anywhere. And there are worse things than to become a pig farmer.'

'Not most people's dream, I suspect.'

'Perhaps not, but then I never had many dreams, beyond escape.'

He frowned slightly, as if that revelation again gave him another piece of the seeming puzzle she presented, then nodded, not ignoring it, but storing it away for later—or never—perhaps.

'How do you know so much about all of this anyway?' he asked. 'Pig-shelters, and crops, and all the rest… I've been trying to get a handle on it since I was told what I was to become, and only understand perhaps half.'

'A house is a house, and a farm, well, I had no notion really, but I read some books after I agreed to marry you. Brought more with me, and there were a few hidden about here.' He quirked his head, smiling a smile she couldn't quite decipher. 'I didn't even have a chance to ask,' she said, changing the subject for the moment felt a little unsettling for her liking. 'How your farewells were. If you managed to sort whatever business you had to.'

A slight shadow passed across his face, and it wasn't due to one of those nasty draughts slipping through the still open door, and moving the flame beside him.

'In all honesty, I thought it would be harder,' he told her. 'Maybe I was just ready to start afresh.'

'Did you have many friends? Or perhaps a sweetheart? I didn't even ask that either,' she realised, frowning slightly.

'I was rather a solitary creature,' he said, with a sad huff of a laugh. 'I had a good apprentice, who became a friend, and I knew people, only I never…created ties, I suppose, despite living in the same cottage where I was born, and being around the same people I was all my life. Strange, isn't it?' he asked, and she nodded, knowing that feeling very well. 'As for a sweetheart… Once, there was a woman. But that is a long tale, and not one for a night when we're both barely still holding on our feet.'

'I'll leave you then,' she said, moving towards the door. 'Good night, Thorn.'

'Is there anything that scares you, Hypatia?' he asked blindingly clearly, and frustratingly simply, before she could fully depart, and close the door.

She thought about giving him a non-answer, or not answering at all. But then she thought, they had a chance, the two of them, that not many had; the chance an odd sort of instinctive safety between them provided, to be honest, to the extent that their own strength allowed them.

'To be trapped in a cage so long it moulds my flesh and soul. Of never taking chances, of waiting any longer, and never becoming.'

'You took a chance, marrying me. The fate which scares you is therefore already impossible.'

'What scares you most, Thorn?' she asked, turning back to him, her heart still smarting from the reassurance and hope of his words.

'You.'

Uncertainty filled her heart, drowning out the rest, as she felt both the wound of his honesty, and the skipping of her heart at his confession.

Knowing she would not be able to untangle the *whole* truth of his meaning, nor have the mind nor heart to face whatever it might be, she nodded, and left to find the comfort of her own bed.

I think perhaps I should fear you too, husband.

Chapter Eight

Though Thorn wasn't unaccustomed to hard work, nor what many would consider inhospitable and gruelling hours, he found that first day at Gadmin Hall had had rather more of an impact on his far from delicate constitution than expected. He might've blamed the diminished hours of sleep he'd been afforded—perhaps three or four, by the time he'd settled into bed, only to be woken by Henry just before dawn—except he'd slept profoundly, and dreamlessly, and had many such a short night before, and never been the worse for wear.

Likely it was just the magnitude of his life's upheaval which was finally impacting him; not aided in the least by the magnitude of the work still ahead, the mounting distraction of confusing inklings resembling feelings towards his wife, and his own apparent new propensity for late-night confessions such as that which he'd made last night. It was naught but the truth, and he'd been attempting to match Hypatia's honesty with his own, to continue their partnership as it had begun—

with such stark and unreserved, refreshing candour—however, he felt somehow he'd injured her, and at the same time, revealed something of himself he'd not had the time to fully consider, or digest.

Which was that Hypatia was rapidly becoming a strong and unalienable presence and necessity in his life, as though she'd always been there, even while he continued to discover new facets and aspects of this stranger he'd agreed to share something of a life with. And her becoming such a strong and unalienable, such a natural and vital presence, was rather unsettling for a man who'd been content his whole life to be as independent as one could be.

Yes, he'd loved Helen, and sought to bring her into his life; however, her betrayal had forced him to face the fact that he'd never *needed* her in his life. It wasn't that he'd thought their life together would just be him, continuing as before, with Helen as some accessory, however, he'd never quite felt Helen's presence as he did Hypatia's—but again, that was likely down to the circumstances of everything, and Hypatia was terribly clever and headstrong, and hard-working, and merely interesting on the whole. As for anyone else in his life, well, beyond his father, Frank, then Malek, well, it was as he'd said. He'd not really sought to create ties with anyone. Before the betrayal, he'd been busy, work consuming most of his days, and well, he'd felt he had *enough* in his life. Few friends, but good ones. And perhaps, yes, there was a sense… He knew what loss could do; how it could transform someone. He'd seen it with his father; with himself, after the betrayal. He'd become someone angry, and resentful, and he hadn't liked himself. All that compounded so that he'd had neither the heart nor need to go seeking out more people to bring into his life.

So really, it was only the fact he'd been alone some time now, along with the circumstances of everything, that was unsettling him slightly, and not that he feared he was beginning to need Hypatia, nor terrified of what it might be like to find himself alone yet again, or worse, betrayed again.

Right. Only the circumstances.

Really, he was according far too much thought to this generally, even regardless of all that needed to be done in order to ensure any and all of them here at Gadmin Hall could eat tomorrow. If Hypatia could appear at breakfast, looking unbothered, annoyingly bright and *en forme*, ready for the day ahead in the best of her few gowns—a horrid creation whose colour fell somewhere between old mustard and eels—well then, he could carry on with his day, and life, without preoccupation. So he had, enjoying breakfast with her before readying themselves to set off on their explorations of Gadmin Hall's estate.

Hypatia had had the foresight—though he didn't want to think of *when* she'd had the time—to prepare a list of parcels, farms, and areas to be visited, in order of priority, with what the ledgers and records indicated they should find at each place. As he'd followed her out to the horses, sliding on his hat which he felt gave him *somewhat* of the air of a country gentleman—if only because he'd chosen to pair it with the best of his everyday attire that he'd once worn to visit gentlemen's houses for work—he'd wondered again what might've become of him if he'd chosen anyone other than Hypatia for a wife, or found no one at all, but as soon as the morning's dew-strewn breeze had hit his face, he'd dismissed such thoughts as the sort of *preoccupations* which he'd previously sworn off.

That dismissal had stood fast most of the morning thus far, as they'd been quite busy indeed, muddling through the mess they found—untidy fields, parcels not where they were meant to be or long sold, mistrusting tenants not so happy to meet them, and fields or pastures being used by mysterious parties yet to be discovered—a mess worse than they'd hoped for, though admittedly, those *preoccupations* crept through with every efficient note, conversation, or plan Hypatia made, leading the charge. Much like last evening, at times she would take the lead without question or hesitation, and at others, she would seem to remember herself, and that he was meant, according to society and certain beliefs, to be her lord and master, so she would wait, and he would nod and smile, and silently entreat her to continue on her productive and merry way. Then they would be off again, in companionable silence as they explored their lands, and enjoyed the pleasant breeze and sunshine, and the preoccupations would be dismissed for a while longer.

Now, as they came upon another tenant farm the preoccupations and gratitude crept in again, as Hypatia dismounted, and led the charge searching for the inhabitants amidst a dilapidated assortment of middling-sized stone buildings, among which fussed some chickens and a mongrel, and the tinkling of goats' bells could be heard.

'Hello?' Hypatia called, as both of them searched for more human signs of life. 'Is anyone about?'

'They might be in the fields like the first,' Thorn offered, and Hypatia nodded. 'Then again perhaps not,' he added, when a flash of something to his right caught his eye, and he turned to find a young lad of about ten staring at them, a bucket of water in his hand. 'Good morning.'

The boy narrowed his eyes, and Hypatia turned to examine him too.

'Hello. I'm Hy—the Countess of Gadmin and this is my husband, the earl. Are your parents or whomever is in charge of this farm around, please?'

'Maaaaaaaaa!' the boy called, and Thorn smiled to himself, as Hypatia quirked her head, studying the lad as though a curiosity. 'Maaaaaaa!'

'Why are you shoutin' down the yard, Theo?'

sounded another voice from behind. 'Have you got that water or—?'

Whirling around, they found a tiny wren of a woman, covered in flour, eyes as wide as Theo's.

'Good day, Mrs Hampton is it?' Hypatia smiled, heading for the woman, hand outstretched. 'I'm Lady Gadmin, it's a pleasure to meet you, and this is my husband. We were wondering if we could have a word with you and Mr Hampton?'

The wren blinked, took Hypatia's hand to shake it, then realised halfway through doing it *what* she was doing, then tried to correct and curtsey, so that it ended up looking like some formal court greeting—or so Thorn imagined one might—albeit with floured hands and muddy shoes.

'Of course, my lady. Theo, get yer father. Lord Gadmin, my lady, if you'd follow me, I can offer you some tea, and I've a rhubarb tart if you'd like, or biscuits.'

'That sounds lovely, thank you,' Hypatia said, a smile in her voice, as she and Thorn followed Mrs Hampton towards the cottage, set a little ways from the main farm buildings.

It was a sweet little home, surrounded by a small wildflower garden, larger planted areas for vegetables, and a few pear and apple trees.

''Tis not really fit for company,' Mrs Hampton hesitated, ushering them through the untidy, but clean space, littered with clothes, tools, and the occasional decorative piece such as an embroidered verse or some such. 'I'll have to have ye in the kitchen, we've set up my brother and his lad in the front room.'

'A kitchen is always the most welcoming place,' Thorn told her reassuringly as they made their way there. 'And closer to the cake.'

Mrs Hampton tittered a laugh, uneasy still, though he could tell she wasn't as uncomfortable as she might've been had he and Hypatia been more...*lordly*, he supposed.

A day if there ever was one that being a jest in earl's clothing—though I've not even the clothes—is a boon.

She led them on into the kitchen—warm with the sun, and love—strewn with all manner of food in various states of preparation—bread, jams, herbs, and so on—and settled them at the slab of oak much like that in Gadmin Hall's kitchen, before serving them some tea and rhubarb tart.

'So you've been here eleven years as I understand it?' Hypatia asked as she did, beginning this meeting much as she had the others.

'Yes, my lady. We were lucky, George—that's my husband—he took on the farm just a few months after I became with child, with Theo. So we were able to get the farm runnin' before we had a young 'un runnin' around if you understand.'

Both he and Hypatia gave non-committal smiles, and nodded, digging into their tart and tea; a welcome treat indeed.

'This is delicious, Mrs Hampton,' Thorn commented. 'The best I've ever had.'

'You're too kind, my lord,' the wren blushed.

'You must give me the recipe if you've the time before we leave,' Hypatia said, earnestly, Thorn realised, and he added that to what seemed to be now continuous mental notes which in time would compose a book: *On Hypatia*. 'I'm not much of a cook myself, but I'm sure Langton would be happy to try his hand.'

'Of course, my lady, I can tell ye, or my husband can write it.'

'Thank you.'

'My lord,' came a deeper voice, and Hypatia and Thorn turned to the doorway to find a formidably fearsome scrap of man. 'My lady.'

He seemed as others this morning had—angry, resentful, and embittered—though he hid it somewhat respectfully.

'Mr Hampton,' Thorn greeted gravely, rising, to offer out his hand.

Hampton appeared confused, but took it nonetheless, before settling at the table, and bidding his wife to do the same, though he partook of no refreshments.

'You wished to talk,' Hampton said bluntly, the *so then talk* contained in his tone; unspoken but unmissable.

'I'm not sure what you'll have already heard,' Thorn began slowly, glancing at Hypatia, who shone bright and steady, her eyes encouraging him to continue and take charge this time. 'Being new to this area, my wife and I are unsure as to how quickly news travels hereabouts,' he jested gently, though the Hamptons didn't react. 'Mr Warren has been dismissed.' Now that got a reaction—a smirk of relief and justice from Hampton, and a slow closing of the eyes in thanks from Mrs Hampton. 'Everything as regards the title, and my inheriting it and the estate, has been incredibly complex, and with the previous earl's illness, as we understand it, Mr Warren was left to his own nefarious devices. My wife and I are seeking to repair any ills done, and see that everyone prospers on these lands. And to be entirely frank, we are looking for help, neither of us being farmers by trade or upbringing.'

Hampton nodded, turning to his wife, who took his hand, and smiled gently, encouraging him as Hypatia seemed to Thorn.

And? How useful is noting such similarities?

'We knew Warren was up to no good,' Hampton sighed after a long moment, meeting Thorn's gaze again. 'But we've been here since my son was born. We weren't ready to leave, and had nowhere else to go. We tried to see the old earl, but couldn't, and we knew Warren had the magistrate's ear, so we did what we had to, and we paid, and we kept our 'eads down, and got my brother and his lad to come last year, and that was that.'

'Warren was overcharging the rents, and before the earl died, pocketing the difference,' Hypatia told the

Hamptons. It had been her *modus operandi* all morning—tell the whole truth—though Thorn was realising it was also part of who she was in every circumstance. 'When the earl passed, he kept it all. My husband and I will see justice done, somehow, once we find the best place to go to pursue it. As for what was taken... We might be able to recoup what was lost in years' time, or we might not, right now, all we've time for is getting things working again.'

'Why are you tellin' us this?' Hampton asked, confused, and angry, though unsurprised. 'Makes no difference now. What matters is what you plan to do next.'

'It does make a difference, Mr Hampton,' Hypatia said, unfazed. 'The calculations will take time, but for those willing to stay on, we will make reparations. Rents will not be collected until such time as the estate's debt to its tenants is repaid. When they are, rents shall return to what is fair. We also hope to discuss the possibilities of engaging help from you, or anyone who might be willing, as there is much to do to set things right. You farm barley and beets for instance?' Hampton nodded, regarding Hypatia as many did—including Thorn—with confusion and respect. 'Would you be able and willing to give us a portion of your harvests for feed? Depending on the amount supplied, we could offer pigs—alive or butchered, as you prefer, and manure of course.'

'Aye.'

'Excellent. There is also a matter of two parcels adjoining your eastern fields—we've not had time to in-spect, but if the trend from this morning continues, I will wager they've been left untended for years?'

'Correct.'

'And they are rather small, but were noted as hav-ing good soil. Were you to consider perhaps tending to them, and growing some turnips or other crops you might suggest, we could include them in the lease in return for a fifth of the harvests.'

'My lady, this is most—'

'Irregular, yes, we know,' Hypatia shrugged. 'As my husband said, we are not farmers. We can learn, but this is your home, as much as it is ours. You know how to tend to it properly, and you have as much a stake in making your farm thrive as we do. We mean to start as we go on. See to it that the whole estate works to-gether, towards the common aim of preserving, and enjoying the land we live upon. Our main focus will be on the pigs, and so we must rely on good people to help with all the rest. If this isn't agreeable to you, we understand, for we are asking a great deal.'

'It is agreeable,' Mrs Hampton said, with an insistent glare to her husband.

'Excellent,' Hypatia grinned. 'We've made similar offers to the other tenants thus far, and will continue to do so. As yet, we have two others who have agreed to stay, and the Greers unfortunately we discovered left.'

'Death in the family,' Hampton said roughly. 'Moved up north last we heard.'

'Most unfortunate,' Hypatia agreed. 'Thank you for letting us know. We will seek to find new tenants, therefore if you have any recommendations, do share. We hope to get as much in order as we can by week's end, so we can all begin anew. Perhaps we could come again, after that, and visit, see where we all stand.'

'We'd like that, my lady,' Mrs Hampton said gently. She glanced at her husband, hesitating, and he nodded after a moment. 'Ye should know, some parcels have been…used by others, we thought it was with the earl's blessing, but now I think…'

'We would appreciate you sharing any names, Mrs Hampton,' Thorn said as delicately as he could. 'We don't seek to make trouble, and would like to come to proper arrangements for the use of certain lands, but have no idea where to begin, and those who remained at the house don't have much knowledge of the situation either.'

'I'll write you a list of what I know,' Hampton agreed slowly.

'Thank you.'

'And, one last thing, if it isn't too much trouble,' Hypatia said. 'Could we borrow a goat or two?'

Thorn thought then, that if he'd had the funds to pay for some fancy portrait artist, he might've commissioned a painting of the scene then: the bewildered looks of the Hamptons, Hypatia's incandescent and contagious eagerness, and his own likely balancing amusement.

But I've not the coin, so I'll simply paint it to memory, just like that day in her parents' home. By the end of my life, I feel I shall have quite the series.

Days like no other; a wife like no other.

Chapter Nine

As they slowly ambled to the top of a gentle rolling hill, in the midst of one of many pastures that had long since been grazed, becoming more of a wildflower extravaganza, a haven for bees, crickets, and all manner of other creatures, Hypatia felt lighter than she had in perhaps her entire life, including childhood.

Their day thus far had been long, arduous, full of talking, negotiating, and disappointing discoveries. It was far from over—it was barely past two in the afternoon—and the next few days would be just as demanding; Hell, looking at how things stood now, it looked as if the next few years would be. And yet, as she and Thorn came to a stop in unconcerted unison, she didn't feel the weight of that demand, of that future, upon her shoulders as she'd felt every second of every day before now. Perhaps that made her callous; perhaps that just made her finally free. Either way, she was grateful for it.

She was grateful for the good people they'd met, not

easy, not forgiving, but good people, who seemed to be willing to join this strange sort of team she and Thorn were trying to form; and she was grateful for Thorn. For his easiness, his support, and his apparent appreciation of her taking charge. Of her, full stop, in fact.

She was grateful for this sunshine, for this breeze, and for this view.

'It's beautiful,' Thorn remarked, his eyes wandering over the rolling hills, pastures, fields, woods, houses, farms, and spires spread out before them as far as the eye could see. 'Essex has its charms, but I'll admit, I like these Downs.'

'They feel…welcoming.'

'Agreed,' Thorn smiled crookedly, glancing over at her. 'Did you always live in the city?'

'All my life. First Birmingham, then London. We'd sometimes go out to the country for this party or business thing of my father's, but never long. And I was not always given the opportunity to enjoy it. I've never seen the sea though,' she added, before Thorn could comment as she felt he might on her lack of pastoral pleasures. 'So in that I am jealous of your upbringing beside it.'

'I thought I'd miss it more. But it's so strange, with every passing minute, I feel more at ease, at home here than I did there. I wonder if some part of me never got attached. If it knew I would leave someday.'

'Destiny?'

'Something like that.'

'Do you miss your work?' she asked after a moment. 'Did you enjoy it?'

'I did,' Thorn smiled, nostalgia and memory filling his eyes as they studied the fast-moving, thickening clouds ahead.

'What kind of blacksmith were you? If that is even a question.'

'It is,' he chuckled softly. 'Though I don't know if there's a proper word for what I did, which was a bit of everything, really. Gates, fixtures, doors… The odd decorative fantasy, and piece of jewellery—though that was more for my own amusement and to work my skills. I could never claim to be a proper silver or goldsmith.'

'I should like to see your work someday.'

'You can now, just take off your glove,' he said breezily, but Hypatia frowned, stunned as she understood his meaning.

She shouldn't take it so to heart—obviously it meant little to him but to be a test of his skill, something perhaps to pass the time, and yet—for him to have made her wedding band…

'You made this?' she asked quietly, taking off her glove, and raising her hand to look at the band upon it, whose intricate ivy design she'd noticed and appreciated from the first. 'How?'

'Found someone willing to lend me their workshop for the night,' Thorn shrugged.

'Why?'

Thorn turned, mouth open as if to answer, then his eyes darted above her head, and a second later she understood, for the skies darkened and opened all at once.

'Into the woods!' he cried over the din of the sudden rain, pointing over his shoulder.

Quickly, they spun their horses around, and sped towards the woods just a few paces from the base of the hill.

The short ride into the relative shelter of the woods felt invigorating, or perhaps merely cleansing of confusion and slight emotional disarray; the rain, heavy and quickly soaking, was warm, and there was no thunder or lightning to contend with.

They slowed as they entered the protection of the ancient wood, where petrichor rose already from the humid and fresh space, populated with all manner of old, wise, and gnarly trees, along with young sprigs, flowers and ferns. Not venturing too far, just far enough for the deluge to become intermittent plops on their heads and shoulders, they glanced at each other, sharing a relieved, breathless laugh before they dismounted, wordlessly tying the horses up as the dim grey half-light suggested they might be there for a while.

Once they had, Hypatia wandered a few steps away to the almost edge of the forest, beech, birch, ash, and oak vying to shelter her as she wiped her face with her sleeve, then crossed her arms, and leaned back against an old oak's welcoming trunk. Beyond the limits of the wood, a blurred curtain obscured most of the landscape beyond save for pops of colour from the wildflowers at the base of the hill.

She felt more than saw Thorn lean against the trunk beside her, close, but not too close, just enough so that she could feel the heat emanating from him.

'I'd offer you my coat,' he said after a moment. 'However, I fear it is more thoroughly soaked through than yours, and would only worsen your state rather than improve it.'

'Perhaps I should offer you mine,' she grinned.

'I'd wager it is large enough. Where did you find that anyway? Despite your gowns, I cannot imagine even your mother or sister subjecting you to such sartorial choices.'

'Henry dug it up for me. Cleaned it best he could. Truthfully, I think it's perhaps the piece of clothing I like most of all in actual fact, so I'll thank you to keep your denigrations to yourself. Especially since it has kept me drier than yours has.'

'Fair point,' he said, before leaning in closer, pivoting almost so he stood perpendicular to her, his shoulder still holding him up against the trunk. Her arms dropped to her sides as his fingers ran along the droopy collar of the oversized and shapeless garment made from, well, she wasn't even certain, especially now, since all her mind could seem to register was his heat, and his proximity, and his fingers, and the sound of his breath. 'I shouldn't have criticised it, for now I see it suits you very well,' he added, his voice dropping to a more serious, sultry tone, not losing its jest, but rather his inherent lightness and spark shifting in melody.

'You don't have to be nice,' she told him, turning to meet his gaze. 'I'd rather honesty than false compliments.'

'I wasn't affording you one. I mocked it before I knew you liked it best, that it had been your choice. Knowing it was, and you do, makes me evaluate it differently. And I'll not lie, it makes you look like a farmer's wife.'

'Which is what I am.'

'Yes,' he smiled, that spark she'd liked from the first in his eyes again, along with a sprinkle of the other thing she couldn't name, and which was beginning to drive her a bit to distraction by its alien nature. 'I think it helped when meeting all those tenants today too. You look respectable, but not as though you're afraid of hard work.'

'I thought it might.' Thorn smiled again, his fingers still toying with various parts of her coat, and though she knew the conversation the heavens had seen fit to interrupt was better left in the past, she couldn't resist the temptation. 'Why did you make my wedding band?'

'And my own,' he said, levity and distraction colouring his voice again.

'Why, Thorn?'

He stopped, his hand not dropping, but fingers clutching lightly to one of the middle buttons on her coat, as his eyes met hers, sombre now, though still full of a life he couldn't contain if he tried; not that she would ever mind.

'I went to buy one,' he finally told her, and vaguely, she registered her breath was shallowing, in time with his; punctuated by the off-beat drip of raindrops from the water-saturated locks of hair, onto the tops of his cheeks. 'I stood in a shop, ready to do so, held some in my hands, but I realised... It didn't matter that we were entering into a business arrangement. The vows I would be taking meant something. I would mean them. I would be pledging my life to yours, and that *meant* something. When I call you wife, and you call me husband, that means something to me, it... I wanted...a demonstration of that. That despite it being business, I would still care for you, and protect you, and cherish you, and I wanted you to have something thoughtful. Something entirely yours. Something of mine.'

'Oh,' she breathed.

She felt, grounded, yet dizzy, caught in this hazy bubble they'd created, swirling in it, yet never more present and alive.

There was desire in that, she recognised it, felt it, warming her veins, tempting her closer to Thorn, but there was something else too, a profound strike to her heart; of having been touched by this man, her husband's thoughtfulness, his sense of care, and duty.

A strike such as she'd never felt before, and much like that unknown quantity that sometimes sparked in

Thorn's eyes, which by its alien and foreign quality, both fascinated and frightened.

'I didn't speak those vows lightly either, Thorn,' she told him, realising her mere *oh* was a bit lacking considering all he'd confessed to her. 'We never spoke of our beliefs, but I'll tell you now that though I don't believe in a grand, higher power, I believe in truth, and honour, and so I meant them too.'

He nodded, relief dancing in his eyes for a second as more drops peppered his cheeks, the light from the storm which may or may not have still been progressing—Hell if she knew—turning his skin almost translucent, like that of some ancient creature who might dwell in woods such as this.

One of the drops from his hair landed on his bottom lip, and she was so very tempted to claim it with her own lips, but she hesitated, her body vaguely leaning in closer to his, then falling back against the trunk, before she realised there was nothing really to stop her. He was her husband, after all, they'd discussed such possibilities, and when she glanced back up at his eyes, she found them affixed on her own lips, so she allowed herself to drift into him, millimetre by millimetre, as he curved inwards to her, the hand that had been toying with her coat drifting across her bodice, along to her waist, clutching her there instead, not tightly, but steadily.

The moment seemed to last forever, distance unchanging yet diminishing as even the drops falling from his hair slowed their pace, and finally she could feel his breath mingling with her own, the air between them warming, making her lazy, drowsy, yet vibrantly alive. And then his lips were there within reach, and she touched them with her own, brushing them against his soft ones, collecting that drop of water she'd longed to claim. She savoured it, and him, that lovely taste she remembered from the first, so tantalising yet already familiar, licking her lips before brushing her lips against his again, their noses bumping gently against each other as they did.

Brushes, and feather-light touches and exploration became tiny kisses, planted on each corner, each dimple, each line and millimetre of his lips—and hers—as their breathing shallowed and stilted evermore. Her tongue darted out between her teeth, and met his—quickly, on the top at first—then with a sharp inhale, and tighter clutch of her waist, as she grabbed a handful of his shirt in one hand, his soaked coat in the other, they deepened the kiss, delving into each other, dancing, teasing, learning, with tortuous slowness and exquisite intention. Mewls and pants and moans punctuated the slow tempo, coming from her, and him, and perhaps the groaning forest too, as he leaned into her, sweat, and sticky heat increasing her light-headedness, his weight reassuring yet unoppressive.

He shifted, stabilising himself better against the tree as he reached deeper into her mouth, and the hand at her waist drifted down, to her hip, then her thigh, clutching and caressing best he could through the layers of clothes—and she was inordinately grateful for the lack of layers, only the most basic for her.

She undulated into him, as he slid closer to her, and—

'Thorn?' she asked as he suddenly broke their kiss, sucking in deep breaths as she did too, though she felt somehow she had less air now than before, with him connected to her.

'You intimated only your portion was untouched,' he panted, licking his lips, and she blinked, her mind needing a moment to return from *lust-filled haze* to *processing*.

'Is that an issue?'

'No,' he grinned dangerously, shaking his head, his eyes, shining like silver in sunlight, affixed on her. 'I want to touch you. Feel your slickness on my fingers. May I?'

'Would you not had I said I hadn't been touched before?'

'I still would've asked, but perhaps more politely.'

'Is there a more polite way to ask that?'

Thorn's grin widened, and his hand shifted, masterfully gathering up her skirts to find that slickness he was apparently so curious about.

'I don't think there is,' he murmured, teasing her by resting his hand on her mound, and leaning in to pepper her jaw, her neck, and the notches by her ears with tiny kisses. 'Just as there's no polite way to ask if you pleasure yourself, Hypatia?'

'Yes.'

'Then show me how to please you,' he ordered, in the softest whisper anyone had ever spoken perhaps. 'Guide my hand.'

Well now.

That was…new. She'd never—

Just do it, Hypatia.

So she did. Releasing his coat, to slide her hand onto his, and guide it to her admittedly *very* slick folds, as he watched her, every tick of her pulse, every change in her eyes.

Parting her legs a little more, she opened herself to him, in every way, as his rough, but long gentle fingers delved into their prize. His own breathing laboured again, pupils dilating as they found the promised honey, running slowly, and mindfully, along her folds, inside, then out, past her bud, along her bud, then around the origin of it all. It was…

Astonishing, decadent, slightly awkward, admittedly, until they found a coordinated rhythm and ease of movement together, but as they carried on, him exploring her, his lips within reach, but refusing to kiss her whilst he learned her pleasure, and drove her on her instruction higher, and higher, to the drippingly sweet pleasures of ecstasy. Fingers tangling together, eliciting more sensation than she'd ever felt—alone or in company—he left no inch untouched, until finally, she guided his fingers inside, pressing them inside her tender flesh, and showed him how his thumb and others in conjunction could finish her.

So he did, with relentless determination, and exhilarating fascination, until her stilted cries echoed in the silent woods around them; her eyes never leaving his. He held her steady, his fingers still inside her, his body keeping her safe and close, until the last waves of delight became memory, and then he slowly removed his hand, letting her skirts fall as he licked his fingers clean.

And though there'd been many prior indications that her new husband was deliciously dangerous, and that there could be much of interest between them, it was only then that Hypatia truly understood just how dangerous, and delicious, this marriage could be.

'It stopped raining,' she said dumbly after a very, *very* long moment watching him.

'So it has,' he agreed, without looking. 'And we've much work to do. However, if you're agreeable, my dear wife, perhaps we should talk tonight of just what sorts of arrangements you might be happy to make.'

'I am agreeable.'

Thorn's smile then seemed to say: *yes you are*, and though she was hardly a girl, or a blushing maid in love, Hypatia felt like all of those things.

I am merely happy to have made a good choice of husband.

So she told herself, as she and Thorn put themselves

somewhat back together, and mounted their horses, and continued on their way, to finish their work for the day.

And I am merely pleased, perhaps, which is not so bad a thing, that my husband seems to...like me. In more ways than anyone ever has seen fit to.

No, that was not so bad a thing to be pleased about indeed.

Chapter Ten

'Have we any milk, Langton?' Thorn asked, likely looking as harried as he felt, given how the cook was regarding him, as he stood in the kitchen's doorway, darkness but for the moonlight behind him, his coat bundled in his arms like a babe, which wasn't *too* far from the truth of his current predicament. 'Having said that, I've no idea if cow's milk is appropriate given the situation.'

'And what situation might that be, milord?'

This one, Thorn said silently, his eyes communicating the loss at which he was, as he pulled back a corner of his coat, to reveal a tiny pink snout.

The things I do for my wife.

'Ah,' Langton said, ushering Thorn in, and pulling the chair closest to the fire away from the table so he could sit. 'I'm no expert on the rearin' of pigs, but I'd think cow's milk is as good as their mum's, though in the little ones it can give them some…upset. Not sure what else to give 'im as I expect he won't take to the teat?'

'Afraid not,' Thorn said, shaking his head. 'We found him beside a dead sow, she must've passed since the feed this morning, and the others had been taken under wing by another, but this little runt refused to go anywhere.'

Langton nodded sagely, and sadly, for no matter how much one knew about the rearing of pigs, it didn't take an expert of any sort to know runts, particularly those who refused to adapt, didn't stand a great chance in this world.

'I'll get a beaker and warm some milk for ye.'

'Thank you, Langton.'

Thorn sighed, his day—all of it, from joy, to desire, to laughter, to work, to confusion, to desperation, catching up with him as the fire warmed him from a chill he'd not felt till now.

Glancing down at the tiny creature in his arms, he wondered if he was cut out for any of this really. Being a farmer, holding a life such as this in his hands, knowing the likelihood of preserving it was slim; being responsible for so many lives lord of this manor as he was, husband to his wife as he was. When it had been merely an intangible idea—this life—even as he'd stood in the House of Lords and gone to balls and all the rest, it hadn't felt quite so daunting. When he'd been alone, unable to imagine what it would be like to take all this duty and responsibility on, in a sense, it had been easier. Now, as he lived it all, he couldn't help but bloody wonder if he was good enough, strong enough, capable enough. Enough, really.

He wondered if he was cut out for this life, for marriage, for—

'Here you go, milord,' Langton said gently, setting a beaker of warm milk on the table.

Thorn took it up, shifting so he could tempt the tiny mite to drink some; he may not know much about rearing babes of any kind, but he'd seen enough mothers of all species feeding their young to know the basics.

'Ye hungry yourself?'

'I am, though I'll wait for Hypatia, she shan't be long, I think. She was closing up for the night, but insisted I not wait to take care of this one. We managed to check on them all, and catalogue about half. Though until the veterinarian comes, who knows if the numbers will stand.'

'I've a pie in the oven, a nice bit of salt beef in it Ian dug up from somewhere b'fore he left, though best not to ask where. It'll keep till the missus—her ladyship— has come back.'

'Thank you, Langton.'

'The vet will be by tomorrow in the afternoon, and Danny an' Fred will be 'ere in the morn to await your orders.'

'Excellent,' he nodded, distracted by the piglet he held opening its eyes with a curious snort, before rooting at the beaker. 'There you are…'

'Her ladyship seems to know quite a lot about them critters, if she'll tell me what's best for it, I can see if I can find what's needed.'

'She very well might, Langton, however, I have taken charge of this one's care. Her ladyship shall not be burdened with it.'

Langton said nothing, but somehow Thorn heard the smile nonetheless.

It bolstered him somewhat, in his conviction that his choice had been the right one. When he and Hypatia had found the mite, tucked away in a corner by its mother, he'd known the choice they faced. End its life then and there, or try to save it. And he'd seen it in Hypatia's eyes, not a lack of courage in the face of mercy, but a hope that the life could be saved, and he'd also known that she'd taken care of enough, of too many, throughout her life already; she shouldn't have to tend to one more. Not if he could ease that burden, take that responsibility for her. So he'd swaddled the thing, and promised her he would do what he could.

So I shall.

His attention was stolen then by the runt, who had summarily finished his milk, and was rooting for more. Raising the beaker, Thorn signalled to Langton, who obliged, and so the creature resumed his meal.

'I suppose I should find you a name,' Thorn commented, as the little thing revived with every drop of milk, and warmth, and comfort.

'Not if ye intend to have 'im serve 'is purpose, my lord.'

'As much as I should say I do, so as not to waste a penny of this *investment* as I suppose he should be considered, I've the oddest feeling that this one... If he survives this, I fear I'll not send him to become bacon.'

Langton chuckled, and moved about, attending to something or other, whilst Thorn continued staring at his new charge, who quickly finished his second beaker and summarily drowsed back to a comfortable slumber.

'I think I'll have to get to know you first,' he told the runt. 'Before I name you. You cannot go through life with a name which won't suit you.'

'If only all this world were as wise,' came Hypatia's voice, and Thorn turned to find her as he'd been, standing at the kitchen door, the night framing her, the glow of the kitchen beckoning her in.

Despite any untidiness about her, she glowed, with vitality, and that same energy that had captured his attention in the garden. Made perhaps even more magnetic by the memories floating behind his eyes, of having seen her, tasted her, and felt her come undone; a delicacy he couldn't wait to experience again, if she would allow it.

'Unfortunately not all are so lucky as to be bestowed names which fit their character,' she shrugged, coming in, and closing the door, Thorn's eyes following, and realising as he did, that Langton had disappeared.

'Maybe it's just that some have their personality

change along the way. Though I'll admit, much too often it is I suspect a lack of care and attention which sees children bestowed with unsuitable names.'

'Or a need to fulfil some societal requirement, like naming your firstborn after your great-grandfather, though the poor thing is the farthest from a Hilary one could ever be.'

'There's pie in the oven, according to Langton,' Thorn told her with a smile, and she nodded, washing up, before dotting about the kitchen to see them served with steaming hot salt beef pie within minutes. 'Thank you.'

'We shall have to thank Langton,' she said between mouthfuls. 'This is most excellent.'

'Agreed.'

'Would you like me to take him so you can eat easier?' Hypatia offered, nodding towards the runt snoring in his arms.

I didn't know pigs snored.

'Not unless you wish to hold him, I can manage with the one hand.'

'Very well.' They both took a deep breath, settling into the comfortable silence and atmosphere, the food doing its work to restore them. 'Why did your parents call you Thorn?'

'Are you asking whether they suspected my character from an early age meant I should become the thorn in either or both of their sides?' he jested, and she chuckled.

He felt again, the pleasure it was to make her smile, laugh; to just…be near her.

You are tired, man.

'As my father told it, my mother's ancestors were Danes. And took the family name because they either lived by a thorny hedge, or a tower. She died in childbirth, so my father sought to carry her legacy on with my name, alongside his.'

One legacy I never truly knew, the other I was forced to leave behind; both of which I fear only the names remain.

It wasn't true, he knew, all his father's lessons, love, the memories shared of his mother, Thorn's own character, forged as surely as anything tangible by his father's hand, all of it and more, was his true legacy, and remained with him, to be upheld and honoured.

Still, some days, grief stole reality, to make itself more potent and powerful.

'I'm sorry, Thorn.'

'It's all right,' he reassured her, though it wasn't, and wouldn't ever be. 'At least I didn't feel her loss, only the lack. Not to say my father didn't try his best.'

'I'm sure he was a good man, for you are.'

Thorn nodded, swallowing the lump in his throat, before swallowing some more pie, and ale that Hypatia had served them.

'He was. Did everything he could so that I would never feel the lack, though I wonder if it is possible not to, past a certain age. He was a simple man, hard-working. I think… Maybe in some ways, I wanted him to know, I was grateful for all he gave me. Appreciated the magnitude of it, rather than merely taking it as my due. And that's why I worked hard to grow our custom. To better myself, my skills, my words, so that I could show him… I don't know.'

'That it would be in good hands. That he'd been a good father, to raise such a son.'

'Something like that. I'm sorry that your parents, your family, aren't…well, that you aren't close,' he said after a while, and Hypatia gave him one of her now familiar sad, but shrug-like smiles.

'They aren't terrible people,' she told him, pushing away her plate, sitting back, and cradling her ale on her lap. 'They never struck me, or mistreated me, and though in many ways they left me to my own devices, they never ignored me, acted as though I did not even exist. Money, success, it changes people. Especially those who know what life can be like without them, which was my parents' case. Though I'll admit, I don't… Some days I think my parents never wanted to be parents, they merely did what was ordained and dictated, hoping for an added layer of security. When I was young, very young, barely out of the nursery, I remember imagining I had parents like in the storybooks. Not the cruel ones who sent their children into dark forests to be eaten by witches, but the kind ones who sent armies to find their beloved offspring. I don't remember them ever feeling like…my parents. More like adults I lived with. I was given the best of everything, but never their…full interest. Perhaps they were disappointed, that I wasn't all they'd hoped to further their advancement in the world, or perhaps they didn't know how to be parents if not as their own had been. Given that my father was one of seven, working by the time he was four, and that my mother worked the looms, like her mother before her, until my father made his fortune… It was different for me, than it was for them. Either way, before long they started talking about the day I would take care of them, good girl that I was, and that day came soon enough though I don't think they saw it as having arrived. Then my sister came along, I was so excited at first, believing…'

'You would have a friend. Someone.'

'Yes. And I took care of her when she was little, and it was good, and lovely, and then I think my parents saw when she was about five or so that perhaps she could be something else, or more to them than I could, and that was that. We grew apart as they spoiled her, and prepared her for another life, but I still don't think… Much as they doted on her, I don't think they were ever parents to her either. She just learned to be what they wished her to as I did. It isn't that they are cruel, just… careless, in many ways.'

With a sniff, Hypatia shook her head, shaking off the thoughts, before sipping her ale; but he held onto them, onto this other piece she showed him, not lightly, he knew.

'At least your parents did you a kindness, with your name,' Thorn offered with a gentle smile. 'I cannot think of one more aptly named for such as your namesake.'

'You're kind, Thorn, though that is a mighty legacy to live up to. I did fare better than my sister, admittedly.'

'Epi?'

'A bastardisation of *Iphigenia*. Daughter of King Agamemnon, doomed to be sacrificed to Artemis. Though in some tales, the goddess saves her after demanding her life.'

'Maybe your sister will learn to write a better ending, and find a way to save herself from a fate I wager you fear for her. As you did.'

'Maybe,' Hypatia nodded. 'I should get ready for bed.'

'I didn't mean to—'

'I know, Thorn,' she reassured him, before rising, and clearing their plates. 'I just realised it's time for bed. It was a long day, and shall be another tomorrow.'

Coming back around to face him, she glanced down at the piglet in his arms.

'I think he's all the company I'll be having this evening,' Thorn admitted, letting his intense disappointment at that show, unabashedly. 'I daren't leave him alone for the night.'

Hypatia nodded, and made to leave, though she stopped at the edge of the three stairs leading up into the corridor.

'Regarding our earlier conversation, Thorn, when your new companion is ready to be left alone at night,' she said, looking him square in the eye, without hesitation or bashfulness. 'As I said that night in the gardens, I shouldn't mind enjoying your company. Given this afternoon's...*taste*, I think we might prove to be rather good bedfellows.'

He might've said something, but his mind had gone completely blank; he could only grin, which made Hypatia smile broadly and teasingly before she disappeared, and well, he supposed that was good enough.

'Now then, you,' he said to the tiny thing in his arms. 'I'd suggest you get well and on your own feet sharpish. For as much as I'm sure I can find time to enjoy my wife elsewhere, I find I've the mighty desire to do so in a proper bed, so that we might languish and lounge and please each other like the newly minted lord and lady we are.'

One day perhaps, I'll feel less odd at calling myself that.

One day I'll feel less odd about many things.

Chapter Eleven

Since the newlyweds' dashing escape to the country, we have been left bereft of any news of our favourite earl and countess, and can give no reports as to how they or the swine some posit were the previous earl's downfall, fare. While some might argue there are, given the recent political happenings and turmoil, more pressing and vital preoccupations, this writer feels a conclusion to their tale would be a welcome divertissement. London, the country, may not lack in entertainment, however one knows London at least is as bereft as I, for one can't fail to notice just how often the name Quincy has passed Society's finest lips of late; the youngest would do well to use her newfound notoriety as her brother-in-law failed to. As you well know, I for one will always champion any arrivistes seeking to summit this country's highest rungs.

Jack the Cat, Londoner's Chronicle, May 1839

The days which followed their woodland interlude, and the discovery of their tiny runt, were, if possible, fuller than the first Hypatia had spent at Gadmin Hall, but then, looking back, perhaps those hadn't been so full as they'd felt. Not that she minded the industriousness, the busyness, the long hours, the sweat, the muck, nor any of it really. Part of her wondered if she should; she'd left her old life to escape a forced labour of care, but she knew it wasn't at all the same.

This new life—despite its surprises—had been her choice, and she felt as if she was working to build something meaningful, that she could be proud of; her forced care of her parents and sister, without choice, without a voice, a say, even true appreciation, or meaningfulness—for no, she hadn't wanted any of it—was not the same at all. No, she hadn't dreamt of being a pig farmer, or a countess, or even a wife, but then as she'd told Thorn, she hadn't really dreamt of much. Once they got their enterprise functioning smoothly—as smoothly as one such could—she would have time, and means to perhaps discover what else she might want from life. For now, she was content to learn, and work, and discover, and solve problems which seemed to arise with every hour. She was content to dream of restoring Gadmin Hall's glory, and perhaps, growing closer to husband.

All in all, they made good progress over those few days, which made every aching muscle, every cut, every bruise, and every day without a proper bath, worth it.

The veterinarian came as promised, and delivered… news. Whether it was good or bad, remained to be seen, as the man himself—a sombre, but intelligent middle-aged man who'd only come to this part of the country a few years prior, and was as glad to see Hypatia and Thorn making changes as anyone else—had decreed. He spent nearly the whole day with them, looking at every pig, and checking not only their health, but also kindly advising on what purpose each would best serve, and how to get them into whatever shape they needed to be to do so. He spoke to them not patronisingly, but patiently, explaining it all as though they were students—which in many ways, they were—heartened each time Hypatia asked a question, or offered some slightly differing suggestion for review, according to what little she'd been able to read.

He took care of what animals unfortunately needed to depart this world, and gave them advice and medicines for others, with orders on general care and well-being moving forward. He didn't say much in regard to their discreet questions about other local owners and farmers, about anything he might've heard in respect to the goings-on at Gadmin Hall, though he did advise them on respectable markets and butchers nearby.

Danny and Fred, who arrived, ready to work albeit somewhat wary of the new, seemingly clueless and *un*-agriculturally minded earl and countess, were somewhat more talkative as the days passed. Hypatia might've taken their growing candour as a testament of trust, and perhaps it was, though she quickly discovered they were simply more of the talkative sort, which suited her very well. In between discussions of which fields to plant, sow, harvest, when and how, or what lands to use for the pigs—the closest first, as the poor creatures would need time to accustom themselves to freedom and fresh air—and what structures needing building for them, they would mention many things of note.

How Warren had apparently spread word that all the terrible things being done on the estate were the old earl's orders—or those of his representatives—including but not limited to the dismissal of any workers who disagreed with him. How everyone had already thought the old earl mad for going all the way to Gloucestershire to purchase thirty pigs, and sell off all he had to do so, and grow his herd, or how the place just wasn't worth the trouble for anyone since there were farms aplenty to be worked. They mentioned more industrially minded neighbours to the north; the older, more conservative aristocratic landowners to the west. They mentioned the best inns, the best shops, the best fairs and events, and even the best malthouses where one could, if one arrived early, be treated to a heel of bread and warm cider.

Hypatia took it all under consideration, just as she took everything those they hired and spoke to in the following days offered. She and Thorn visited the remainder of their lands and tenants, and with help from them, along with Danny and Fred, soon they had not quite a *full* roster of workers, but very nearly. Langton's niece Mary arrived from Tonbridge, with her young daughter Niamh, an adorable little sprout with a penchant for helping Langton in the kitchen, and a mop of blond curls Hypatia knew many would envy. Mary took charge of the house without hesitation nor question, apparently determined to prove her worth and skill despite her young charge, who others might not have welcomed so easily; however, as the saying went—not that Hypatia liked it in the least, the saying, that is— beggars could not afford to be choosers. And though Thorn and Hypatia weren't beggars yet, they were having to work extremely hard to ensure what funds they had were invested best they could be, be it in the farm, or the house.

So they did, making plans for each and both, working off their lists to deal with the most urgent matters— the roof, proper tools and equipment, more books to learn their new trade, workers, food—and also ensure they had some measure of security if they failed most spectacularly in their endeavours. They set aside some portion of funds in reserve to merely garner interest, another small portion to engage the solicitors to handle the Warren situation, and Thorn insistently set up an allowance for Hypatia, also paying back her five pounds already spent; a frugal life did not mean severely limited financial freedom for her, or so he vowed. They set aside some money in their minds for those matters less pressing—a new coach, some additional furnishings for the house, etc.—but otherwise, every penny was accounted for in accordance with the plans they'd agreed on.

It was a strange thing, though it grew less strange and disconcerting every day, to make plans *with* someone—or many *someones* depending on the conversation. To be part of this partnership, working towards a common, and meaningful goal. Hypatia tried not to think too hard on it, merely to enjoy it, and being heard, respected, and looked after, and indeed, the amount of work meant she had little time to do so. However, some moments, like at breakfast, when she and Thorn—and sometimes Henry or Mary—would discuss their plans for the day, it would strike her, the loveliness of the change. The ease of it; the relief and joy of it. No more did she have to run a household, care for others, manage everything, with unspoken demand yet without being seen lest they feel somehow less. No longer did she have to squash her own thoughts, and opinions, lest she be ridiculed, or dismissed. And she would thank whatever fate or sprite of luck had seen her sit in that garden the night of the party, and take a chance on Thorn.

One thing which turned out to be an urgent investment—according to Mary, and many others—was new clothes. Neither Thorn nor Hypatia's wardrobes were suitable for being seen about various towns, markets, or even church—the latter a continual debate, as Hypatia preferred not to go, Thorn cared little, his faith in his words, *personal*, yet both knowing it was part of their newly acquired station. There was also a return to London in their eventual future, Mary had pointed out, though one look at each other, and Hypatia and Thorn had silently agreed to put that out of their minds for now. They would need face that eventuality at some point in future, but for now, the consensus was that Gadmin Hall was the priority. Hypatia knew why she didn't want to think of London, after they'd only just got here; she liked Kent too much. This place, who she was here; who she was with Thorn, and getting to know him without any pressure or curious eyes. She wondered if he felt at all the same, and made a note to ask him sometime, if she found the courage.

But yes, new clothes were non-negotiable, even for their country life, particularly not since their old ones worsened with each day of work, regardless of Henry digging up more pieces from who-knew-where for them to use. Despite a *little* excitement at the prospect of getting new garments that she would've chosen, Hypatia was quite minded to just ask Mary—a talented seamstress according to a begrudging Langton, and less begrudging Henry—to do the work, or to merely do it herself, however, she was dutifully reminded that patronage of local businesses was an important part of being Countess of Gadmin.

So here she and Thorn were, in Sandham, the closest village-almost-town which had a draper-cum-haberdashery-cum-tailor-and-dressmaker. It was a charming little place, not as busy as one near a rail station, soon-to-come rail station, or on the main road. However, it was on one of the more travelled roads traversing the countryside, and boasted therefore a small but respectable inn, a variety of shops to serve the local populace—a grocer, a butcher, a baker, the clothier, an ironmonger, and so on—and some bright little cottages and homes, set around and below from the small green and Gothic-style church.

Having finished their sartorial business at *Wilson's*—covering the Mister Wilson, the Mrs Wilson, and their assistants, the Mssrs Wilson—which had taken far longer than Hypatia would've liked, though not nearly as long as they'd planned for, which was a pleasant surprise, Thorn and Hypatia wandered about Sandham, trying to get their bearings, and in a way, she supposed, introduce themselves to their new neighbours.

It had been a move made like so many, she realised, since Thorn's arrival, in concert but without need for consultation beyond a glance.

'Are you pleased with your choices?' Thorn asked, as he led the way towards the green.

'Yes, thank you. At least I will be if Mrs Wilson heeds my orders, and manages to deliver them without any of the ribbons, lace, bows, or other unnecessary adornments she was so set on convincing me I needed.'

'Well I don't know, I thought the pink flowered lace for instance, would've been just the thing to bring out the grapes on that extraordinary bonnet she had you try on.'

Hypatia glanced at him, to find him just as serious as his tone suggested; all except for the tiniest hint of a dimple above the left corner of his mouth.

'You think you're amusing, don't you?' Hypatia chuckled, tugging and pulling his arm gently, teasing the smile and jest from him until finally he laughed heartily. 'Actually, come to think of it, that bonnet would've looked most fetching had I worn it whilst you sported that waistcoat Mr Wilson proclaimed the height of fashion—remind me, was the colour seaweed, or pickle?'

'Well now we *must* go back for that bonnet, for I'll have you know when you weren't paying attention, I ordered that waistcoat, with embroidered pigs too.'

Thorn wiggled his eyebrows, and Hypatia laughed this time, drawing the looks of the few passersby, though perhaps that was merely the general curiosity they'd faced since arriving in Sandham, that reserved for *newcomers*.

She didn't have long to ponder it though, for in a trice, Thorn had stopped them, swinging Hypatia around so they faced each other, standing indecently closely, his hand sliding down her arm to take her hand as he so seemed to like to, and which she didn't mind for that very reason.

Not that she was averse to touch, only as she was dis-covering—having not truly had a proper opportunity before—though she liked her husband's touch in certain situations, she had no need of it as he did in other less *sensual* moments.

'I am glad you will have clothes that you like,' he said, gentleness washing away any jest, and warming her heart. 'If we achieve nothing more than that in all of this, I'll be glad of that. And admittedly, I will be rather…excited to see you in that gown with the *superbly* dropped shoulders,' he said, tantalisingly marking the invisible collar line over her current one. 'And that dark puce will be an excellent colour for you.' Hypatia wrinkled her nose, stifling a grin, and he sighed. 'It was *puce*, wasn't it? Ruined my attempt at seduction.'

'Was that what you were trying to do?'

'You asking that doesn't bode well for my answer.'

'I suppose not,' she grinned, letting her enthusiasm for his attempt, and indeed, any further engagement in any manner of seduction or bedsport, shine in her eyes.

They hadn't had occasion to…continue where they'd left off so to speak, work being what it was, and their exhaustion creeping in further with every passing day, only she needed him to know, the days since their last encounter had only served to increase her own enticement.

As they had his—at least as far as she could tell from the smouldering gazes he'd sometimes throw her across a barn, or field, or table. Even at times whilst they were covered in muck and other things best left unsaid, such as when she'd slipped and tumbled into a pile of it, and he'd laughed until she'd tried out her skills at tossing handfuls in his direction. They'd both ended up worse for wear, though laughing, and still, his gaze had been smouldering, which she supposed said something of their rather exciting compatibility.

A compatibility whose longevity she didn't know— just as she didn't know what their married life in general would hold once life assumed a more gentle, less hardy pace—but which she wished to enjoy whilst she could. The rest, the future, could wait to be discovered and adapted to in time; no use fretting over it.

Though I doubt adapting to not having Thorn in my life someday will be as easy as adapting to having him in it.

'Soon,' she promised with a smile, tapping his lapel, and moving them onwards. 'When we've more than a couple hours to shut our eyes, and perhaps enjoyed proper baths, and then there's the question of your current nighttime companion. Of whose health and nomenclature I haven't inquired.'

'He is growing apace,' Thorn told her, an affectionate smile on his face as they circled the green slowly. 'The doctor said to keep on as we had been, and I was thinking I might see if he would like to come with me tomorrow, when we bring out the next group to the woods. He seems very curious, staring out the window at every chance, though I don't think he knows quite what to make of the goats.'

'Ah yes, of course. He'd be able to see them now they're trimming the back gardens. I think you should bring him tomorrow. Langton for one will be glad to have him out of the kitchen, he keeps finding the runt rooting around the pantries and even found him in the cellar this morning.'

'He has good instincts already, and actually, I've been thinking… Truffél would be a good name.'

'As in the French? *Truffle?*'

'Somewhat reminiscent, but actually *Truffél*,' Thorn clarified, spelling it out. 'It is sophisticated, and has a little twist.'

'I think it suits very well,' she smiled, shaking her head slightly, wondering what would happen the day the pig grew, and Thorn couldn't treat it quite so much like a pup. He'd taken to it greatly, and though she wondered some days why he hadn't wanted her to help in its rearing, he loved the little beast, and so, she was glad for him. 'We should stop by the butcher's,' she said, changing the subject. 'See if he'll take care of those Dr Gideon mentioned were at their time. Danny did mention he rears his own, but perhaps he would have an interest in ours for a change.'

'Agreed. I'll not do business with the one in Horings, as he was Warren's pet, and it would save us going five miles for the other Hampton mentioned.'

'Perhaps we could find some small things to purchase at the other shops too. Langton mentioned needing a new saucepan, and Henry could do with some proper shears if he's going to continue replanting and tending the gardens.'

'And Niamh might do with some rhubarb sweets or something, if there are any to be had.'

'Rhubarb? Did you eat those as a child?'

'They were my favourite, as it happens, madam. What kind did you have?'

'I—'

Hypatia was about to admit that she'd never had sweets as a child, nor many as a grown woman—likely unwisely, for he'd buy her a boxful of twenty varieties—when she noticed a rather well-dressed man of middling everything, hailing them with a stick, and calling *hullo* from across the green.

'Thorn...'

Thorn followed her gaze, and along with her, plastered on a somewhat awkward, but mostly polite smile.

'Good day there, Lord Gadmin, Lady Gadmin!' the man said, coming to a halt before them, looking very energetic indeed. 'My apologies for hailing you unceremoniously, however I've been meaning to come by Gadmin Hall for days, and was just on my way there, when Mrs Bowles, the baker, told me you were in town, so I simply had to find you!' Thorn and Hypatia blinked, waiting for the man's name, or purpose, and he paused, only realising after a rather long moment that he'd missed out such pertinent information. 'My apologies again,' he chuckled, offering his hand out to Thorn. 'Simon Reeves, I've a sheep farm a mile or so to the east of you, and I heard you were looking for me. My flock have been grazing some of your lands, according to arrangements made with your previous bailiff, Mr Warren.'

'Ah, Mr Reeves, a pleasure,' Thorn said jovially, doing as he had with everyone else in a similar position they'd tracked down until now—giving them the benefit of the doubt. 'I'm glad to finally put a name to the sheep.'

'Ha! Very clever,' Reeves chuckled, before turning to Hypatia. 'Lady Gadmin.'

He made to bow, but she offered her hand instead.

'How kind of you to come find us, Mr Reeves,' she said, when he finally found it in himself to shake it.

She watched him carefully, but saw none of the usual telltale signs of it being out of some sense of male superiority, but rather shock, because of his own technically inferior societal position. Which boded well in his favour as came to giving him the benefit of the doubt; as did the fact that so far none of those they'd managed to track down as having used Gadmin Hall lands had done so knowing Warren's deceit and treachery. Hypatia suspected that if there were any some such, she and Thorn would only eventually hear of it through the gossip mill, and be able to do nothing, as they would've likely taken their beasts, crops, or whatever else, by then, or merely cut their losses.

Or so we can hope; the last thing we need is any manner of fight or war.

'Let me assure you both,' Reeves continued, what looked like sincerity about him, though Hypatia would have to rely on Thorn for his thoughts and reactions. 'I had no idea my use of your lands wasn't condoned by the previous earl, or his agents. He was a strange old fellow, and everyone around here knows he went a bit…enthusiastically into the pig business, without much success, so I thought he was merely seeking some additional revenue. Since I heard that wasn't the case, I've of course taken my flock elsewhere.'

'We appreciate your honesty, Mr Reeves,' Thorn said, throwing her a glance, and she nodded. 'However, there is no need. We are not farmers by profession, but we are learning, and having a variety of visitors and crops on the land is naught but beneficial as we've heard. We are more than happy to continue to welcome your flocks, perhaps you'd be so kind as to visit us at the Hall one of these days, and we can speak of which pastures are best now. And discuss what other arrangements we might come to. We are neighbours after all, and all want, I think, the best for this land.'

'Well said, my lord,' Reeves said somewhat bombastically. 'Couldn't have said it better, in fact. I will do just that, and thank you very kindly. I wish all around these parts shared such sentiments, but they've been caught by the fever of profit, and call from the cities for *more.*'

'There is greed and a love of money in every trade, Mr Reeves,' Hypatia said, with a mellowing smile, and he tipped his head, touching the brim of his hat.

'Wise, my lady, very wise, the both of you. Well, I'll be off, then, it was a pleasure to meet you both, and I shall call upon you at Gadmin Hall very soon indeed. Good day!'

And with a bow, and flustered half wave, he was gone.

'That's one more down,' Thorn commented. 'I hope I did right, and said what I should, I assumed you were in agreement when you nodded.'

'You did, husband,' Hypatia smiled, taking his arm, and turning them back towards Sandham's main street. 'However, there is one minor complication.' Thorn frowned, quirking his head, and she smiled. 'We're going to need some furniture for at least one receiving room.'

Laughing, Thorn nodded, and off they went again.

And Hypatia couldn't help but feel as though she'd arrived somewhere she'd always meant to be.

Chapter Twelve

As Thorn led Hypatia along the paths to the south-west of the grounds, behind the gardens, where woods met untamed wildflower fields—though at one time, he wagered, the patches of land had been more *parkland* than *rural* field, as suggested by the peppering of trees in some manner of order and design—he realised that though in many ways, it might be incredibly inadvisable, he'd somehow become entirely smitten with his wife.

There were worse things, he supposed, and had he been in another situation, alone, and not quite as anticipating of the near future as he was, he might've allowed himself slightly more thought, and even fear. But in consideration of his current circumstances—leading Hypatia slowly, his hands over her eyes, her very enticing self pressed closely to his front—he merely allowed himself a quiet *hm*, and smile of amusement at the turn of events. It was freeing, he realised, the sensation of being smitten; it had been a long time since he'd felt the melted butter of excitement run through his veins, or the easy smiles that popped and rose like champagne bubbles. Of course, he knew one need always exercise some manner of caution, so as not to be swept away by the pleasantness of it, to a land of unwanted infatuation, but so long as one did, there was no harm in revelling slightly in *being smitten*.

Holding fast to those feelings and sensations, at the very least, a welcome respite from the toil, and concern at the prospect of potential failure, he led Hypatia on to the spot he hoped so she would like, and that Henry had directed him to today, whilst Mary and Niamh had been his aides in ensuring it was all he wished it to be.

'How much further?' Hypatia asked, an eagerness in her voice that gave him heart.

'Not much,' he told her, pausing to do so, and catch her ear gently between his teeth as he did, her rambunctious curls teasing his nose.

So it wasn't; soon enough they descended the tiny hill that was more like a bump, and arrived at the shores of a tame, but fresh and sprightly creek—more of a pond where they were, widening as it did, before tightening again as patches of trees and woods contained it to either side.

'We're here,' he said, stopping them by the blankets, covering baskets—one with food, the other with washing necessities—and removing his hands from Hypatia's eyes.

He stepped back, and came to stand beside her,

watching as her eyes travelled over the view, hoping she saw the beauty he did, and liked it just as much.

He saw the honey-green eyes—afire like magical flames in the setting sun's light—travel over the quietly bobbing stream, so clear you could see the rocks below, and the dancing leaves of the trees in slight breeze, and the golden reeds and grasses across the way and around them, like the waves of the sea almost. The pops of movement—bees, dragonflies, and butterflies going about their evenings—and the buzz of life, nearly, but not quite, as vibrant as hers. The scents, of a sun-baked day, of summer, and vibrancy, and wildflowers and the earth herself.

Thorn waited, until finally, she exhaled so deeply he felt his own shoulders relax.

'It's...wonderful, Thorn, thank you.'

She turned to him, but something told him he wasn't quite ready to see all her eyes held, so he grinned, reaching for the blankets, and uncovered the treasures below.

'I have it on good authority the water is clean, and fresh, but not frigid,' he told her, opening the basket full of soaps, towels, and even a dressing gown and change of clothes—well, a shirt and loose trousers for both of them. 'And if you wish to be left alone, I will leave you, and go beyond view until you are done, and then return so we can have our...candlelight dinner,' he added with a flourish, opening the second basket.

Then, he had no choice but to see all her gaze held,

for she dropped on her haunches before him, and there was so much light, and joy, and surprise, he felt like the mightiest man to ever have roamed the earth.

And not to compare, for no love was equal, he had to admit he'd never felt so purposeful with one look from another.

'You don't have to leave,' Hypatia breathed, licking her lips, and glancing at his own, before a wicked smile split her face, and she rose out of reach. 'Though if you stay, I will need some assistance with these garments.'

Smitten, I say.

'This is Heaven, I think,' Hypatia said, half-floating, half-sitting in the deepest part of this stream—which, when standing, was about waist-deep—her naked form torturing him as it remained somewhat concealed beneath the gently lapping water, various limbs and outlines of her features making themselves known in a sensual game of hide-and-seek.

As much as Thorn had been tempted to devour her whole and become acquainted with every inch when he'd assisted with her disrobing, he'd satisfied himself with languorous brushes of his fingers against her warm skin, effervescent in the sun's light, along with whispers of kisses every so often to it. He'd promised her a bath, and wouldn't distract her, or himself for that matter, for he was admittedly mightily eager for one too.

It felt as if this was the first time in days, weeks,

months—Hell, perhaps even years that he'd truly relaxed. Not without a care, but with a more profound sense of perspective; that in this moment, those cares and concerns mattered not, or at least not enough to mar this time.

And for all that her floating and bobbing felt like tortuous teasing, there was a knowledge that Hypatia wasn't intentionally being sirenic, she was merely comfortable, with herself, and him, and perhaps that was what was most tantalising of all; her continued trust and ease.

'I'm inclined to agree,' Thorn smiled, leaning back slightly, to wet and refresh his hair again.

They'd washed themselves—with exceptional relish and dedication, the need to scrub clean greater than that to turn it into a perhaps seductive game of washing each other—some time ago, but neither of them seemed inclined to leave the cool and invigorating water, even for food.

And so as much as there existed a sensual charge between them, humming beneath the ease and simplicity, as much as Thorn was tempted to discover just how Hypatia felt when every inch of her was wet, he was enjoying just being with her.

Whether we be mucking out pigsties, or lounging in streams, it seems to be so.

'Do you know, I've never bathed in a stream before.'

'No offence, but I might've guessed. I cannot imagine either Mr or Mrs Quincy for that matter, condoning such uncouth and common behaviour.'

Hypatia laughed, and he let the melody of it, perfectly tuned with the rest, fill his heart.

'They'd have to notice to care. I suppose it is I who never went searching for streams to bathe in in London.'

'There must be some, though I don't believe that is something London is on the whole known for.' Taking a breath, he hesitated before continuing. 'I know… things are complicated between you, but should you wish to visit your family in time, or merely for me to gather news discreetly…'

'Soon, perhaps, I shall enquire for news. I thought I could just leave, and never look back, and in many ways, I can, but in time, news, an exchange of letters perhaps, even if only for the important markers in life, would be good. I wish them no ill, but I… I don't think I love them as one should family. I love them, in a sense, and care for them, only I…can't explain it. Do you find me callous?'

'No. I find you disarmingly honest.'

'Sometimes those can be the same thing.'

'Not in this instance. You speak your heart, not something to injure another. And I think, maybe you were never given a chance to love them, as a daughter or sister would. Never given the chance to *be* family. You were asked to grow up, to fulfil duties not yours to bear, and so you could never be true daughter or sister.'

'Perhaps.'

'Are they…a reason you do not want children?'

Frowning, Hypatia made her *I am thinking seriously before I answer* face.

'In part, it is likely I suppose. A fear of having to care for another creature, or a fear of repeating my own up-bringing. But I never dreamt of being a mother. Never felt the urge others do. Whether that ties into knowing it wasn't what was planned for me, I cannot be certain, but I think not. Rather, I've never wanted it enough, and one should, truly want it. If one has a choice. So perhaps there was freedom, in never believing it was my inevitable fate or duty, but being allowed to make my own choice. What about you?'

'I thought about it many times,' he admitted, quieter than he'd meant to, which was telling, he supposed, not that he minded, he found. 'I was prepared to do it, I could see myself doing it, yet equally, when…certain things happened, when I was alone again, untethered, I found, I didn't mind, having lost that possibility of fa-therhood. Like you, I realised I had a choice, and mine wasn't for a child. I realised I had been ready to *more seriously* consider the possibility because others wanted it, expected it, even my father, and I…well, part of me hadn't wanted to disappoint. Then, when I inherited all this… I may not have wanted it, but I wanted to commit to it, in a manner I hadn't wanted to commit to many other things before.'

'The woman you loved once…' Hypatia began tentatively, watching her hands ebb and flow beneath the surface, and Thorn sighed.

He hesitated, knowing one word would stop her, but that eventually, they would need speak of it, and now was as good a time as any, he supposed. Naked as he was, he felt safe, and though it wasn't about a *tit for tat*, he had to give as well as he got if he wanted this relationship to have solid foundations, to carry them through to a future he now saw he wanted.

A lasting one, of friends, at the very least.

'Will you tell me of her?'

'She's called Helen,' he began, trying to find the beginning, the end, the middle; the various parts which would answer all the questions contained in Hypatia's sole spoken one. 'Her family were involved in all sorts of business—fishing, markets, and so on—and I wouldn't say we grew up together, but I had a very early awareness of her, as I did of most in our environs. About a decade ago, after a few years admittedly *enjoying* myself around town, my best friend Frank—who I had grown up with—and I ran into her and a friend of hers at a fete. And I think… I fell in love right then, or at least, I had a profound sense she would *matter* to my life. We began courting, we met each other's families… We made plans, or at least…' Thorn frowned, leaning back again to draw some inspiration from the passing copper and pink clouds above. 'I thought we did, but in all honesty, I realise now, I don't think we ever did. Not together. It was more a sense of yes, we'd marry someday, and build a life, but looking back, we never truly said or spoke of what we wanted outright. I suppose… Well, her parents were very successful, and I had built up my business well enough, but I think I worried—despite never hearing them say anything of the sort—that they wished for someone able and willing to take over for them in time. Or really, just someone worthier. They are also Catholic, and not until a few years ago would marriage have not been complicated, and my father died four years ago, and I took quite a while to grieve, and years passed… I say all that, but the core truth is, we were together for eight years, and in all that time… Many things happened except us speaking properly, or me asking what she wanted. I just thought we were happy. That it would all fall into place or work itself out, or… I don't know.'

Sighing heavily, Thorn straightened again, shaking his head, and throwing a glance at Hypatia, who merely looked back at him, without judgement, without anything but pure invitation and openness.

'She left me for Frank,' he told her, no easy way he supposed to cut to the end of the tale. 'Rather, I caught them together, about two years ago, and I've no idea how long it was going on for, but I imagine that's telling, that I didn't ask. She told me she wanted more, that she wanted commitment, and more than the life she'd had up until then, or that of a blacksmith's wife. I'd thought she was happy to be such a wife, to live such a simple life, but then, looking back, I think she was fooled by my ambitions to grow my father's business and thought, I don't know, that I'd build a smithing empire or some such.'

'I wonder what she thought of your change in fortune,' Hypatia commented.

'I've no idea, though Frank came to visit when I was back there. He said they were happy for me, and I wished them well, and in truth, I do. Their betrayal cut deeply, and I don't condone it, though I might have forgiven them—I'm not quite certain yet,' he said with a grin that Hypatia mirrored, understanding in her gaze. 'I suppose I am coming to realise that though I loved her deeply, there was always a sense of disconnect. Of not being partners.'

The weight of that realisation was compounded by another; that he and Hypatia had learned to communicate and become partners with ease and rapidity. Whether it was a lack of expectation—of love, of being happy, of their marriage being romantic—or because their characters more readily matched, he wasn't sure, and didn't rightly care, so long as they continued as they'd begun.

'And I suppose, your character hasn't changed, so there is that,' Hypatia noted, and he smiled, broadly.

'It doesn't bother you, my lack of ambition?'

'I don't believe you lack in ambition, only your ambitions are simple, and liable to change with time. Right now, your ambition is to see this place thrive, and that is more than enough.'

'My ambition is to see all of us thrive.'

'As I said. More than enough.'

For now. Yet I cannot help but wonder if someday that will not be enough for you.

And I would not blame you. For you deserve more than this world itself.

'Would you have married? Given the choice? Regardless of expectation? Need?'

'I don't know that I would've. For myself. Committing to another…gladly. After…their betrayal, I had no intention of ever doing so, and less of committing in any manner to love. Risk, choosing wrong again. Learning I had to marry, well, I was not pleased, and I still feared choosing badly, however, it felt like less of a risk.'

'You wouldn't be risking your heart.'

'Precisely. Only my great fortune. What of you, Hypatia?' he asked, rather than lose himself in pleasant, but useless meanderings of the mind. Rather than admit: *I am glad it was you I married in the end.* 'Has anyone ever captured your heart?'

'No,' she smiled gently, paddling her hands and feet softly, moving, but not to distract, to feel the water's flow around her. How he knew, well, he didn't know. 'But then I never sought it, nor was I open to it. My life was planned for me, and once, when I first came of age, and was told of my dowry, I think I hoped someone might take me away from it. Then I learned what the truth behind the mirage of freedom was, and I accepted my fate, finding pleasure where I could. I'd long read about the promise and wonder of more sensual delights, and was already very much interested in discovering them for myself, and so I found them discreetly where I could—a handsome groom here, an interested party at a gathering there—but I knew I could never have love.'

'Your parents didn't...'

'There was control to a degree, they read my correspondence, dictated much of what I was to do or not, but it was as much a farcical mirage as the rest. So long as I did what was asked of me, and maintained my role... Like with the streams, and everything else, they would have had to truly care to notice, to mind anything I did. I always knew, however, that love was off the cards as that might've taken me from them, as grander dreams might've, but as for the rest... As I said, I was discreet, and it wasn't as if I was spoiling goods they hoped to sell off.'

Thorn grimaced, hating the wording as much as Hypatia's tone told him she did. Hating much of what she had lacked as concerned her family too, though that was nothing new. And in the end, it had shaped her, even if only by forcing her to shape herself into something incredible, and so he could not hate it with all his being.

'I've shocked you, Thorn.'

'Your words are harsh, but the truth as many see it. I am not shocked, merely...'

'Do not say sorry for my life.'

'Sorry that you could not even dream of love.'

'Perhaps it is for the better. I've seen too many twisted by such dreams, then disappointed when they do not find it. When life appears but a sham facsimile of glorious dreams. Too many others twisting themselves into unrecognisable forms in the pursuit of love. Losing themselves to the duty they feel towards it, whilst never being rewarded by it, for they are no longer themselves at all.'

'Is there nothing you dreamt of then? No profession, no far-off land, nothing?'

'I don't… I couldn't imagine myself as something other than I was. Not specifically. Perhaps I did not know my own mind well enough. My own self. Perhaps I merely understood my circumstances too well, and so did not wish to be yet another disappointed dreamer. Or perhaps it was freedom I lacked to do so. I dreamt of that. Freedom, escape. Not enough to seize my own fate.'

'Until we met in a moonlight garden one summer's eve.'

'And so I changed my fate,' she agreed. 'Or it was changed, if you believe in such stuff.'

'I like the idea of it,' he told her, knowing her comment to be somewhat leading. 'Fate, Destiny, Predestination. I like the idea of a powerful being, or beings, putting order to the world. Believing that what we can't find in this life, we might find in another, be it justice, or peace. But as for God as he is described in many books, I don't think I quite adhere to that. Good wisdom and lovely poetry though.' Hypatia nodded, grateful for his words; he didn't ask, for he knew her thoughts on the question of faith. 'Why did you decide to take a chance on me that night? Every day since?'

'The alternative…scared me more than trusting you. If I hadn't, I would've continued to be all everyone said I was. All they tried to make me. I found that a more terrifying prospect than the unknown for once in my life.'

'And my eyes sparkled,' he grinned, not diminishing Hypatia's confession, but giving her some levity he felt she needed then.

'And your eyes sparkle,' she nodded, a grin splitting her face. Slowly, it disappeared, and her eyes turned to examine the glinting waves around her. 'What does it feel like? To be in love?'

Something within Thorn revolted at being asked that question, at having to find words to describe such an ephemeral thing; such tasks were appointed to poets, or artists, or great thinkers, not blacksmiths-cum-pig-farmers in the midst of a pleasant evening stream bath.

But something else inside his heart melted, and twinged at the open, vulnerable, and somewhat heartbreaking question.

'For me, with Helen, it was…rather like drinking a good whisky,' he said, trying not to feel so terrible nor stupid for making such an analogy. Others compared it to great things, and he compared love to alcohol. *Tell-*

ing, perhaps, of many things. 'It was exciting, sparked my senses, then surprised me, and finally, filled me with a warmth and disconnection from the world but for that warmth. When it ended, quite a while after the betrayal I will add, it felt as if it had reshaped parts of me. I don't know if it was the manner in which it ended, or the price paid for such a thing as love, for my father, good and kind and loving as he was, he was destroyed by my mother's loss. Almost as if love, when taken away, highlights the worst parts of yourself. It made me angrier. More solitary, more...resentful. Then again, some find they can remain the people they became through love. So maybe it is not so very dismal. It's not very romantic a view on the whole, I know, but that's the best I can do.'

'Thank you, Thorn.'

'Are you hungry?' he asked, rather than ask the question he wished to: *do you want to fall in love someday?* Primarily for he wasn't sure he wanted to hear the answer. He didn't want to ask himself if he was ready to love and lose again; if he wanted to. For he did believe in the stuff—*love*—he'd seen too much of it, felt it, to be a non-believer, yet perhaps that was why he was warier of it than a younger man might be. 'The sun's nearly set now, and I am well-pruned.'

'I could eat,' she nodded, a dangerous grin he didn't know yet on her lips. 'You get out first. 'Tis only fair considering you watched me submerge, that I should be allowed to watch you emerge.'

'Whatever my lady commands,' he said, enjoying her bluntness, and this new...was it a game?

If so, he was surely enjoying it.

So he rose, ensuring he got proper footing before doing so lest he fall back into the water and make a complete fool of himself, rising as slowly and seductively as he could manage, giving his wife time to appreciate—he hoped—to her heart's content, all his mortal coil was.

Her grin widened, and so did his, and he stood, imagining himself Poseidon emerging from the great waves of the sea for a moment, before turning, and making his way back to the bank and their belongings; again, ensuring his lady had as good a show as she wished for.

When he reached the bank, and turned back to her, hands on his hips because *why not*, especially since he felt absurdly tall and proud, as her hot eyes devoured every inch of his dripping self, he wondered again what great fortune had seen him have Hypatia for a wife, and not solely because of her sensual interest in him, and forthright manner. He might've thought more, pondered his luck more profoundly, had she herself not risen from the stream just then, a siren herself; or perhaps something older, more dangerous. She was something...a phoenix, afire in the last rays before dusk; a rainbow, shimmering and glistening with a thousand hues. She was also herself, breathtaking and resplendent, and confident, and alive with that light inside her that put the sun's rays to shame.

Dumbfounded, his arms dropped, and the only coherent thought in his head was that at least she was able to see him at his *full* height—the cold stream perhaps not showing off his assets to their full extent—and that if he was going to watch this tantalising show she was treating him to—and there was no doubt she was using her body to tease him now—he might as well sit. Besides, in truth, his legs felt shaky, and he couldn't imagine standing on them much longer.

As slowly as he had, she approached the bank, and he leaned back, elbows on the ground behind him to appreciate every glint, glimmer, and spark; every curve, every bump, every hair and every bounce of delectable flesh. Until finally she stood at his feet, and he was just about to move, to take her hand, and pull her down to him so he could feel all his eyes had just devoured, when she raised a brow. He quirked his head, trying to understand the silent command, and then she moved again, touching his feet with her own, gently tempting them apart, and so he parted his legs, and he waited, his breath shallowing, anticipating...whatever came next.

If there had been any coherent thought left in him, it surely departed, and all he saw were curls the colour of a thousand of the brightest sunsets coming towards him, because Hypatia stepped between his legs, then dropped to her knees, and his body knew, and reached towards her, even as his seemingly leisurely position didn't quite change.

Until his head fell back, and his toes curled when his

wife took him both in hand, and in her mouth, without hesitation, and then all he felt was the wet heat of her mouth, and her tight grip, and the bumps of her tongue, and the slightest whisper of a scrape of teeth every now and then, and her other hand, clutching and caressing his thigh, and the softest place where it met his groin.

As he'd learned her, she learned him, as he moaned, and made noises he thought resembled approbation—hoped, really, for his mind was just full of mind-bending pleasure, the sort which came after hours, or days, or centuries of anticipation—and an occasional shift or buck, as gentle as he could.

Another man might've seen it as some sort of mark of a lack of manhood, how quickly she had him spilling himself inside her mouth, hands clutching the blanket beneath, teeth biting into his bottom lip, toes curling, and incomprehensible noises escaping him as he saw beautiful, white blankness behind his eyes; however, Thorn knew even if it were an acceptable measure of *manhood*—which it wasn't—his expediency was solely down to his wife's talented mouth and fingers.

He let himself fall, and drift, and it wasn't until he could lift his head again, and peek open his eyes, that Hypatia released him, dropping back on her haunches, licking her lips as he had his fingers, and he thought that truly, he'd been right from the first, this woman commanded him. Somewhat—*entirely*—overwhelmed by precisely how that felt, and all she'd made him feel till then, he encircled her loosely with his legs, and leaned forward, and captured her lips with his own, and kissed her far longer than he would ever know.

All he knew, was that it was dark by the time they made it to the food; though luckily he'd had the fore-thought to call it a *candlelight* dinner.

Chapter Thirteen

There were some things Hypatia had, if not expected from her arrangement with Thorn, then known were a distinct possibility; that sense of possibility had in turn largely factored into her decision to accept his proposal, and risk all the comfort and safety she'd benefited from previously—for no matter how unfulfilled her life was, she had possessed those things.

She'd known from their few minutes together it was likely they would get along, have lively conversations; shared a certain sense of wit, and plain sense.

She'd wagered he was in essence, a good man; respectful, kind, *not a wastrel*.

That wager had meant she'd wagered something far more important; that she could trust him, that he wouldn't injure her, mistreat her, or abuse his power over her once he'd gained it.

And finally, she'd suspected after their kiss, and discussion of the matter, that they would do well together as regarded intimate affairs, and that in all likelihood, she might enjoy some sensual time, at some point in their marriage, with him, and that it would be very pleasant.

However, Hypatia had to admit two things to herself, as they, well, there wasn't really any word for it but *mauled* each other messily, making their way from the kitchen—where they'd left their baskets, devoid of anything but crumbs, blankets, and linens—clutching at each other, at the bundles of clothes in their arms, at walls, door-frames, and eventually, banisters.

Firstly, she had to admit that she was very glad she'd married this man with a house devoid of furniture and baubles, for it made their progress much smoother than it might've been otherwise, and resulted in no damage but to their shins and shoulders as they bumped and rolled against uneven wooden surfaces when they got too carried away and lost their balance.

Secondly, she had to admit that she'd gotten far more than she'd bargained for with Thorn; in the very best ways. She'd found all she'd wagered she would—kindness, respect, good company—but also all she hadn't truly dared hope for, such as profound care, understanding, and true partnership. She'd trusted him with her future, and her person, and also found someone she felt she could trust her whole self to, as she had, with every word, every question, every confession, such as those spoken tonight in the stream. She'd found someone who trusted her with parts of himself she was sure he hadn't before, and that was something extraordinary, and potent, and vibrant.

And if she was honest, though she'd expected any intimate encounters with Thorn would be good, pleasant, and somewhat satisfactory, she'd not quite expected their compatibility to be quite so potent. She'd not expected to become quite so quickly addicted to his taste—to all of his tastes—to be set quite so afire by the look of him in full natural state, or when he lost all composure and control, *because of her.* She'd never been desired, felt wanted so insatiably, and desired so insatiably.

Perhaps most discombobulating of all, was that she'd not quite expected to need him so much—she'd expected to want him, not to *need* to feel his hands on her, or to know what he felt like inside of her, or how his whole body might feel above, or below, or—

'Why did you stop?' she asked, somewhat petulant, likely glassy-eyed, and very out of breath when Thorn broke their kiss.

'We have arrived at our rooms.'

Blinking, she turned to discover that they were in fact leaning against the wall between the doors of their rooms.

Looking back at him, she found him breathing exceptionally hard, dried strands of hair both falling dangerously over his forehead, and sticking up in the oddest manner, while sweat beaded at his temples, and his eyes glowed in the semi-darkness of the moonlit corridor.

'Would you think me presumptuous if I invited you to my room, under no pretence but that we continue this, and with the reassurance I did happen to buy a preventive in Sandham?' he asked, determination and desire laced with hesitancy.

'I likely should,' she grinned. 'However, considering I too acquired such an item during our outing to Sandham, it would be most hypocritical.'

'I am beginning to realise just how much I've underestimated my luck on finding you in the garden,' Thorn sighed, shaking his head desperately, and claiming her mouth once again.

Hypatia lost herself in that fierce and deep discovery for a few moments, before initiating a half-roll, half slide towards Thorn's door, fumbling around with her free hand for the latch, before finally finding it, and throwing open the door.

Making a sound that resembled both a growl and sigh of relief, Thorn followed her as they stumbled in, thankfully having the presence of mind to not fall in too far before closing the door, not that she thought anyone would come spying.

All bets were off then, as the bundles they'd somehow managed to keep hold of fell to the ground, and liberated of those burdens, they put their hands to better use, tearing at each other's dressing gowns, shirts, trousers, and at their own boots—thankfully only slipped on—then skin, hair, fingers, hips, chests, breasts, anywhere really, they could reach, still refusing to end the kiss, tongues winding and darting in exploration in between every sharp inhale they could muster.

They left a trail to the bed they managed to find—Hypatia only realising they'd found it when the back of her knees hit the mattress, without enough warning to prevent a reflex from having her break away from Thorn, and sit upon on it. He remained somewhat frozen before her in mid-air, leaning but not looming, as surprised as she was, until his eyes refocused, glinting in the moonlight streaming in, and a slow grin divided his face. His chest heaving as much as hers, he slowly straightened, letting his eyes catalogue and drift over every inch of her much like they had at the stream, sure and sweet as a caress; and she did not resist the impulse either.

In fact, to better aid both of them, she slid back on the coverlet, leaning back on her forearms to better see, and be seen; and because she felt safe, and appreciated, and unjudged, she tantalisingly slid her legs slower and slower apart, so that he could see all of her. Thorn made a strangled sort of noise, focusing in, his own private self certainly appreciating the view.

And with every breath, every glance, every second, I find myself hungrier, and more in need of whatever this man can give.

What he gives me now.

'If I ever think to get the shutters on these windows repaired,' he breathed, licking his lips, that little dimple above his mouth teasing *her*. 'Please remind me of what a foolish notion that would be.'

'Certainly, husband,' she said.

Why...

She wasn't entirely sure. All she knew, was that she felt the impulse, and Thorn certainly seemed to appreciate, eyes flashing wider for a second, before his jaw tightened determinedly.

He stepped forward, but Hypatia was confused when he then leaned down to his left; at least until he slid a case she recognised well from under the mattress, and tossed it on the bed beside her feet.

'Any preferences?' he asked, raising a brow. 'Once I've ensured you're positively dripping with need, of course.'

I already am, but perhaps I am mistaken, Hypatia thought, shivering against her will, swallowing hard, the way he spoke, his presence, his beauty and that terrifying, screaming need she had for him, conspiring to make her behave and react in ways she never had.

He accused her of commanding him, but she found, he commanded her body just as frighteningly; he scared her just as much for how everything within her clamoured for him to touch her again.

'Once you've assured yourself of my readiness, we can discuss,' she managed to get out, and if it sounded breathy, well, she didn't rightly care.

A quirk of his head in assent, and he was kneeling before her, then sliding his roughened and deliciously calloused hands up her legs, from ankle to knee, where he grabbed hold, and slid her back towards him, until her bum was just on the edge of the bed, her quim was in his face, and then his hands slid up the tender inside of her damp and sweaty thighs, and he spread her legs even further apart.

He inhaled deeply of her scent, while she scrambled to inhale at all, his eyes drifting closed for a moment. Then, having taken what he would, he held her right leg where he wished for it to remain, resting his other arm on her left thigh, curling his hand around so he could spread her intimate, already drenched and dripping lips apart, and without further preamble, licked her in one wide and masterful stroke from cleft to bud.

Hypatia's shoulders slid forward as her back bent upwards, and her toes curled, and everything tightened deliciously.

'Damn it, Hypatia,' he gritted out, the vibrations tickling every already sensitive nerve. 'I'll not last long with you tasting like this.'

'Who said you had to?'

Another growl was his answer, and Hypatia found that when Thorn set his mind to do something well, he did so, a sense of time-pressure adding to his focus and mastery.

He remembered every spot she'd shown him previously, and laved succinct, but lavish attention on it, swiping, licking, and teasing with flicks and grazes of teeth. He explored every part of her intimate self, whilst she fought not to buck and move too much; clenching, and tightening her belly as she waited for his next move. He kissed, and delved deep into her, drinking and making the most otherwise disturbing noises, which somehow made her pant and moan even more. He brought her to the very edge, and the blasted man knew it, for he stopped, and rose to his feet, and she gazed up to find him waiting for an answer to her previous question.

In response, she slid back up the bed whilst he found the preventive case in the mess of bed linens—a miracle in itself—and covered himself. When he had, she turned over, the coverlet scraping tantalisingly at her sore and peaking nipples and tender flesh, and tucked her arms beside and somewhat beneath her, knees nearly to elbows, and slightly spread, and waited.

Another pitiful moan escaped Thorn, and she grinned, her cheek flaming against the bed, which dipped without much ado as he clambered on.

'You'll be the death of me, woman.'

'Only a little death.'

And then he was cursing, and right behind her, tucking himself against her flesh in every way possible, and she managed to get in one stilted breath as he filled her, and took hold of her hips in one spectacularly smooth and determined move.

Closing her eyes, and letting herself fall into this dizzying, mind-splitting, and mouth-watering connection and incandescent compatibility, Hypatia clenched and released him inside her, moving with him, yet trusting his hold, his control, his everything.

She breathed in the old coverlet, and his sweat, and their scents, as she scraped and slid against the bed, his grunts and sounds of approbation and pleasure true music to her ears.

'More,' she breathed, feeling his nearing his own peak.

So he grasped her tighter, not shifting his position, but pulsing into her harder and deeper, before finally one of his hands did shift, following the dripping trail her body gave him, and he found her bud, and then she was muffling screams by twisting her head into the coverlet, and grabbed it tightly too.

The most incredible pleasure she'd ever reached, by her own hands or another's, blinded her; sending stars and dancing magma into every corner and reach of her. And with a few final thrusts, Thorn surrounded her with his body, having reached his own height of pleasure, and once he'd released himself into the preventive, encircling her with his arms, he guided them into a side and backwards tumble so they could lay back to front, and catch their breaths.

'That was far from a little death, Hypatia,' he chuckled lazily after quite a few minutes recovering, sliding the rest of the way out of her.

'Yes, you're very good at that,' she grinned, and he chuckled again.

'Happy to serve.'

They remained there a few minutes longer, at which point Hypatia's last echoes of pleasure had dissipated into chill, and she began to feel the stickiness, and the sweat, and the heat of Thorn's body, and feel all of it in a way she didn't like. For though she enjoyed sensual encounters, she'd discovered early on that there was something about the *after*, about the reality of others' bodies and her own, which was entirely uncomfortable, and marred the entire preceding experience if she didn't separate herself from it. And much like with the hand-holding or touching, Hypatia had never really found but that she slept worse with someone else in her bed or chamber; that more generally she was entirely happy and more comfortable in solitude than in company of any sort.

Besides, it was late, and she needed some rest—especially after that—so she rolled away from him, and he grunted discontentedly.

'Thank you,' she smiled, turning back to kiss him gently, and swiftly. 'Good night, Thorn, and rest well.'

And though he looked somewhat surprised, he neither said anything, nor moved much at all, while she threw on her shirt, and made her way towards their interconnecting door.

'Good night, Hypatia,' he finally said.

So she smiled back at him, and left, cleaning up before tucking into her own bed.

Thinking all the while, how well suited they were indeed, since he didn't seem to be of the sort who minded she didn't stay—but rather of the sort who liked their pleasure, and their own personal space as she did.

Much more than I expected.

Chapter Fourteen

A fortnight, or so, later

The sun was merely a promise, hues and hints of orange and pink mingling with purple and turquoise at the edges of the sky, proper sunrise still a couple hours away, but already, this part of the city was alive, buzzing with life and excitement, for it was market day. Pens, covered spaces, carts and signs vied for attention amidst the mass of bodies—human and animal of all varieties.

A thousand cries—bleats, snorts, yells, and everything else one could imagine—mingled and punctuated the complex aroma to be expected in such a place—dung, sweat, and feed every so often offset by a hint of perfume or lavender soap—and though this one didn't quite rival the greatest city markets, it was enough be a proper example of such a place as humanity had seen for millennia.

The hum and energy was admittedly helping Thorn

gain in liveliness and enthusiasm—otherwise stymied by a two a.m. departure, so they could arrive in time, and not have to pay for lodgings for the night, or someone to undertake this endeavour for them—and he took a long deep breath, letting everything, pleasant and unpleasant, penetrate him fully.

This...this too is part of who you are now.

'So this is a livestock market,' Hypatia said, now they had a moment to breathe, settled in their allocated spot as they were, somewhat awed.

A sentiment which, if he was honest, he shared; on many counts.

Surprisingly, it was also Thorn's first visit to such a place—not just a livestock market, but a market of this scale. Perhaps he might've, to give demonstrations of his skills, or drum up new clients; however, he'd been lucky in inheriting a solid business from his father, with enough well-paying and faithful clients—who also admittedly brought more custom through word-of-mouth—and any further patrons he sought, he did so discreetly, and personally. So while he'd been to markets before, fetes, and fairs, this was another beast altogether for him too. His awe and fascination, akin to Hypatia's, was also likely due in some measure to being in the thick of it, of not being some browsing potential buyer of whatever wares or produce was on offer, or curious onlooker of all the same, but instead being here to sell. Not being a visitor, but instead an integral part of this strange new world.

*Which someday might not feel so strange at all; as all
the rest of the novelties in my life have become normal.*

'We did well, I think,' Hypatia commented, glancing at those others around them; their pens, their signs
and general presentation, including their clothes. 'Especially given the time in which we prepared.'

'Yes. We'll have to thank Reeves.'

Indeed, when they'd finally sat down and begun to
organise, they'd realised…they had no real idea of how
to organise, of the way things were done, what to do,
really, and it wasn't the sort of knowledge which could
easily be acquired from books.

Equally, no one they knew well enough to ask had
much to offer on such things, being mostly experienced
with other manners of trade or markets. And it wasn't
as if Hypatia and Thorn particularly cared to go knocking on doors, asking for help. So it had been a boon
when Reeves had turned up at their door—with a lamb
in tow for Hypatia, which Henry had thankfully taken
charge of, and who had since become fast friends with
Truffél, wreaking havoc on poor Langton's kitchen garden, amongst other tomfoolery. It had thankfully been
a sunny day, so they'd been able to invite Reeves for
tea in the garden, where Henry and Mary had set up
some wrought iron garden furniture they'd found who
knew where; Thorn had learned to be grateful, and not
ask questions.

In any case, over tea, Mr Reeves had advised them
on this market—Maidstone, a city with a long history

of trade and commerce, and featuring the closest and best market for their purposes—as well as given them a detailed idea of how things ran, and how to prepare. So they'd followed his advice, gathered as large and varied a selection as they could transport themselves in three carts—Thorn, Ian, and Danny each driving one—and packed their supplies, including a simple wooden sign marked *Gadmin Hall Farm* Thorn had made, and here they were. Dressed in their new clothes—Hypatia's dress sans adornments in the end—looking the part of well-to-do, but not too out-of-their-depth aristocratic landowners and farmers. Now, all there was to do, was…wait.

And pray someone wanted what they had to sell.

A wait which grew rather exponentially as it happened, hours trickling by, though potential buyers were aplenty. Except none seemed interested in what *Gadmin Hall Farm* had to offer, though they would stop at the farmers around them.

Thorn and Hypatia watched, trying to discern how to better attract clients, only there seemed to be no fixed method. Some would engage, others let their pigs, goats, chickens, cows or geese do the talking. The only commonality seemed to be ease and familiarity.

'Oi, Joe Morton, I got them chickens ye wanted!'

'Why, Mr Banner, ye'll be pleased with these bucks I have today!'

'Susan still making that nice cheese for you, Mr Waters?'

It wasn't that Hypatia and Thorn didn't try to engage with a *hello* here or a *good day* there—if anyone dared come within a few feet as opposed to leaving wide enough a berth the *HMS Victory* might pass—and sometimes would be afforded a look, but nothing more. A dismissive glance, a judgemental up-and-down, a quick, unjustified measuring-up of the swine on offer, and they'd move along. Soon enough, the sun had properly risen, and it wouldn't be long before it would come time to clear out; at this rate, they'd be going home worse off than they'd come.

Thorn glanced to Hypatia for perhaps the millionth time—Danny and Ian having been sent to do some shopping, and fetch some tea, the four of them certainly not needed at present—to see if the despondent look they'd both sported progressively more obviously with each hour whiled away, remained, but instead he found his wife's gaze focused on a large man across the way, who was well, but not expensively dressed, and engaging in haggling the price of hogs.

'We've hogs here, at good price, Mr Fairchild,' she said, not shouting, but not *delicately* either, taking a step forward.

Thorn wouldn't say the market quietened completely, but he would've said there was a definite hush, as heads turned, including that of this Mr Fairchild, who raised a brow, and Hypatia smiled.

'Lady Gadmin, of Gadmin Hall Farm,' she said, extending a hand, which the man took an age to shake, though he finally did, approaching slowly. 'If I heard correctly, you're looking for some well-priced hogs to expand your herd. A butcher such as yourself will appreciate the quality of these very unusual animals. We've porkers too, should you wish to trial the meat with your customers first.'

Fairchild watched her for a moment, before turning his attention to the pigs.

Jumping into the small enclosure, blessing his good fortune again at having such a clever, forthright wife, able to do what he'd not been, Thorn coaxed forth one of the porkers Hypatia mentioned for the man to examine.

'How much?'

'Six and a half per pound for the porkers, half crown for the hogs.'

'I'll give ye a joey for the porker.'

'I can perhaps go down to sixpence, but not a joey.'

'A joey and a ha'penny.'

'You'd offer another a shilling per pound, Mr Fairchild, so a sixpence is more than a fair price. These are good pigs, of a kind not oft found these ways, and the meat will speak for itself.'

'I heard about Gadmin Hall, and the mad earl who went to Gloucestershire to fetch his precious pigs, and spent all he had of money and mind on building a herd. Last I heard, they were rottin' away, and bein sold for feed.'

Fairchild glanced at Thorn, as though he might be

the mad earl in question, and though Thorn was beginning to feel like he might fit that denomination given enough time, he wasn't the aforementioned.

'As you can see, reality and gossip often diverge greatly,' he said, holding the man's gaze. 'The past is the past, and those who contributed to any veracity such tales might hold had best examine their own actions before vilifying others,' he continued, wagering Fairchild had either heard the truth, or that scum Warren flung muck at the Gadmin name as he departed the area. 'The animals all have a recent clean bill of health, and as my wife says, the meat will speak for itself. As will you, with your expert eyes.'

'Or this gentleman's,' Hypatia chimed in, roping in another unsuspecting passerby, who'd demonstrated too much curiosity at the goings-on. 'What do you seek, sir?'

'I'm in need of some sows,' he said, realising he'd been caught, and not a little charmed by Hypatia; a sentiment Thorn understood all too well.

Another like I who dared glance too long at this woman and was ensnared.

'Six and a half it is then,' Fairchild sighed. 'I'll have three porkers for now, if you have them, but mind you, one complaint from any of my customers, and ye'll not do business here again.'

'Excellent, Mr Fairchild,' Hypatia grinned, gesturing for Thorn to come complete the sale.

Which he did, half an eye and ear on his wife, who

continued to work marvels, attracting more and more, if nothing else, curious souls; tempting a few more here and there to part with coin, and take some of their animals away.

Danny and Ian arrived not long after, helping where they could, and in one of the quieter moments, Thorn permitted himself to lean against the enclosure, and merely watch his wife work, pride filling him to the brim.

At least, until one of the neighbouring farmers came to stand beside Thorn, watching Hypatia as he leaned on his walking stick that more resembled half an oak's trunk.

'Had one like 'er once,' the older, grizzled man said, and Thorn might've thought it in pleasant reminiscence had he not punctuated his statement with a hack and spit. Thorn frowned, turning slightly to the man, who shrugged. 'That woman wouldn't peck, she'd drive, and nearly drove me off a cliff, till one day I said: "Woman, I'm yer 'usband, not yer servant." And she said she didn't need me, and I'd see just how well I got on without 'er, and 'ere we are, seven years later, and I've never been so 'appy. But 'twas my own doin', lettin' her think she could run the place. Ye mind yerself, son.'

And with a tap to the side of his nose, and what Thorn supposed was meant to be a wise man's knowing gaze, he hobbled off. Thorn shook the comment off, and turned back to his wife, and thought something along the lines of *some men just cannot abide a strong, capable woman.*

Except, the man's words were like poisonous, thorny vines, wrapping themselves and clutching to already dark ground. He thought about how the man had said he'd never been so happy; yet he looked unkempt, sallow, and frayed. He looked like he had needed his wife; was lost, bereft, without her.

And perhaps that was what held fast to Thorn most of all, as they finished their time at market—having sold a good half of their stock, which was disappointing but far from disastrous—and too exhausted and frankly penniless to do anything else, they began the three-hour trip back home, in quiet silence; a silence he knew Hypatia noted, but took as mere tiredness, though she bounced with energy and satisfaction on the cart beside him. Through every mile travelled, that man's transformation in the face of love's loss, held fast to him. For Thorn had realised early on, he needed Hypatia. She was the strong, capable one, and there was certainly nothing wrong with that, but as he grew to need her more every single day, in ways he daren't even think on, she seemed to need him less and less.

Oh, she enjoyed his company—in every way possible, or so she'd demonstrated since their first true evening together—and welcomed his thoughts, and opinion. But she still left him every night, having gotten the pleasure she sought, and she made more and more decisions without his consultation—not that they were bad, or his consultation was required—and he was always the one to initiate any sort of sweet touch, and in every way, she thrived, and would, with, or without him in her life.

It was part of her charm, part of what he liked about her, part of what astonished him every day. And yet, from the first, that divide between them—her thriving and adapting so easily to *everything* whilst he struggled and felt an imposter—had been felt. Though it had been hidden, diminished by gratitude, respect, and yes, to a degree, his besottedness, it had remained. And now, more than ever, he felt his own lack in comparison to her. As he had, admittedly and not, with his father, who'd built a business, not been given it, with Helen, who'd wanted more than he ever had, with strangers even; and though it was unfair, and he knew it well, he began to feel angry. He began to feel resentful with Hypatia for that, for not sharing his need, or indeed, his feelings. For being strong, and secure in herself, and needing no one really. Nothing but books, to fix roofs, and sell pigs, and charm idiots like him.

It would only get worse too. Here, it was noticeable, the chasm of competency, but how would it be in London? How would it be when came time to fulfil all those societal and political duties he'd already been overwhelmed with—and that was having only dipped his toe into the murky ocean? Would he be forever asking Hypatia to tell him what to do in the House? Letting her lead the charge at parties and other such nonsense?

How long would she remain by his side? Endure being the better of them both, before she grew tired, restless, resentful? How long before her freedom sparked her to have dreams, and she realised she dreamt of more than merely *him*, and what little he could offer? Where would he be then?

He wondered, and that resentment grew, for knowing, for having always known, she would be better at any and all of this than he ever could; more of a countess, worthy of his inheritance than he. By the time they arrived home, all that putrid resentment had truly festered, and so he told her that he and Danny would see to what beasts remained, and not to wait for him, for dinner or bed.

So she didn't, and well, that just made it worse.

Chapter Fifteen

Since they'd returned from market, Thorn had become quiet, and distant, and Hypatia wasn't entirely sure what to do about it. She'd tried talking to him directly, asking if all was well, or if there was anything preoccupying him, but he'd begun some new sort of behaviour which involved grunting, and moving along, or saying most unconvincingly: *'I'm fine.'*

They still worked the farm together, executed their plans together—making deals with brewers and dairies for their scraps and such, managing to hire one more worker for the farm, and a maid for the house, as well as purchasing some furniture for one drawing room and a bedroom—but it felt vastly different. Not only because Thorn seemed to have lost his sensual interest in her, not growing cold, but neither reaching out for her, seeking her proximity as he had, but mainly because they'd lost what had felt like a certain synchronicity. Hypatia tried not to take it personally, though it seemed to be directed mainly towards her, even if his grim mood carried over onto his dealings with others. She tried telling herself that he was likely just disappointed their first escapade to market hadn't been a roaring and tremendous success, and that the weight of the estate, and all those other responsibilities he had were simply catching up to him, except none of it really seemed to stick to her heart, as the calming balm it should've been. So, at a loss of what else to do, Hypatia simply carried on.

It wasn't as if their life had somehow become less busy. There were still pigs and fields to tend. Accounts to be done, rents to be collected, harvests to plant, and a house to run. There was still a lot to be done to transform Gadmin Hall's estate into something prosperous, and well-functioning, and so she strived every day to do so. Each day too, brought its own little surprises, its own challenges, and its own little joys.

Truffél was growing apace, and following Thorn—and sometimes her—around like an eager and surprisingly well-trained sheepdog, which she knew first hand from his control and taming of their lamb, who Niamh had named simply: Lamb.

The embankments near some of the fields along the river crumbled after a significantly tempestuous day, and so crops were lost, and solutions to drainage and flooding needed to be found.

New piglets were born, and they and the sows needed extra care and looking-after.

The Hamptons came over to give some advice about

autumn and winter plantings, and Theo let it slip that some of Hypatia and Thorn's clothes—those Henry had unearthed from who knew where—had actually been his parents', and hadn't in actual fact miraculously sprung from *who knew where*. With some gentle coaxing and investigation, Hypatia discovered that in fact anything Henry and Mary had brought into the house since her arrival, be it clothes, garden furniture, tools, or doilies, had been donated by kindly tenants, families of workers such as Danny and Fred, and even Mr Reeves. And while others might've taken that gesture poorly, as an insult, Hypatia couldn't help but be touched, beyond words. In time, she vowed to repay their kindness, and that thought actually brought about the one thing she had managed to talk with Thorn about: tonight's dinner, to which all on their lands, all those neighbours who had helped them thus far, such as Reeves, were invited.

Though in actual fact, she hadn't talked *with* Thorn about it, rather, she'd told him what she'd discovered, and what she wished to do, and he'd said, '*do what you will*' in a tone she wasn't certain how to decipher. Instead of losing any sleep over it, however, she'd merely put her plans into motion—regarding the dinner, and the surprise she had for Thorn too, which she hoped might make him feel more himself—learning just how far one could stretch a penny or what one could put on the menu when one hoped to feed a rather large crowd without declaring bankruptcy. She, Langton, and Mary worked as terrific allies in getting it done, and Hypatia learned yet more skills.

Making daisy chains, arranging wildflower bouquets, and finding things which might be used as tables and chairs in the unlikeliest of places. I certainly cannot say my life is dull.

No, she certainly could not. In fact, if anyone had asked, she wouldn't truly have had a bad thing to say about this new life of hers, in which, for the first time in perhaps ever, she felt truly happy. The only thing marring it currently was Thorn's grimness, but then, hopefully a nice festive evening, and her other surprise, and he would be right as rain again.

Restored, and—

'Looks beautiful, my lady,' said a voice, and Hypatia turned away from the lantern she'd just lit, to find Mrs Hampton, a basket in her hands at the dining hall's door.

It was perhaps the most majestic room in the old house, large enough to receive the numbers they hoped would come; all high ceilings, and exposed wooden beams, fit for a king.

Or friends.

'Delia,' she smiled, going towards the woman, who'd insisted she call her by her Christian name. 'I'm so very pleased you could make it.'

'The boys have gone to see if Langton or Mary needed help,' Delia told her, holding out the basket for Hypatia. 'Well, my husband and brother have. Theo and his cousin went to find Niamh and Lamb.'

'You are all meant to be guests tonight, not helping, and you certainly need not have brought—well, actually, I take that back,' she amended with a laugh. 'Neither Thorn nor I shall ever say no to your rhubarb tart. Thank you. Will you mind though, if I add it to our puddings tonight? Share with the others?'

'Of course not. Where I come from, that is how a meal is made, by all.'

'Words to live by. Come, I'll set it on the sideboard, and you can tell me of any news.'

'No news, milady. Beyond this place coming alive again,' she added, staring around at the dusted, clean, and flower and paper fanion chain-decorated hall. 'D'you know, they used to say Bess herself came here to stay once.'

'Now that must've been a sight. And expensive.' The women laughed, and Hypatia gestured to the crates of drinks set beside the sideboard full of puddings. 'Would you care for something, Delia?'

'Thank you, a cider if you've one, Lady Gadmin.'

'Hypatia, please. I feel no more a countess than Lamb might, and we are friends of some manner now I hope. I've a dearth of those, so if you'd indulge me, I'd be forever grateful.' Hypatia waited, and finally Delia smiled, bowing her head. 'Thank you. And as for the cider, we have some of Kellerman's, which I've heard is either the best, or inferior to Jones', though we felt it was a safe bet since as Mrs Wilson advised, the north of this area prefers Kellerman's, whilst south of Sevenoaks road, 'tis Jones'.'

'Aye, so it is,' Delia chuckled, while Hypatia opened a bottle, and poured them each a glass of the stuff.

They sipped for a moment, making appreciative noises, Hypatia for one enjoying the calm before the proverbial storm—the descent of all their guests—wondering vaguely where Thorn had gotten off to, before shaking that thought aside, and merely being grateful she'd had the foresight to change into one of her nicer, but not new, gowns before finishing up this room.

Speaking of which, she glanced around at what they'd managed in here. A long table made up of doors, tables, slabs and random pieces of wood, covered with enough cloths and coverings it looked like a mighty quilt, and that wasn't to mention the mix of crockery and tableware; tables, stools, benches and barrels for seats, some with mite-worn cushions, others not, flowers aplenty, candles, lanterns, and lamps warming the space, all surrounded by those lanterns, fanions, chains and other homemade decorations, and she thought, it was beautiful.

'Will yours or his lordship's family be visiting soon?' Delia asked, not knowing what a sharp topic indeed that one was, and Hypatia had to try her very hardest not to grimace. 'Or are they in London now, awaiting your return? We'll be sad to see you go when you do.'

'I'm afraid Thorn has no family to speak of. And I

am not on the best of terms with my own, so visits are not to be expected.'

'I'm sorry.'

'Thank you. But you needn't be. I have made peace with it, and I am glad to start afresh here. As for a return to London, Thorn has duties and responsibilities there now, as do I, I suppose, however I'll admit, it's not something we've discussed in great length yet. There's been so much to do here...and in truth, I am not eager to return. I like it too much here.'

'Aye, 'tis a good place, this.'

'Yes—'

'Ma! Look what Niamh and I found!' Theo cried, coming in, hands cradled around something that neither she nor Delia could see, yet which made Delia's eyes go wide with dread nonetheless, as Niamh trailed behind him, looking like she'd just found treasure.

And so she had, they discovered as they found a beautiful toad in Theo's hands—a toad which promptly escaped, and so ensued a merry chase around the hall, ending only just as other guests began to arrive. Any further conversation with Delia was curbed, which Hypatia regretted somewhat. She might've liked to try and gain some wisdom, about life, and marriage, and the world. Perhaps in time, she might, over a lovely cup of tea; under the shade of Delia's fruit trees.

For now, she would greet her guests, and see them fed and watered and having a jolly time, and when Thorn appeared, he would help her, and they too would have a lovely evening, and all would be well.

I have decided life here can only be well; even at its worst.

Thorn did appear in the end, entering the hall with Mr Reeves, and a small brace of other tenants, looking much more jovial, and in good spirits, though to Hypatia's eyes, shadows and a certain stiffness prevailed amongst the smiles, laughter, and general air of bonhomie. She said nothing of it, however, merely smiled, as he did, and went on about having a wonderful evening.

This evening, the surprise I have planned, hopefully those will clear the cobwebs of his mind; or at least afford us a proper chance to talk, as we haven't in some time, and which I find I sorely miss.

In any case, Hypatia—and from what she could see, Thorn, who was sat at the other head of their very long and pleasantly animated table—did go on to have a very pleasant evening. Drinks flowed, the roasted hogs appeared to complement the myriads of other dishes they'd managed to prepare—everything from warm lentils to salads of cress and cucumber, to fire-caramelised apples and pears—and more drinks appeared and were passed around. Children ran amok and played at knights and kings, Truffél and Lamb appeared, and made generally polite requests for scraps. There was laughter, and good conversation—ranging from local news to the true effect the Corn Laws had had, and how they hoped a repeal would pass—and there was warmth and gaiety such as Hypatia had never known. Acceptance, and *life*, such as she'd never felt before.

As the puddings disappeared, along with the harsher spirits, a pleasant dimming swept over them all, at least until the songs began, accompanied by a flute someone produced from a pocket. Though some got *moderately* ribald and jolly, neither did they completely extinguish the pleasant settledness in the hall, which Hypatia revelled in, leaning on her hand, smiling without end.

Delia finished a lovely duet with her husband—a song of summer loves and spring children—and Hypatia smiled all the more, clapping along with everyone else.

'Your turn now, mistress!' Fred shouted from halfway down the table, waking Hypatia from her pleasant reverie.

She was about to try and refuse, and even began to wave his suggestion away, when cups banged against the table, and other voices joined in, saying: '*Yes, my lady, a song!*', '*Tradition, Lady Gadmin!*', and so Hypatia chuckled, relenting. She'd never been overly talented at the exercise, but neither had she ever been told on the few occasions she'd tried her hand at it, that she was no good at all. Besides, hesitating, holding back…that was old Hypatia. Not Gadmin Hall Hypatia.

Rising, she tried to think of her best choice, and it wasn't until she met Thorn's gaze across the table, both magnetic and somehow sorrowful, that she decided.

'There once was a girl who lived by the shore,
And made castles and kingdoms of shells and sand,
Dreaming of horizons and homes not known but longed for,
Calling to the waves to sweep her to those dreamed of lands.
Oh take me, sea maidens and beasts, she would call,
Take me to see those I've yet to meet,
Oh take me, oh take me, I'll wait till nightfall,
Take me, Poseidon, so I ye entreat.
But the gods and sirens and waves left her there,
For years till the girl turned to woman,
And the shores of castles of shells and sand remained bare.
She lived her years, neither mother nor maid, growing wan.
In dreams she'd still sing: take me, sea maidens,
Take me to see those I've yet to meet,
Oh take me, oh take me, I'll wait till night be fadin',
Take me, Nodens, so I ye entreat.
Then one day a ship on the horizon was seen,
And the woman of silver and grey knew 'twas the sea that had sent it,
So into the waves she walked, serene,
And swam to the ship, reaching it as the waters winked, moonlit.
As anchors were raised, she sang to the sea, arisen!
Thank ye for taking me to those I've yet to meet!
I'll wait no more nights to see those horizons,

You're taking me home, life'll be sweet.
You're taking me home, life is sweet.'

The last notes hung and echoed, stillness and continued silence from the congregation allowing them the time to drift and wander to the furthest rafters. Cheeks burning, from Thorn's steady and heady gaze, so like that she'd missed of late, yet still plucking at the strings of her heart for its dash of torment, she sat back down, forcing herself to smile to everyone gathered.

Finally, they seemed to wake from hypnosis, or stupor, a great wave of cheers, congratulations, and banging cups meeting her ears. Reassured, she smiled wider, meeting her husband's gaze again, and trying desperately to let him know that whatever was bothering him, she could make it better.

They all can, this night can, if you'll only let it.
Let me.

Chapter Sixteen

Thorn was entirely aware that since their unsatisfying, yet admittedly somewhat fruitful trip to market, he'd been something of an ass. Skulking, grumbling, retreating, from Hypatia, and anyone else who dared come near. He'd become himself as he'd been in the days, months, and yes, to a degree, years, after Helen and Frank's betrayal; a mood, a melancholy, an anger, a feeling, whatever one would term it, which he'd only conquered through industriousness, and admittedly, a hardening of his heart.

He was also entirely aware that Hypatia had done nothing so treacherous, or repugnant; that all she'd done was work to the bone to help him make their home, their livelihood, a success, or like tonight, to make their neighbours and new friends, feel welcome, and thanked, for all the good fortune and grace they'd shared. He was entirely aware that it was his own fault, his own problem, that he'd let some idiot he knew not one whit of twist his heart and mind with laughable and ridiculous words and opinions, said in passing, and that he himself was a better man than this—the thoughts, or the ensuing behaviour—*and yet.*

He couldn't seem to stop any of it—the thoughts, or the behaviour—though he justified his recent behaviour on a strange case of preservation; distance meant he could sort out his mind, and his heart, and go back to the loveliness that had been, without saying or doing anything that might injure Hypatia, or anyone else for that matter. He told himself that, all while he knew distance, silence, just made the thoughts rot and boil ever more.

She doesn't need me.

She doesn't want me.

I'm not good enough.

I could leave tomorrow, she'd be fine.

Does she even like me?

I suffer without her near, and she thrives, as ever, carrying on as if nothing were wrong.

Though of course, nothing truly was *wrong.* There were minor catastrophes, and problems, with straightforward solutions. Still, Thorn couldn't snap out of it.

Tonight's dinner, or party or whatever they were calling it, might've done the trick, had Hypatia not been so damned *glorious.* Transforming their house into a welcome home, making it all so beautiful, and taking care of all the arrangements, and even *thinking* of doing it to thank all those who'd showed them kindness. All he'd been able to think was: *she didn't need me but to supervise the butchering of the hogs, and their cooking, man that I am, those are my only duties.* He conveniently discarded the reminders his mind gave him that he might've very well made daisy chains with her if only he'd asked, *talked* to her, said one word; she wouldn't have cared one whit, or perhaps she might've been happy for him to do so.

The evening had revived him in many ways. It was easy not to maturate in one's own poisonous thoughts when one was distracted by good food, good drink, conversations and games with children. Except that one glance at Hypatia across the room, and how she held everyone's attention, and shone so bright, and laughed so magnetically, and he would want to be there, by her side, soaking it in. Soaking her in. He wanted her perhaps more than he'd wanted her thus far, and not just her body, but her heart, and her soul, and her thoughts, and her sorrows, and when she'd sung that song, he'd been transfixed, and yet so very sad, because she wouldn't let him have any of it, and rightfully so, he had no business having any of it, he didn't deserve it, her, not given the thoughts he was harbouring, and also he had no right, not given the nature of their relationship, agreed and shaken upon, and the fact they'd been married, what, just over a month now?

I can't even recall—what day is it today?

And to make it all worse, Hypatia hadn't allowed him to go back to his room and sulk further once the last of their guests departed, *oh no*, she had to lead him through woods, and paths, and fields, to who knew where, glancing back so often with hope and mischief in her eyes he wanted to get caught up in, but refused to be ensnared in, stubborn bastard that he was.

So he remained sulking, sullenly following through darkness, until finally Hypatia and her little lamp stopped bobbing, before a middling-sized stone cottage of some manner.

'We're here,' she said, breathlessly, waiting for him to be excited, but quickly finding herself disappointed, so turning to open the door instead.

He followed, because something inside still refused to not obey her commands; refused to injure her and tell her he was going back to bed. Stepping inside, his nose began to recognise scents, and then she was lighting candles, and he realised...

'This is a forge,' he breathed, stunned, blinking as his eyes found the hearth, the bellows, the tools, the anvil, the tables...

'Mrs Siddows mentioned there was one here,' she told him excitedly, her eyes still searching him, hoping for approval, or excitement, or *something* he couldn't find it in himself to give, as a turbulent whirlpool of feelings swept his insides bare and raw. 'She said it hasn't been used in years. They used to have a smith for the farm, but he was one of the first to go when the old earl was making cuts.'

'These tools, they're new...'

'I hope they're right. I asked around, and read what

I could, but if they're not right, Rowan at the ironmongers said you could switch them without issue. As for the rest, gathered where I could, and Danny and Ian and Fred helped, cleaning it all up, and getting it back into shape.'

'You used your money for all this, didn't you?'

'Of course. This was my surprise, for you.'

It was…

So much.

Too much.

Thoughtful, and kind-hearted, and wonderful, and excessive, and the most incredible gift he'd perhaps been given, and it filled him with such joy, wonder, and marvel, and bewilderment that guilt, remorse, and self-hatred, also reared their ugly heads.

And in their true destructive fashion, they dimmed the rest, until all Thorn could see, or taste, or speak, was the worst of himself, and his mind.

'Is this your roundabout way of telling me I should go back to what I'm good at?'

'I don't understand.'

'Surely you can't have failed to hear them at market,' he spat, rounding back on her, her dumbfounded expression worsening *everything*, rather than forcing him to take a proper step back, and look at himself, and his egregious behaviour. 'If such things were said to me, I can't imagine what was said to you. And I expect everyone on this bloody farm, on this estate, and in the village, is thinking such things. Saying such things. That

I've no idea what I'm doing, that you're the one who knows everything, who's out there negotiating prices, and fixing roofs, and handling pigs, and running things. You've been doing so from the first, without any aid from me, and so I must wonder, what purpose do I serve beyond being the imposter of an earl?'

'I didn't think you minded,' Hypatia said quietly, searching her brain he could see for examples to prove his point. Part of him knew she would find none; the more cruel part told him she would find countless. 'I've asked you, I thought we were working together…'

'But we're not doing it together, are we?' he near shouted, throwing up his hands like the petulant, insecure child he knew he was. But he just couldn't *stop*. 'You do it all, and I'm just here to sign papers, or say *yes, Hypatia*, or lift pigs from the muck, and even then, how many times have you done *that* yourself? You make the decisions, and you know what's best, and why shouldn't I just step back, and go back to my old work, and let you save my legacy and restore the title, and do it all, and there we go.'

'You don't just… I want to do it *with* you,' she told him, her earnestness chafing as she took a step towards him.

'Why? Do you even *like* me, Hypatia?' That one stopped her, and he saw a doubt, a questioning, an examination of her mind that fuelled his anger. 'You leave my bed when you've had your pleasure, and you never touch me otherwise, I am always the one holding your hand, or caressing your cheek, or…*anything.* Some days I wonder if you even like me touching you, or if you're just enduring it to get what you want.'

'I don't mind it—'

'You don't *mind* it?'

Aghast, her answer proving him right on all counts, even if it did no such thing, he shook his head, laughing bitterly.

'Thorn, please, don't misunderstand me.'

'Actually, for the first time, I think I understand you very well. It was my mistake again, believing something other than what was before me.'

'Thorn—'

Even if he hadn't waved her off, like some dismissive arse, and walked out into the warm, but cold to him night, her words would've been stopped by the crack he heard in her voice; a complement to those heart-wrenching tears he'd seen dancing on her lashes before he'd turned away.

Another man, a better one, worthier one, would've immediately turned on his heel, and marched straight back in there, and begged forgiveness for having injured her, as he knew he had. Not only by spouting some ridiculous nonsense he'd allowed to fester inside him, not only by saying very cruel things, but mainly, by being unwilling to *talk*, as they had so readily until now. Certes, he had valid feelings, doubts, questions— *does she like me, do I serve a purpose, does she need or want me*—but he'd not taken the time to open himself up to her. To be vulnerable, to express it all, and *ask*, in a civilised, cool, and *ready-to-hear-the-answer* way. For that sin, and perhaps, many others, he'd likely be punished with what might prove to be the worst fate possible; the loss of an incredible woman. One he cared for so deeply, and he…

She'd be better off. What have I to give?

And perhaps, that was truly at the root of it all, that very question; or so he purported, and pondered, as he attempted to find his way home in the dark, having paid little attention to where he truly was.

This is going to be a long night. Mayhaps the longest of my life.

Chapter Seventeen

If there was one thing Hypatia couldn't be accused of doing very often, it was getting lost in melancholy, or sadness. Most of all, it was crying. It wasn't that she didn't purposely do so, bottle it all up like some, force tears away for the supposed weakness they demonstrated, or anything thus, it was more that it had been a long time since she'd experienced emotions desperate enough, great enough—good or bad—to need to dwell in them, or have them be so overwhelming they couldn't but be bodily expressed.

Whether it was a fault in her making, or her upbringing, or indeed, a fault at all, was neither here nor there. The point was, she had from a very young age learned that while others might ponder, and ruminate, and dwell—or rot, depending on one's perspective—revel, or enjoy, certain feelings, or get caught in dark chains of thought they couldn't escape from, she didn't. It wasn't that she'd always been content with her life— if there were powers above, they knew well she hadn't been—but somehow her mind, or her heart, or whatever ruled her, allowed her to simply move on. Or not *dwell*.

So she would in all likelihood never leave her parents' house, no use crying on it, if it could be changed, she would seize the opportunity. If one such never appeared, well, dwelling on her sad fate would not change it.

So what if Epi had broken her one and only doll? Screaming about it wouldn't change it. Either the doll could be fixed, or it couldn't, and if it couldn't, well, its loss would be mourned promptly and succinctly.

That wasn't to say there hadn't been moments of despair, of sorrow—like when Granny Quincy, Hypatia's only friend and who was like a true granny to her, died—but after a satisfactorily cathartic few days of sadness and crying, Hypatia had moved on with her life. When her parents had taken more interest in Epi, and denied Hypatia her sister lest they need her to assist with care or education or dressing or whatnot, well, she'd mourned that loss, and done what she'd been asked, and hoped her sister would be happy.

Only, as she discovered standing in the middle of the forge that night, she'd never quite been hurt as Thorn had just then. Part of her knew a great portion of the sorrow piercing her chest and threatening to rip her heart from it was due to the fact she'd been *so* excited to show him this, thinking it was just the thing to make him better, and more himself again. That she'd been so excited to do something for him, full stop; though why, now that remained a mystery, beyond the fact that she'd felt the need, the desire to, and not *solely* to make him feel better, and bring back the Thorn she'd missed of late. Another part of her was crushed, disillusioned, and hurt, as it had believed he knew, saw…so much she'd *not* said; and yet another part desperately wanted to try and untangle it all, find answers as to how and why it had all gone wrong, and examine everything he'd said properly, to find a way forward.

Instead, she did as she felt she must, and stood there, and cried. She cried until her throat was hoarse, and her chest hurt, and there was a big trail of salty tears and other liquids running down her chin. For the first time in a very long time, she let herself feel the tremendous hurt—not only from Thorn's words, but also from her confusion, and disappointment, and perhaps too all the strain of the past few days, and months and years. And when she had, she heaved in a deep, stilted and shaky breath, and wiped her face with her sleeve in the most unladylike way imaginable, extinguished all the candles and lamps she had lit, and took her lantern, and went home.

For a moment when she arrived back inside, she pondered cleaning up what was left of the mess in the hall—having told the others to simply go to bed and leave it until the morning—but she realised that would not be as beneficial as a proper night's rest. So she climbed up the stairs, and hoped that Thorn had made his way home, or would, safely—she daren't check—

and cleaned herself, changed, and fell into bed, straight into a dreamless sleep.

A sleep which didn't turn out to be particularly restorative, but was satisfactory enough to have her up at her usual early hour, dressed, and down to breakfast without any noticeable delay. Thorn wasn't there, and Hypatia asked Henry if he'd been down already, because no matter what had passed between them, she still cared what happened to him. Henry told her he'd been down an hour prior, and was already out on the farm. So she ate her breakfast in quiet solitude, glad that no harm had come to him, and no search parties need be sent out. Then, she went on about her day, managing to not encounter Thorn—likely by his design, as there hadn't been a day since he'd come she hadn't seen him—for which she was glad, for it gave her time, and space, to sort out if not everything, then most of everything.

Not only for herself, but also, for whenever she spoke to Thorn, she needed to know where she stood on many things; what had happened to bring them to this, and how they might move forward. If indeed Thorn wished to speak to her about it all, find a way forward. Everything about him until now gave her hope he would, but then last night, he'd behaved in such a way she might not have believed him capable had she not seen it with her own eyes; felt it with her own heart. It was such a radical departure from all she'd known him to do and say and be, that she would never have wagered on it being possible. Even though she supposed, she'd always known he had to have some bad for all the good; as everyone did. Only she'd never expected it to be thus.

And so she worked, and she thought, and she ruminated, and pondered, and worked some more. By the time she was doing her evening checks of the pigs out in the pastures—Truffél and Lamb aiding as they seemed to prefer her company to Thorn's—she'd come to a few conclusions, or revelations, or answers, or whatever one preferred to term them.

Firstly, that Thorn had behaved very badly indeed, and that she deserved an apology for such ludicrous, and vicious behaviour. In fact, she grew angrier the more she realised just how cowardly he'd been, ruminating for nigh-on a bloody fortnight, avoiding her, keeping all his doubts and fears and all to himself, without even bothering to ask for time to sort through any thoughts that plagued him. Although she understood how difficult it might've been to be so honest and forthright, well, they'd spoken of many things openly, and without reserve since the beginning of their acquaintance, and really, only so many excuses could be made.

Secondly, she had to admit that in many ways, though she didn't like it, she understood where his fears and sense of inadequacy were stemming from, and such feelings were natural. She may not like them, she may know that it wasn't up to her to engage in behaviours which might make him feel more useful or purposeful, it wasn't up to her to make him feel like a *man* which

she supposed was what this boiled down to in many respects; however, she did understand. He'd been brought
up with certain beliefs, a certain path, and now was
struggling to find worth and a place; after having been
left by a woman who in essence said he, his dreams,
his future, weren't enough for her. After being forced
into a role so many purported he was unworthy of. And
so much more.

Thirdly, she realised that—

'I'm sorry, Hypatia,' Thorn said from behind her,
giving her a start as she closed the gate to the pasture
she'd been in, Truffél and Lamb scrambling beneath it
to stand at her feet.

Turning, she found him standing there, covered in
exhaustion and dishevelment, which weren't from his
day's work, looking as contrite and annoyingly as handsome as anyone could but no one should have the right
to for how it could melt hearts, in the pale pink glow
of a long drawn-out sunset.

'Go home,' she told Truffél, pointing in the general
direction of the house. He looked up at her for a moment, then at Thorn, then snorted, and deciding he'd
do as bid, set off, Lamb trailing and bleating behind
him. 'Go on,' she told Thorn, as invitingly as she could.

'I was an ass. A cruel one at that. My…sense of
worth, my uncertainty and self-doubt, are not your
fault, nor yours to bear the brunt of. All you've done is
stand by my side, fight every battle, offer me yourself,
and I threw it back in your face as though it meant noth-

ing. And I am so very sorry, for all of it, and I know I've no right to ask for forgiveness, for you to want to take me back, but I am asking, because I care for you too much, for this, for us, to not ask. I never expected any of this, but I'll be damned if I wish to lose it, to lose you now. I should've turned back last night, and fallen to my knees, but I was so caught in a horrid storm of thoughts, however I will do so now, if you wish.'

'Tempting an image as that might present, Thorn, I don't want you on your knees,' she said, the attempted humour and playful jest marred by the sincerity of her statement, and tears pricking her eyes again. 'I want us standing, together, as we have been. I accept your apology. I don't condone the manner in which you expressed yourself, and should you ever do so again, I might not forgive you, but in this instance, perhaps it was a good thing. I did a lot of thinking today.'

'As did I.'

'We never courted. We never spent time together before we married, and though we discussed some things, there is much we didn't have time or occasion to speak of. I suppose that is a problem that plagues many,' she said, offering a small smile, which Thorn took, with a grateful nod. 'I for one didn't imagine all that would happen between us. I don't just mean the intimacy, but everything being...*good*. It felt easy, and simple, and I think we got swept up in it, and never really spoke of who we were, and what we need. I thought I was helping, taking certain things in hand, and I see now, how that might've made you feel without purpose. So I am sorry too.'

'You've nothing to be sorry for,' he said, taking a step towards her, then stopping, realising perhaps it was still too early for proximity. 'Whatever I felt, however inadequate I felt, that was my problem, not yours. I should've come to speak to you, I know it's because of things I heard as a boy, about what a man should and shouldn't be, and how I felt, being handed my father's trade, and all Helen said about my lack of ambition, and all the world has to say on what a proper and right *anything* is, and my own skewed views. Because of old wounds, and new ones too, and a sense I've always held that my worth depended on how well I controlled things, and handled things, and bettered myself, and supported others, but you've no blame in that. There are no excuses to be made.'

'You should've spoken to me, properly,' she agreed. 'But I'm not making excuses for you. I happen to like explanations. They help me understand. And I think they can help us find ways to be better together, if you want that.'

'Of course I want that,' he promised vehemently, and she smiled, relieved.

'Do you want to take over things with the farm?'

'Not unless you wish me to. We continue as we were, together. With you mostly in charge, as you've the better grasp.'

'If you're sure.'

'I am.'

'Do you want the forge? I hoped it would make you feel at home, I thought you were upset about the market and our lack of sales, and that it would make you feel more like yourself. I know you missed it.'

'I do want it. It was a beautiful gift, Hypatia, thank you,' he breathed, his exhaustion and dishevelment not gone, but replaced with relief, and hope which matched her own. He stepped closer, and so did she, a testament to her desire to make things good between them again. 'It touched my heart, and that scared me, along with all the rest. But I loved it, and even last night, the whole party, it was wonderful. You're wonderful. In case I haven't made it clear yet, I don't want to lose you.'

Reaching out with his clean, soil-stained hand, he made to take her hand, then thought better of it, and dropped it again.

'I do like you, Thorn, very much,' she said, taking it in hers, and twining their fingers. 'More than I've ever liked anyone. To a degree which should probably frighten me, but strangely doesn't. I am more myself with you than I've ever been with anyone, I've not felt I need to hide my thoughts or how I see things, that I was…that you accepted it all. And because of that, I thought, you saw things I should've spoken with you about. What I said, about not minding when you touched me, when you held my hand—'

'You don't have to—'

'I do,' she said, holding his gaze, still contrite, but

less troubled. It heartened her, as every word, every gesture, every breath did. 'Lest it drive a wedge between us again, which I don't want. I can't have you thinking… I enjoy being with you, in every way, Thorn, know that. I leave when we've finished because I don't like sleeping with another. I don't…know how to explain it, but I don't particularly care for sharing, talking, not like that, and I don't like bodies in the aftermath, or not having my own space. Me leaving, is merely because I like waking alone, and not having to share the blanket, and not being subjected to, or worrying about horrid morning breath. There are so many reasons, but it isn't because I've had my pleasure, and I am done. I simply need a space, for myself. I always have, and likely always will. And I know you express yourself with your touch, but it isn't something I do. I think you know I enjoy being *with* you, but I don't need you to hold my hand, to feel something. Maybe I'm broken in some way, but I just don't *need* it. I don't mind it, but I don't initiate it, not because I don't care, but because I don't feel an urge. But if it's that important to you, I can remind myself to do it, and I can try staying with you after our time together for a little while, and we can find a way to make it work. I want it to work. I for one found so much more in this partnership than I expected, and I don't want to lose you either.'

'I don't want you to do anything which isn't…yourself, Hypatia,' he reassured her, caressing her cheek with his knuckles, as if to say: *I understand you, I won't ask for you to go against yourself, but if you don't mind me touching you, I shall.* 'Perhaps some talk, or time together, half an hour or something would be nice, if it doesn't trouble you so much. With a blanket between us, or time to clean up, if that is better. And if touch isn't something that comes naturally to you… Words, kind words, every now and then, a reminder that you are here, and I am here, and we are together…'

'I can do that.'

He smiled, the past day or days catching up with them both.

Hearts sore, but mending, hope alive again in both of them, he touched his forehead to hers, and closed his eyes, and so did she, grateful for this moment, for him, for not having seen it all go to wrack and ruin.

Though someday, it might; someday, life might make them drift apart. No matter how good things were now, it was likely down to being thrust together, and sharing so much compatibility. Given some weeks, or months, or years, a more sedate life, a return to London, other interests, whatever it may be, the likelihood was they would return to what they'd agreed to be; business partners. Friends too, if they were fortunate. That's all they had promised each other, all either wanted, and that was that.

For now, they had whatever this was, and she for one, would treasure it.

'Let's go home,' she whispered, feeling the strength of all that sentence held now.

'Yes, I suppose we best do so, before Truffél and Lamb drive Langton to terrible deeds,' Thorn agreed, standing straight again, but keeping hold of her hand as he led her onwards. 'I will say, I am looking forward to some of what's left of the food tonight. I know you let everyone take some, but I'm not ashamed to say I was glad to hear some rhubarb tart remained. We did well with that hog too. You weren't lying about the deliciousness of our meat. It is rather special.'

'We should try and win a prize!' Hypatia said excitedly, stopping them again. 'I can't believe I didn't think of it before! It's the thing to do for well-to-do gentlemen, some even have portraits painted of their winning beasts!' Thorn said nothing, merely watched her, somewhat bemused, but she continued. 'It's more about size with swine I think, rather than lineage or breeding like horses, but we've both! Belinda would be good, or perhaps Clyde, they would just need some extra care for a month or two, and we could see what fairs might have prizes, and then that would cement our reputation, without a doubt! Hell, that horse farm in Sussex was nothing compared to what it is now that groom—well, the viscountess—won that race last year!'

'Did Langton not warn you of the dangers of naming the pigs?' Thorn finally drawled, his bemusement spilling over into a dangerous grin; one she'd sorely missed.

'We all end up leaving this world, one way or another. Giving something a name denotes respect, and care for it.'

'I suppose you're right. As for your idea… Maybe we should see if Reeves has any thoughts on the best fairs,' he said, tugging her hand gently, and getting them walking again. 'But you'll have to tell me which ones Clyde and Belinda are, though I suppose I could hazard a guess…'

So Hypatia made him guess—which he did after a rather long game, that took them nearly the whole way home.

And as they stepped back into Gadmin Hall, though she knew the road ahead remained uncertain, and full of obstacles, she thought, if they could just continue as they were learning to now, there were a thousand more possibilities before them than there had been yesterday.

Not merely in regard to the farm, but in regard to this marriage, which felt truer than ever before.

Chapter Eighteen

How long such a tradition will last in a new world such as that we see dawning is a matter of speculation I am ill-equipped to engage in, however undeniably it remains true that the time for our illustrious to make their fashionable retreats to the country is fast approaching. While this writer was disappointed the Earl and Countess of Gadmin were not to be seen in Oxford among the other agricultural delights, whispers posit that all is rather quiet and successful for them on the southern front. Rather a boon for the unsuccessful Miss Quincy, who failed to capitalise on her notoriety before it was born of tragedies with ducks, dukes, and treacle tarts, and finds herself with a dearth of invitations. If the doors of Gadmin Hall remain open to you, Miss Quincy, do share with us news of your sister and brother-in-law.

Jack the Cat, Londoner's Chronicle, July 1839

'This is entirely and utterly irresponsible, Thorn,' Hypatia grumbled, almost in time with the grumbling of the carriage, as they sped onwards to the south. He grinned, and waggled his brows, telling her silently as he'd told her on the twenty or so previous occasions today she'd uttered such sentiments, what he thought of her protestations.

'You're impossible,' she sighed, crossing her arms, and making a great show of pouting, and not staring out the windows, for he'd made sure they remained covered, so as not to ruin the surprise.

'Yes, but you rather like my impossibility in this context, I think,' he argued, raising a brow she saw, for she couldn't resist a peek. 'And you'll enjoy this surprise more if you let it *be* a surprise. You know I'm right.'

A *harumph* was his answer; which translated in Hypatia speak meant: *you're right but I won't admit it out loud just yet*.

Though she would eventually; that was something else he'd learned of late. Hypatia was attentive to ensuring her feelings, thoughts, unspoken meanings, and admissions of things such as *you were right*, were clearly spoken, even if it took minutes or an hour for her to do so, depending on the day. It was one of the many things he'd grown to appreciate and love about her in the past month, which had been, if not carefree, then splendid in its boisterous simplicity, and unpaved normality.

Their life had continued on much as it had been progressing—*sans* vicious outbursts, or great misunderstandings. There had been moments of chafing, of annoyance, of things rising unexpectedly to the surface—frustration at not succeeding instantly at this whole *saving Gadmin Hall* enterprise for instance—but Thorn and Hypatia had both learned to just say it outright. Sometimes to leave it, or the other for a day or night, but to return, with a cool head, and care of how to share. It was novel, and terrifying, yet restorative and comforting in ways Thorn had never experienced.

Their work generally continued apace, returns to market if not filling their coffers, then making more or less of a mark, depending on the day, somewhat in great thanks to Mr Fairchild, who had returned for hogs, and spread the word the meat and pigs were good. Neighbours continued to help and become friends; fields were planted or leased, new tenants found. Bits of furniture were bought for the house, repairs made to windows, doors, floors, and everything in between. A couple more workers joined them—a few lads for the farm, stables, and fields—and plans were made for the autumn. Reeves helped them make plans for a fair in late September in a nearby town—small, but of reputational prestige—and Thorn and Hypatia worked hard to get Belinda and Clyde both to exceptional weight and presentation without harming them. They were good animals, who only needed additional tending to show off their interior excellence.

Thorn, when he had a moment to spare, which wasn't often, went to the forge, and made things which were needed on the farm, in the house, or merely for plea-sure; like the other surprise he had for Hypatia. It re-stored him, cleared his mind, and reminded him, as she'd hoped, of who he was. As did, in many ways, all the time he spent with her, learning every detail, every facet of not only her body, but her mind and heart. Her intricacies—such as the way she always brushed her hair two hundred times, though it made her look like a poodle until after a night's slumber—and her prefer-ences, and her everything. He shored it all up, loving every detail, every morsel, just as he loved every bath they shared in the stream, every passionate kiss in the middle of the pasture, every night he lost himself within her; in every way possible. It showed him what kind of man he was, and wanted to be; reminded him his past, his hurts, his no longer useful ways of thinking were not all he was. But that he was kind, and passionate, and free, and hard-working, and could make Hypatia smile after a long day, and take care of others, and not be crushed by expectation or disappointment.

It taught him that he was a man who could, and wanted to, love again, with his whole heart, in a manner he'd never thought possible. Not selfishly, not demand-ingly, not with any aim but to be with another, and make them happy, and feel life coursing through their veins every second of every day. It wasn't at all like a good whisky; it was like coming home, and being in your favourite chair after a long absence. It was working to understand and learn another because you couldn't be but fascinated, and needed to know who they were, that made you feel so yourself.

In many ways his love for her terrified him, for all that it might, could, hurt and change him if ever he lost her entirely; however, he worked every second to become the sort who loved unreservedly in spite of the fear. Who saw the possibilities of life even if love should be torn from them, for they'd have had the chance to experience it. It was far from easy, but he knew what fear, and anger, and insecurity could do, and he never wished to succumb to them so easily, so readily again. He knew his growing love had played a part in his earlier resentments, cruelty, and anger towards her; some part of him had been terrified of acknowledging his love, lest he accept how terrible a loss of Hypatia, or a wound, cut, or betrayal from her might be. Worse, perhaps, in its difference to that of Helen's, just as his love was different; not that he liked comparing.

He hadn't told Hypatia, of course. It wasn't that he wasn't communicating as he'd promised, it was that he wanted the time and space to do so properly. To do so without making demands. For whatever Hypatia might feel for him, and he knew she felt many things, though she guarded some closer than anyone might expect, he didn't want her to feel the need to reciprocate, or say she did, to make him feel better. He knew how complex a subject love was for her. It would not mean that he was unworthy, and truly, he accepted that if she never loved him as he loved her, well, that would be just fine. He had enough love in him for them both to have a happy life, even if in time they became platonic friends. Hypatia was the most important thing to him, and their marriage meant something beyond a mere business deal; always had, but even more so now. In time, at the right place, in the right time, he would tell her so, tell her all of it, and see if perhaps, she might be ready to renegotiate the terms of their initial agreement.

Perhaps she might risk taking another chance with me.

So yes, the past month had been exceptionally simple, tedious, difficult, lovely, and special, and they'd all been working hard, therefore, this break was just the ticket; for Henry, Mary, Langton, and their maid, Finny, too, since Thorn had forbidden them to work.

I can only hope they follow the edict. As for us, it seems...

'We're here,' Thorn said, grinning in anticipation as the carriage pulled to a halt, and Hypatia straightened eagerly.

'And where precisely is *here*, Lord Gadmin?'

'The sea, Lady Gadmin,' Thorn told her as Ian opened the door, bright sunshine flooding into the carriage and temporarily blinding them, until finally, their eyes adjusted.

Hypatia slid to the edge of her seat, and stared out, and oh, what he would've given to call upon that fictional painter again, to commission them to immortalise her face then, so full of wonder, astonishment, and fascination.

'It's…incredible,' she breathed after a long moment. 'I cannot find words, for it defies all those written about it these past millennia. And the air…so extraordinary,' she grinned, taking a lungful of it, before turning back to him. 'Thank you, Thorn.'

'You're welcome. Shall we?'

'Yes, please!'

Not waiting for him, and barely taking Ian's arm, she descended, unable to wait a second longer, and chuckling, Thorn followed, popping on his hat.

'Enjoy your day, Ian,' he told the man with a nod, watching his wife stand like a statue among the rest of the visitors, workers, and inhabitants making their way along the seafront. 'We'll see you outside the hotel in the morning.'

'And you, my lord,' Ian said, with a bow of the head, before jumping back up to his post, and setting off for his own adventures; funded by Thorn, but of which he needed to know nothing at all.

'So, my lady,' Thorn said, turning his attention back to his wife, and slipping her arm in his. 'We have many choices to occupy our time—and we have a room nearby for the night. There is, as you can see, this delightful shingle beach. There are baths, I'm told, an arcade, some half-timbered houses, a fish market, more shopping, some fascinating boat launches, games, entertainment and walks of all sorts, and a castle. What would you like to do?'

'Everything,' she smiled, broader than he'd ever seen, her eyes alight with joy. 'But first, I want to put my feet in the water.'

So, tugging him along, she set off to find a path to the sea, and Thorn had to mark this moment down too, as one of the happiest of his life.

In the end, they didn't do everything. They wet their feet in the sea, Hypatia frolicking like a child, Thorn frolicking alongside her, to the amused and sometimes disapproving stares of others. Then, when the sea rose past the patches of comfortable sand, they went back and sat on the shingles, and watched the waves, the children, the other lovers, the fishermen.

When Thorn asked if she was hungry, or wished to go explore elsewhere, he saw enough hesitancy and lack of enthusiasm in Hypatia's otherwise bright face, that he knew she didn't. So he went off to find them food, obtaining a mix of sea produce from a fisherman's hut further along, and they feasted on it right there, watching the waves, the children, the other lovers, and the fishermen.

They didn't speak much either, which he didn't find he minded at all. They didn't need to talk today, or any day, to enjoy each other's company, and share in something. Eventually, he rose again to fetch them some shaved ice, but beyond that, they didn't move, until the sea began its descent again, at which point they went to soak their feet, wandering along the length of the shore, and back again. And they held hands, and swung their tied-together boots between them as one might a small child, and they watched the children, and the fishermen, and looked at the huts, and the castle on the cliff, and the other lovers, and the new buildings along the seafront, and watched the sunset.

Thorn, for one, found it to be perfect, and amended his earlier thought; *this* was the happiest he'd ever been.

Eventually, a chilly evening breeze, conspiring with exhaustion, drove them to seek the comfort of their hotel, so, somewhat reluctantly, they put their socks, stockings and boots back on, and made their way there, stopping for some hot buns full of crab on the way, which they devoured without delay or ceremony, before continuing on, weaving through visitors like themselves, and locals of all ages and dispositions, half admiring the architecture, half merely soaking in the atmosphere.

Finally, they arrived at *The Old Beech*, and were brought up to their small, but delicately decorated room, overlooking the seafront, and which featured one specific amenity: a screen between two single beds.

'I hope it's all right,' Thorn said, once the attendant showing them up had departed. 'I couldn't quite justify getting two rooms, but if you wish me to, I'm sure they'll have something for me.'

'This is perfect, Thorn,' she reassured him with a

grateful smile. 'Thank you for thinking of this arrangement. For a perfect day.'

'You're not disappointed we didn't see or do anything else?' he asked, smoothing one of those rambunctious curls from her forehead; just an excuse to touch her really. 'We'll have some time in the morning, but not much.'

'I'm not disappointed at all.'

The way she looked at him then, honey-green eyes so full of joy and light; if he hadn't already been in love with her, he would've fallen for her then.

No one wouldn't have.

He might've told her, found that moment to be the perfect one to say as much, yet something stopped him, and he simply leaned down instead, and kissed her, with a slow, languorous, and profound depth that made everything within him calm, still, and settle.

After a moment, or perhaps a hundred, they broke apart, and he smiled.

'We should get cleaned up, and in more comfortable attire.'

Hypatia nodded, and he released her, so they could go about doing just that.

Seizing the opportunity while she was busy behind another screen, he placed his other gift on her pillow; the bed by the window of course, which he suspected would be open the night through, despite any noise of nighttime revellers below, to allow the briny air and seagulls' cries in. Settling on top of his own bed once properly refreshed and changed, he laid back, and stared at the mouldings on the ceiling, remembering the day, and every day which had led up to it, wondering how he'd gotten here, how extraordinary life was, to have conspired by myriad events, choices, and chances, to bring him to this.

To a wife so extraordinary, to love, to—

'Oh, Thorn...'

He grinned, hearing admiration and pleasure in her voice, and seeing it a moment later when she came around the screen to stand beside him, cradling the iron rose in her hands like some fragile treasure, eyes darting along every millimetre.

'You like it?'

'It's incredible,' she smiled, and he didn't take her surprise at him being capable of such work badly; rather, it filled his heart with pride. Thorn shifted, sitting up, and making room for her beside his legs if she wished to join him, which she did. 'It looks as though you've plucked it from the garden, and dipped it in metal. I mean look at this,' she breathed, running her fingers over it now, along every thin petal, every leaf, every move and wave and twist of the metal. 'This must've taken you days...'

'Only a couple,' he shrugged, blushing slightly.

'I don't mean... This isn't to say you're not good at doing what you are, but Thorn, this is artistry.'

'Do you know, I think I enjoy it more now that it isn't my profession. I used to count the hours, rage sometimes at the time it would take to make such intricate, lifelike pieces for some gentleman's gate, or lady's fire-place shield, whereas making this…'

Was a labour of love.

He didn't say that, and wondered why his lips and tongue refused so to speak such a confession, even in a sideways manner, smiling softly as if to merely say: *you understand.*

'I understand,' Hypatia said, with a mirroring smile. 'Can I ask you a strange question?'

'Lord, you do frighten me at times, Hypatia,' he chuckled. 'Go on, then.'

'That first day, when you arrived at Gamin Hall, and I saw you after my confrontation with Warren, and just now, when I told you this rose was incredible, what were you feeling?'

Frowning slightly, he thought back, not truly being one to catalogue his feelings as they passed through him; recognising them, yes, however, the practice of storing away a notation of their arrival and departure not being something he typically did.

He wasn't entirely sure *why* Hypatia was asking, or if he wanted to know, but he would answer, regardless, as she had asked, and that was reason enough for him.

'Pride,' he told her finally, meeting her gaze, troubled and searching now. 'Of my work, and that day, of you. Beyond how I'd ever felt it before, in truth.'

'Hm,' she nodded, turning to look back down at the rose and biting her lip.

Ask her.

'Thank you,' she said after a long while, rising. 'For that, for the rose, for everything, Thorn. Good night.'

A swift but sweet kiss, and she was gone to the other side of the screen.

Ask her.

He heard her open the window, grinned, then heard her slide into bed, and so he did the same, and extinguished the lamp beside him, before she did hers.

Ask her.

'Why did you ask me that?'

'I didn't recognise it, and so it troubled me.'

Oh, I shouldn't have asked, though I can't truly regret it, for now I understand so much more.

Another chapter for The Book of Hypatia.

'Good night, Hypatia.'

I love you.

'Good night, Thorn.'

Chapter Nineteen

Many would likely disagree—surely those who had to face such sounds every morn of their lives—however, Hypatia found that waking to the calls and cries of the gulls, mixed with those of the other typical birds, be they sparrows or tits; the crash of the waves, and the crisp, salt-laden air, was one of the most pleasant ways to traverse from the land of dreams back into reality.

Though today, she couldn't complain about reality; since she'd married Thorn, and particularly since he'd come to Gadmin Hall, she hadn't found much about reality to disparage of, as she had too often before. Most of it was due to a change in circumstance, in scenery; in gaining her own independence, and autonomy, even whilst being ruled by the necessities of her—*their*—current life. However, so much of it was due to Thorn, like today, like yesterday, because that man, her husband, quite literally made her dreams a reality. He gave them priority, over fripperies, or even necessities; over

work, and need, and made one of her greatest wishes—
to see the sea—come true.

Not only that…it was just *him*, how he was with her.
How he'd been, yesterday, content to merely sit with
her for hours, getting food and comforts when required,
but otherwise, satisfied with keeping her company. And
this room, finding a way to give her some measure of
the privacy and solitude she'd expressed were vital to
her, while keeping somewhat within their means. He
continuously surprised her, with his attentiveness, his
understanding, his open acceptance, and his enduring
tenderness. Every day he worked to prove his heart to
be true, and his worthiness of her trust in him. The
most profound gratitude flooded her heart, her entire
self again, as it had so often with his deeds and words,
for she knew such behaviour to be rare. Such kindness,
and compassion, to not be the rule sadly, and perhaps
not quite an exception, but a rarity. He wasn't perfect,
as she herself wasn't, but he worked so hard—and she
did in her own ways—to demonstrate that he didn't
take her for granted. That though their marriage had
begun as one of conveniences, greater, deeper bonds
had been forged, and he wished to maintain them thus.

Life, time, might take them further from each other
than they were now—she didn't like to think on such
things, as she didn't particularly want to envisage a life
without the comfort of his presence, support, and partnership, however she knew it was a possibility—and
even if they stopped being lovers, and went to tread

separate paths, still, she knew, that respect, that tenderness and protection, would remain.

And that too, is such a rare thing.

Dust motes danced on the growing shafts of light as the dawn turned to that of nigh-on full morning. Hypatia turned to glance at the ceiling, smiling to herself at the realisation they'd slept in well past their typical pre-dawn hour.

Truly a holiday; though I've admittedly not much comparison.

On the other side of the screen, she heard a shift of fabric on fabric, and the change in Thorn's breathing from that of sleep, to quiet but awoken rest. Spurred on by the growing cries, and crashing waves, voices and carts and shouts for fresh fish outside, Hypatia decided she knew well how she wanted to enjoy this morning; what she wanted to share with Thorn in this place too, to add another shell-like memory to her bursting seaside collection of them.

As quietly as she could, she slipped out of bed, rummaged in her bag until she found the case containing what she hoped she might soon need, and went around the screen. Thorn was lying as she had been, on his back, staring up at the ceiling, both hands behind his head, only his waist and baser self covered by the thin linen sheet, whilst his legs tangled in the rest, and his strong, hearty chest remained bare, in all its glory for her to appreciate.

Slowly his eyes made their way down to her as she

came properly into his view, and he smiled lazily, eyes sparking and glittering as hot metal did when he struck it, as she divested herself of her nightgown, and tossed it to the floor.

'What is your preference today, Thorn?' she asked, raising a brow, repeating a now ritual they'd gained since their first night together.

'For you to come and take a nice ride, and your pleasure.'

A nod, and she stepped closer, tossing the sheet aside, and settling herself astride his legs, whilst he—well, most of him—moved not an inch, simply watched, and felt, and let her take care of him.

Which she did, taking some of her already ample wetness to tease him to his fullest with her hand, while he watched, sucking in tight breaths, as teeth held tight to his bottom lip, and his belly quivered, though he refused to look away. And when he had fully risen to the occasion, beading wetness himself, clinging to his own hands and not merely resting anymore, arms bulging as he fought to keep himself together whilst still enjoying the pleasure she taunted him with, she sheathed him with the preventive, ever so slowly, and then guided herself slowly onto him, seating herself precisely where they both wanted.

Sucking in a breath whilst releasing a semi-strangled noise of fulfilment when she was seated and full to brim with him, she took a moment to let her head fall back, and clench her inner muscles, making him twitch and buck.

Letting his pleasure and appreciation fill her every pore, she met his gaze again, intent on not breaking it, and began to do as he'd requested, rising and falling; clutching and releasing, every stroke decadent, sweet, and as slow as she could manage. She took in all she could feel of him, having learnt so many of his tells, his shifts and stilts in breath; the change in his eyes, the appearance and disappearance of those dimples. Sweat and slickness mingled where they joined, the tenseness on his thighs beneath her supporting, and tantalising.

They'd learned much about each other's bodies, how they liked certain moments, such as this, but Hypatia felt her breath and heart skip some beats of their natural rhythm as she continued to draw out both their pleasures, and watch him. Her cheeks flamed more than usual, nipples peaking higher, as though reaching out to him evermore, for something else was in the thick, sweet air between them, something she'd never spied there before; not that she could identify it.

Only that it all felt rawer, more serious, and she mentally tried to swat it away, focusing on her fullness, and his, and the delicious sparking growing in the depths of her inner self, blooming outwards until even her fingers were tingling. Except she couldn't quite, and it was harder to keep pace, and it was still delicious, and delectable, but something pinched inside her chest, and Thorn must've seen it, for in a flash he was there, surrounding her with limbs, holding her tight, and tucking her head into his neck.

Her fingers tightened and dug softly into his ribs, and she nestled into him, as he finished their quest for pleasure, driving up into her, but keeping her tight against him, reminding her how to breathe with his own slick skin rising and falling against her body, soothing her with fingers in her hair, and light squeezes of her flesh.

Until she was dizzy and hot and whining against his skin whilst everything inside of her reached the realest, strangest, most honey-like and terrifying ecstasy she'd ever experienced. Thorn lost himself within her and another wave of pleasure made her cling even tighter to him, so she had no idea whose skin was whose and whose breath was whose. She felt scraped open, torn open, and stitched back together with salve; stitched into Thorn.

And she remained in his arms far longer than she usually could, unable to unstitch herself, or comprehend that what they'd just shared wasn't a dream, but instead the realest thing she'd ever known; all whilst he stroked her, and murmured nothings in her ear, and placed kisses in her hair, and they listened to the waves, and the gulls, and the sea.

Chapter Twenty

By the time their carriage was bumping its way back up the road towards Gadmin Hall's drive, Thorn had decided that purchasing a *new* carriage had made its way to the top of the *urgent things to spend money on* list. No carriage would ever offer an entirely smooth ride—especially not given the state of some roads—and this carriage had admittedly served them well thus far.

That being said, the next time they rode in this carriage together, and wished to cuddle, Hypatia neatly tucked into his side as he held her tight, he didn't want it to become an exercise in avoiding her skull hitting his chin, or vice-versa, or anything else of the sort, because their carriage shook them as though they were in a barrel floating on a bouncing river.

It shall be my own fancy; my one extravagance. Mayhaps I shall have pigs painted on the doors, or ask they be integrated into the Gadmin coat of arms. I don't think the old earl would've minded; quite the contrary.

And in all honesty, he didn't think Ian would mind

something nicer either; just as he likely wouldn't mind a younger lad to share his knowledge with, and quite literally pass the reins to.

Yes, Thorn was in a supremely good mood. And not merely because of the rather spectacular wake-up Hypatia had treated him to this morning. He was in a good mood, because he was damned and bloody well *happy*. His life was far from perfect, and as before, he knew struggles and turmoil lay ahead—they always did—but it was good. Full of everything he'd ever wanted—some of which he never thought he'd have again—and he could now see a future not simply of toil, of duty, of responsibility, partnership, and friendship, but one where he could share his life with someone he loved. He could see himself growing old with Hypatia, here, at Gadmin Hall, and in their oldest years, still going down to bathe in the stream. He could see being happy for many decades to come, and that was not something he'd expected. Not something he'd even thought he'd have the heart for.

Even his life as a farmer, as an earl, he was beginning to see, or beginning to accept, just all the happiness, purpose, and satisfaction it could bring. He'd thought at the start of this whole adventure—or ordeal, as he'd considered it then—that he would have to become something so far from himself, he'd never be satisfied. Now, he saw he was more himself than he'd ever been, and though he missed some aspects of his former life and profession, he didn't miss them enough to not see the boon with which he'd been bestowed.

How strange life is...

'I've been thinking, about the old earl,' Hypatia said, staring out the window, at a rather awkward angle considering her head still rested—or bounced—on his shoulder.

'Have you now.'

'I've been thinking how we merely call him *the old earl*. I don't think I know his name, or even where he's buried. I feel… I don't like saying that I feel sorry for someone, there's a sense to it, a tone, I don't know, I don't like it, but I do feel sorry for him. Being ill, being so alone here, being much as you were, left with mountains of debt, and tasked with doing better, and being so right about so many things, yet everyone thinking he was mad, or old, when I think in many ways, he was just as lost as we were.'

'I think of him often too,' Thorn nodded, gazing out at passing trees and fields which were so familiar now, as though they'd been etched into his heart upon birth, then covered with dust until it was time to come home. 'Not only because he was some distant relative I never knew of. He was as much a stranger to me as anyone else, but perhaps, I suppose, I imagined he didn't have to be. I asked the solicitors about him, but they didn't really have much to say. All I know, is that he was called Ford Harris, and inherited the earldom from his father, who'd tried to restore it from ruin after his grandfather drove it there. He was buried in London, at Tindal's. I went there, and planted some myrtle. I like to believe, that somehow, he knows his pigs are taken care of now. His people too. I think he was trying to save this place, and simply couldn't find the path, so took some others. And lest we forget, Warren played his part.'

'If we ever do win a prize, or fully succeed in making this work… I hope it'll change how people saw him.'

'As do I.'

'We should… I would like to get to know him better too. Perhaps Langton, Henry and Ian would care to share stories some time. Or something.'

'Yes. We'll speak to them.' Sighing contentedly, Thorn turned slightly to kiss the top of her head, just as Ian took the turn onto the drive, so it resulted in him squashing against her somewhat. 'Sorry.'

'Ian takes some of these turns, and I think we shall surely tip over,' she chuckled. 'Or fall apart.'

'Don't worry, a new carriage has, after this journey, made it to the very top of our list of expensive priorities.'

'How very irresponsible, my Lord Gadmin.'

'I know, my Lady Gadmin. However, I have decided we should become extravagant, like the aristocrats we are.'

'I suppose we can allow ourselves some extravagance, and a new carriage is an investment, after all. Besides, until autumn, we should be fine with what workers we have, and no one at the house seems to want us to hire anyone else. I offered Henry some help—maybe another footman or a valet—and he seemed very reluctant. Then again, I promised no matter how many staff we had, he would never have to share a room, and he seemed *less* reluctant.'

'Perhaps we should just promote him to butler,' Thorn suggested, and Hypatia nodded against him. 'He deserves it, and he might be more comfortable in those downstairs quarters. I suppose it is a testament to their sense of duty and position that he and Langton stayed where they were supposedly *meant* to.'

'I don't think they wanted any excuses for a dismissal. I don't know what Langton's past is, but I don't suspect it was all innocence and roses, and Henry is Henry. I can't see many accepting him in grand houses, unless for some other purpose, or for sport, which is repugnant.'

'Indeed. I think old Ford was rather fond of giving people chances or opportunities others might not.'

'I hope we've continued that tradition too, by taking on people like Mary—who is the best housekeeper I've ever known, and Niamh will be a tyrant if ever she decides to go into the profession.'

'Quite,' Thorn chuckled as the carriage slowed, and came to a stop before the hall. Hypatia straightened, and *this* he decided, was the moment, now that they were home. 'Hypatia, I—'

'My lord, my lady, thank goodness you're back,'

Henry said in one breath, tearing open the carriage door before Thorn could finish any romantic declarations.

Both he and Hypatia straightened, the alarm and sheer terror in Henry's eyes making both their hearts skip a beat.

'Is someone injured?' Thorn asked, and Henry shook his head.

'The pigs?'

'No, my lady—'

'Warren?'

'No, my lord—'

'What is it, Henry, by God's teeth, you're scaring us!'

'You have guests, my lady. Rather a collection of them.'

'Who in the bloody Hell is visiting us?' Thorn asked, turning to Hypatia, who seemed as bereft of clues as he.

'I think it's best if you see for yourself, my lord.'

God's teeth, indeed.

Who in the bloody Hell it turned out to be was Mr Quincy, Mrs Quincy, Miss Quincy, Malek, and Helen; the queerest assembly of persons no fool would've ever devised, by Thorn's summation. When he first saw them, gathered in the one receiving room they'd somewhat furnished, perched and sat on the sole old—but not moth-eaten, only frayed—settee, armchair, and footstool, he admittedly gawked.

No one actually said anything—nor were conversations interrupted, only a thick, awkward silence—for quite a long while after he and Hypatia appeared in the room, eyes turning to them in accusation—and apology as concerned Malek—as though he and Hypatia should've known guests were coming.

And there goes my jolly good mood.

As well as Hypatia's.

Indeed, his wife had paled, stiffened, and looked as politely uncomfortable as one possibly could. He cursed them all silently, taking her hand, cursing himself too, for purchasing any furniture whatsoever; though unfortunately given the assembly, he doubted they would've simply left at such a discovery. He hated them all just then, for ruining his wife's and his mood; for interrupting their bliss, and forcing them into whatever this was.

In fact, he hated them all more for what effect they had on Hypatia—*dimming her light, her brightness, so blinding of late*—more than for what effect they had on him. Which was rather insignificant he found, oddly. Malek, he was actually pleased to see—curious too—whereas Helen…he was mostly dumbfounded. No old sentiments, good or ill, sprang forth, merely a sort of quiet blandness.

Progress, forgiveness, a chapter closed.

'Well, isn't this a surprise,' Hypatia finally managed to say, cutting through the silence, though it still held heavy, like walls, parted only to allow voice for the briefest moment. 'Mother, Father, Epi…'

'Helen Linnaman, or so I believe it still to be,' Thorn said flatly, and if Hypatia deduced *who* that made

Helen, or felt anything about that, she showed nothing, merely bowed her head in acknowledgement; as did Helen. 'And Malek Smith, my old apprentice.'

'My lady,' Malek said, recalling his manners, and rising to bow.

'A pleasure,' Hypatia said. 'Well, now that we are all introduced...'

She trailed off, and Thorn realised she was at a loss of what to say next; as in truth, he was, really he just wanted to ask *what the bloody Hell they were all doing here*, but such wasn't done in such varied company, and therefore, he barely refrained.

If Hypatia can, so can I.

'We've been on a bit of journey,' Thorn said instead. 'So if you would allow us a few moments to refresh ourselves, we will join you in the garden for tea. Which Henry will have laid out by now, I'm sure.'

Helen looked as though she wished to flee, and speak to him alone, but he ignored her, and made to turn, taking Hypatia with him.

'We had your things moved to your husband's room,' Mrs Quincy informed them, and Thorn gritted his teeth, tightening his hold on Hypatia's hand. 'Honestly, Patty, I have no idea what you have been up to here these past months. It truly is unbelievable the state of this house, and there was nowhere else for us to go, with Epi taking the only guest room apparently available. What did you expect, for us to sleep in the eaves like servants?'

To sleep anywhere but here, Thorn thought. Instead

of saying it, or anything else uncharitable he was close to, he simply led Hypatia on, and out of that room. He—they both—needed a moment, to gather information from their treacherous servants, and centre themselves. Luckily, he found Mary waiting for them at the bottom of the stairs, looking verily apologetic.

'I didn't know what else to do, my lord. Her ladyship's family…the others, we had no idea if perhaps an invitation had been forgotten, or a letter lost…'

'You did fine, Mary,' Hypatia reassured her. 'There were no invitations lost or anything of the sort. It's not you, but them. Though I cannot speak for his lordship's kith, only my own kin, and in either case I cannot speak of whatever has conspired to bring them all here at once.'

'Yes, when did they all descend?'

'The Quincys, not an hour after your departure, my lord,' Mary told them. 'Miss Linnaman, this morning, with Mr Smith. Both indicated they hoped to be on their way as soon as they'd spoken to you, and were therefore unsure about requiring a place for the night, particularly as they understood the quandary of accommodation. Mr Smith insisted he would find his own way, however Mr Reeves had stopped by, and overheard, so he is airing one of his cottages should it be needed. There are also rooms available in Sandham should we need them, depending on everyone's needs and preferences.'

'Thank you, Mary. Please secure a room in Sandham for Miss Linnaman, as I fear no matter how quickly we get to the reason for her visit, it will not be quick enough to have her back on the road today. And unless my wife voices any objections, her family are to be settled into Reeves' cottage, while her things are to be returned to her own *bloody* room. The guest room will remain available to Mr Smith should he require it. Hypatia?'

His wife fully met his gaze then, tumultuous, and confused, but grateful.

'As his lordship says. Please, Mary. We shall have tea, and see…where we go from there.'

'Yes, my lady. If required, we have dinner and breakfast enough for the lot of them.'

'Thank you.'

With that, Thorn took his wife's hand, and led her upstairs, and to his room, and then, he just held her, for as long a time as he could, before Mary knocked on the door to move her things, and then he let her go.

All the while, whilst he was changing, and splashing cold water on his face, and trying to rein in his anger and frustration, all he could think was: *this is merely an obstacle like any other.*

We can get through it; together.

Chapter Twenty-One

‘Such a lovely garden,’ Helen said tentatively, as though she might be struck by a thunderbolt—or indeed, one of their other guests—for daring to disrupt the suffocating and tense silence which had carried out here from the receiving room. Hypatia was grateful to her however, for daring to initiate small talk which would tide them through until they could discover precisely the reason for all these unexpected guests.

Beyond that gratitude, Hypatia wasn't entirely sure how she felt. Utterly disbelieving of these coincidental arrivals, knowing they were nothing but that, yet still wondering if she had injured some sprite of luck in the past, and he'd thus sought to reward her with ill-timed arrivals of hers and Thorn's past lives. Disoriented, shocked, lost; all and yet none seemed to cover the wide array of emotions brewing and knotting together inside, made worse from the calming, restorative, and extraordinary day she'd spent with Thorn at the seaside. From all their days with few exceptions since they'd begun their new life here, really. From him standing up to them all just now, by rearranging potential sleeping arrangements, and taking her hand, and...

Everything.

In terms of her own family, the greatest emotion was *wary*. They wouldn't have come without a reason—which could be said of anyone, really, but which in this case meant they wanted something from her, and she doubted it was money, and she had truly nothing left to give them, or so she felt. She was entirely Hypatia now, not Patty, and so there was a measure of gratitude in her heart for at least that certainty, that strength.

As regarded Malek, Thorn's old apprentice, she was actually somewhat excited; he seemed a nice fellow, had kind eyes, and Thorn had spoken so highly of him, whatever he wanted, she felt it would enrich all of their lives somehow.

Finally, as regarded Helen, Thorn's former love, well, perhaps that was the most complex of all. Some part of her wanted to be angry, to throw her bodily from this house for her sheer presumption; especially since she was an exceptionally beautiful woman, fineness and grace woven into every perfect line, thick, ruly brown hair, and rather sweet smile. Yet another part of Hypatia was immensely curious. To know if she was here for the obvious reason—to try and win Thorn back, as she'd heard no rejection of her maiden name, but then again that meant nothing at all—or something else. She was curious whether Thorn would be amenable—she tried to see how he felt now, but couldn't spy anything beyond upset. They'd spoken of her, and he seemed to have moved past it, but Hypatia knew close to a decade of love was not so easily swept away, even with betrayal and a new life. She and Thorn might get along mightily in many respects; however, love was not part of their agreement, of their marriage—unless it was solely defined by respect, like, mutual appreciation, kindness, tenderness, sweetness, joy, and so on—and even from the first, she'd accepted that someday, he might leave her to find such wonder elsewhere.

Though I find now, I had begun to dream of more time together. Not solely as partners, but as husband and wife.

So yes, *complex.*

'Thank you, Miss Linnaman,' Hypatia said graciously, patently refusing to look at anyone but her, and be as polite and kind as she could. 'It still needs much work, but we are pleased with what we've achieved, and we have everything we need.'

Hypatia recognised the *harumph* she heard as her mother's but ignored it, and thankfully so did Helen.

'Yes, what a delightful vegetable patch you have, and such herbs and wildflowers as I've never seen. I expect this was once an exceptional apothecary garden.'

'We suspect so, given the history of the house—'

'Ah!' Epi cried, leaping from her seat, as they all turned to hear in alarm.

A snort and a bleat quickly followed, and while Epi

gained some distance from the table in fear and disgust—her mother rising to comfort and protect her dramatically—the rest of them leaned over to spy what had caused such alarm, and found Truffél and Lamb. Which might've been an adorable visit, had the two not been far from babes anymore; Truffél weighing about three and a half stone now, and Lamb being the size of a small sheepdog.

'Truffél, Lamb, come here,' Hypatia ordered, rising, and working hard not to be amused. 'Don't fret, Epi, they are well trained. Go find Danny,' she told them, which they seemed to ponder for a moment, before deciding to obey—though not without greeting their master first.

Hypatia glanced at Thorn, who appeared to also be working hard not to be amused.

'You heard your lady,' he told them after a pat, and taste of his cake. 'Out.'

With another bleat and snort, they were off, trotting through the garden to do as told.

'That's quite impressive,' Helen offered with an unsure smile. 'They are very…sweet.'

'This is a madhouse, Hypatia!' her mother shouted, still shielding Epi as if Truffél and Lamb were about to return at any moment, and devour them whole. 'An absolute disgrace! How can you even think to receive guests in such conditions?'

'I wasn't thinking to receive any.'

'Do not speak to your mother thus!' her father exclaimed indignantly, joining the fray, and rising to reprimand her. She might've rolled her eyes, had she not been so...disappointed, and sad, and returned instantly to the young girl who'd only wanted their approval, their attention, their support, and their love. It cut through her more than the anger and distance she'd felt from them all these years, surprising her by its hurt. *I thought I had moved forward, but it appears hope I thought I had long abandoned lived on still.* 'She is entirely correct, this place is a disgrace! A house in disrepair, no furniture, nothing but chipped crockery and a pigpen for a garden! Have you any idea how hard it has been for us, to have your sister find an acceptable match, to show our faces in Society, when all they will speak of is our daughter, the pig farmer? And that writing weasel at the *Londoner's Chronicle* seems incapable of letting all the infamy die out as a gentleman might? That isn't even to speak of your supposed household! Your housekeeper is unwed with a child, I'm quite certain that cook of yours spent some time in *prison*, and that footman shouldn't even be called that—'

'Enough!' Thorn declared, rising to his feet, not shouting, but not quiet either. 'You will not speak one more word against any of my household, and that includes your daughter.' Hypatia looked over at him, a bright, sparking and irrefutably powerful Ares, her heart full of gratitude, and something else, for him doing what he was. His eyes were on her father, a brow raised in challenge, but he held out his hand to her, and she took it, feeling better at once. 'Why precisely is it you are here?' Thorn asked, simply, but leaving no room for polite divagations and excuses. 'All of you, let's out with it, for I'm tired of this supposed civilised nonsense. Everyone, sit down, and have out with precisely why it is you have come to Gadmin Hall so we can be done with it, and move on with our lives.'

Anyone standing was too afraid to disobey, or too shocked by the uncouth bluntness perhaps, and anyone sitting was too caught to flee, so they all returned to the table, and sat, and sipped tea, and played with forks and pieces of cake, and Thorn pulled his chair closer to hers, and set their linked hands on his thigh, waiting.

'Who's first?' he asked.

'I came to ask if there might be need of a smith in these parts,' Malek said quietly after a very long, tortuous moment, when everyone had stared, glared, and looked intently at each other, as if to prompt another to go first. 'I don't wish to be ungrateful, after all you've done for me, after what you entrusted me with, but I could not find my place without you. The work was good, but in truth, you were my only friend, and perhaps that isn't reason enough to leave what you'd gifted me behind, but I did, and now I am here, asking for more. Though I can pay my way, I sold the forge, and took what I could with me.'

Hypatia glanced at Thorn, spotting a mix of disappointment, sadness at the loss of what he and his father had built, yet heartfelt understanding. When he turned to her, she nodded in response to his unspoken question, tightening her hold on him.

'It so happens my wife gifted me a forge,' Thorn told Malek. 'And there is need of a smith in these parts, and beyond. We can speak of details later, but you are welcome to stay.'

'Thank you,' Malek said, bowing his head. 'Both of you.'

Thorn and Hypatia both smiled, taking a moment to acknowledge this new chapter, for all of them, before Thorn turned to the rest of them.

'Next?'

Thorn's gaze alternated between her family, and Helen; while she alternated between wishing her family would speak first, so that she would never hear what Helen had to say, and that the latter would do so, and put an end to her torment.

'It has been months since we had any word of our daughter,' her father said imperiously, while her mother and Epi looked anywhere but at anyone. 'We were naturally concerned, and couldn't wait another day before ensuring her well-being.'

Thorn raised a disbelieving brow, and waited.

The crickets and bees in the garden entertained them for those long minutes, growing louder and louder, as if sharing the table's anticipation.

'This is absurd,' her father finally said, breaking under the pressure; sweating from it, or the growing heat from the very bright sun, Hypatia wasn't sure, but would wager on the former. 'You must surely see now, Patty,' he continued, turning his gaze on her, her mother and sister joining in, knowing their cues. 'This was an utter mistake. A catastrophe. You cannot live like this. You've had your…fun, made your point, or whatever this was all about, and now it is time to return to your family. You owe this man nothing, we need you, and we cannot do without you. Your sister needs you, and you must distance yourself from this abhorrent life or she'll have nothing, be forced to marry some viscount rather than the duke she deserves, and everything is a mess without you.'

'I'm staying, Father,' Hypatia said simply. 'And I should appreciate it if you called me by my name. Not Patty. I did always despise that moniker.'

Her father started to grumble, searching for words, whilst her mother and sister began with the sniffing and tears. Thorn squeezed her hand, and she looked over at him, to find him silently asking if there was anything more she wished to add; she shook her head.

'There is a cottage available to you for the night,' Thorn told them, and that cut the hysterics, effrontery rapidly replacing them. 'Mary, or one of the others, will see to it you find your way there, and are well looked after.'

'But—' her father began.

'You will remain there tonight, and depart tomorrow, by whatever means you came. And that is the end of it.'

Her father looked about ready to argue, but instead recognised the defeat, and stood, throwing his moth-eaten napkin onto the table, and gesturing for her mother and sister to rise as well.

'Never in my life, have I been subject to such egregious treatment. You, *sir*, are the furthest thing from nobility one could dredge up from the gutters in St Giles.'

'Good,' Thorn said, smiling proudly.

And so her family stormed off, back into the house, voices and cries echoing in their wake.

Then there was only one left...

Malek looked about ready to leave too, but Thorn gave him a warning look, and so he focused again on moving the crumbs in his chipped plate around.

'Your turn, Helen.'

Helen's eyes danced between Thorn and Hypatia, and though she was minded like Malek to leave Thorn and Helen to this, Thorn was giving no sign he wanted her gone, or to do this alone, and so she remained, bracing herself for whatever came next.

'It was admittedly rather rash,' she said, as airily as possible, though Hypatia could tell there were a thousand other serious words dancing between every syllable. 'I heard Malek was coming, and so I begged him to take me. I couldn't... It wasn't until you left, that I realised I couldn't leave it all as it had been. I might've written, but that seemed the move of a coward, and I've been enough of one. I cannot move on without asking you again for your forgiveness.'

That wasn't everything, but for the sake of them all just now, Hypatia, and she felt Thorn too, wouldn't press the woman further; besides, she'd eviscerated herself enough publicly.

'You have it,' Thorn said unhesitatingly. 'I'll never be happy with what you and Frank did, but I forgive you both. As I hope you'll forgive me, for how I failed in being… In taking you for granted, and so much else.'

Nodding, Helen wiped the bottom of her shining eyes.

'Thank you, Thorn.'

'We've secured you a room in the village for tonight,' Hypatia told her, and she smiled graciously. 'I'll accompany you, and advise you on travel arrangements for your return home.'

'Many thanks, Lady Gadmin.'

'Of course.' With a nod, and a squeeze of Thorn's hand, she rose, releasing it. The gentlemen rose too, as Helen did. 'Thorn, we'll leave you and Mr Smith to speak of your further arrangements.'

'Are you sure, Hypatia?' Thorn whispered as she turned to go, and lead Helen on. 'You don't have to do this. Henry, or one of the others can go.'

'I'm sure, Thorn.'

Steadying herself with one final look in his steadying grey eyes, she smiled reassuringly, and made to go again; this time he stopped her with a blatantly possessive, and not unwelcome kiss, before finally releasing her.

'Until later,' he promised, raising his brow in a manner that suggested many things.

So she smiled, wider, truer, and led Helen on.

What a day this has been; and it is far from over.

'This is truly beautiful country,' Helen said, a few moments after they'd set off, Hypatia driving them on at a quiet, but determined pace in a cart, as Ian had taken her family in the carriage; their own not prepared, and Ian having been advised that his priority was to get the Quincys off the grounds by any and all means. 'I can see its appeal.'

'Yes, I find that I have quite fallen in love with it,' Hypatia said, with an ease she didn't expect to have with the woman.

But then, away from her family, from Thorn even, she found she was better able to focus on what truly lay in her heart, and the simple truth was, she bore this woman no ill-will, though she was still immensely curious about many things, some of which she might gain answers to if she had but the courage to ask; others that she would never know, yet be at peace with.

There was an understanding of her now, here, alone on the road to Sandham, in the blinding summer sunshine, a light breeze restoring both their spirits, and bruised hearts.

'It is very good of you to take me yourself,' Helen

said, somewhat sheepishly after a long moment watching hedgerows pass them by. 'I could've made my own way.'

'I know.'

'You're not at all what I expected.'

'From a countess or from the woman whom Thorn married?'

'Both. Either,' Helen said, a smile in her voice, and Hypatia smiled too.

'You're not what I expected either.'

'I'll take that as a compliment.'

'It's meant as one.' They fell into silence for another mile or so, Hypatia dipping her head in greeting as they passed some workers they knew, then finally, she spoke again, seizing the opportunity she doubted she would ever have again. 'Did you come in hope of rekindling things with Thorn?'

'I…'

Glancing over, Hypatia found the woman gaping as she searched for words; guilt in her eyes.

'It's all right,' she reassured Helen, who only seemed more flustered at that. 'It's natural, you two shared many years together.'

'It isn't because of his change in circumstance,' Helen said after a while, realising surely, that Hypatia bore her no ill-will, and that such answers and talk were needed.

'If it was, you might've tried to win him back sooner,' she commented, and Helen laughed.

'True.'

'Are things not going well with Frank?'

'It is…difficult,' she sighed. 'But it feels so strange speaking to you of all people about this…'

'Who else have you to speak of it with just now?'

Another sigh, and Helen relented fully; when Hypatia glanced over again, as they turned onto another lane, she found the woman somewhat deflated, and resigned.

'We are both affected by the loss of Thorn, by our own guilt at our actions. And things… Well, in many ways, nothing much has changed from how it was with Thorn, and so I find myself looking to the past, wondering if I made choices for the wrong reasons, or asked for too much.'

'I asked Thorn about you. He regrets, or regretted, I'm not certain, how he treated you. You should know that. He told me, he only realised recently, that he'd never truly spoken to you, asked what you wanted, worked *with* you, to achieve and obtain what both or either of you wanted. He made excuses in many ways to preserve things as they were, since he found them to be just fine. What you and Frank did injured him, but he admitted he had his own large part to play in your relationship not being all it might've been before. I probably shouldn't be sharing this with you, but I'm not sure Thorn ever will, and I feel as you've the right to hear it.'

'Sometimes it is up to others who understand us better than we do ourselves, to speak our truths to those who need it. So thank you.'

Slowing the cart to a halt in a small verge, Hypatia stopped, and turned to Helen, admiring her perspicacity, and appreciating her words fully.

'Do you love Frank?'

'Yes,' Helen admitted quietly, shame marring her joy. 'He loves me, fulfils me in ways…'

'Thorn never could.' Helen nodded, and so did Hypatia, taking a deep breath.

'I don't seek to excuse myself, but I don't think I would've done what I did had I not, much as I regret it.'

'Then you should fight for what you have, and be honest with Frank in ways you and Thorn never were. Be clear about what you want, and when, and how, and if he cannot give you that, and you cannot give him what he wishes for, then perhaps, love isn't enough.'

'You're very wise, my lady.'

'Am I?' Hypatia shrugged, and got them moving again. 'If you say so.'

'You're quite…odd, if you don't mind me saying,' Helen chuckled, and Hypatia shook her head. 'But I see you and Thorn, you suit in ways we never could've. You've done him good, I see the change in him, and he is happy.'

'We are doing well with the house, and the farm, and things are looking up.'

'*You*, make him happy. He loves you very much, and all I can say is that I am happy for you both.'

Hypatia smiled non-committally, not bothering to

refute the woman's assessment, particularly since she didn't want to debate its veracity.

That Thorn was happy, that she was, was undeniable, and yes, they contributed to each other's happiness, and liked each other, and cared for each other deeply, but as for love, romantic love as Helen suggested, and Hypatia being the predominant source of Thorn's happiness... It simply couldn't be true. For many reasons, including and not limited to the fact that Hypatia couldn't... couldn't bear the weight of that. The responsibility, the weight, of holding another's happiness, it was too much. There was a difference, between care, and sacrifice, and duty, and twisting oneself into what the other needed, and knowing that one wrong word or move or choice could mar another's joy or damn their soul to torment. It was wrong, and couldn't last, and to hold such power over someone like that, it was madness, and irresponsible, and terrifying, and so it couldn't be true. It couldn't be love, because Thorn himself had said what could happen to one who loved—so many had over the millennia since man's existence—and that was the cost, and neither of them wanted it, and they barely knew each other, and it didn't feel like whisky, and so many other reasons.

Patently ignoring that Thorn might very well be a predominant source of her happiness and joy, and without him, she wouldn't quite have so much of it, or that she'd not twisted herself into anything but herself for him, Hypatia drove them on into Sandham.

'Are you sure you won't return to Gadmin Hall for dinner?' she asked Helen, having introduced her to Mrs Jennings, whose room she would be taking for the night, and explained the best way to get back to Essex. 'You are welcome, I am sure there will be plenty of food.'

'I don't think that is the best idea,' Helen said graciously. 'But thank you.'

'Well, then, I suppose this is goodbye. I wish you all the best. I hope things work out for you and Frank, and perhaps, someday, Thorn will bring me to visit, and we can all meet again.'

'I would like that, my lady. And thank you, for everything.'

'You are welcome. I'm glad you came.'

'So am I.'

'Good day, then, Helen.'

'Good day, my lady.'

With a smile, the two parted, and Hypatia got back on her cart, and drove it all the way home, taking her time, as the solitude was just what she needed to return to herself.

To give Helen's words their proper perspective, and cast them off, and not worry anymore that she or her husband had somehow fallen in love with each other. It had never been part of their agreement, and though she shouldn't find it so terrifying at all, she certainly did, and so she rescinded an idea she'd toyed quietly with for some time since coming here, that perhaps it was worth the trouble, and that she might like to try it someday.

For I find now, it isn't a prospect I delight in any longer.

Chapter Twenty-Two

'You should entertain more often,' Malek said wryly, perking up from his otherwise silent spectatorship, once Hypatia had disappeared with Helen; and Thorn had had enough time to silently pray nothing might be said, or happen, to distress Hypatia. He might've handled this all better, given Helen the private audience she clearly wished for, and yet he found he had no regrets. 'The strangest, yet most interesting afternoon I've had in a long while.'

'You were always a worse hermit than me,' Thorn pointed out, turning back to his once apprentice, now... whatever he would be. *Friend and associate? Friend and...?* 'I can only imagine you didn't improve much after I left.'

'I don't know what you mean. I hosted dinners and balls, and bonfires, and garden parties every day and every night after you left.' Thorn grinned, and Malek sighed, apology shimmering in his eyes. 'Are you angry?'

'With the Quincys, yes. With Helen…no. Unless she injures Hypatia. With you, no.'

'I should've written before I made any decisions, consulted you, asked your opinion—'

'I gave you the business, what you did with it was your decision. It is bittersweet, I will not lie, and yet, perhaps it was time. What my father built is not lost, and I understand that not everything works out in the manner we hope it to. Today is a prime example,' Thorn grinned. 'Basking after our outing, I was looking forward to ending the day with my wife in bed, but instead we came home to a houseful of guests, only one of which I was admittedly glad to see, though I'll not regret saying that which needed to be to Helen.'

Malek smiled softly, and downed the remainder of his cold tea.

'You should speak to them,' he said quietly, gazing up onto the house's facade. 'Her family. I may not be an expert, and I know speaking of important matters is generally not your preferred activity, however from what little I saw, there is much to be said, and I don't get the impression your wife will be heard were she to do it.'

Thorn nodded vaguely, knowing Malek was right; he'd already felt that impulse plucking the strings of his heart since their harried departure.

Were he to remain silent now, either they would attempt such a supposed rescue again, or an unbreachable gulf would grow between the Quincys and Hypatia, and knowing what little he did, remembering what she'd shared, he didn't think that was something she truly wanted. He was just beginning to wonder if there wasn't some veracity to her father's words—that Hypatia would be better off elsewhere, that living as they were featured some absurdity and dishonour—but Malek interrupted him before he could fall too far down that path; one which he knew was the furthest from the truth as possible.

Our life is good. We are happy, and though much needs improvement, we are working on it. Together.

'I like her,' Malek said. 'She is kind, and very clever.'

'Far cleverer than I,' Thorn agreed. 'Far more everything than I might've hoped for.'

'I am glad for you, that your marriage turned out to be one of love in the end.'

'I don't... I don't know if she feels thus for me,' Thorn admittedly quietly, realising he'd not really had anyone to speak to about this, his doubts, his questions. He might've spoken to any of the workers, or his staff, but it was too close to home. And in all honesty, Danny and Fred for one were some of the worst gossips, so that was the last thing he needed. 'She... We care for each other, and I certainly love her more than I thought I ever could. But she is so strong, so independent, so... everything, which is wonderful, I don't think she needs me enough to love me.'

'You believe that a necessity?'

'In my experience, yes.'

Malek made a non-committal noise, which Thorn was about to ask him to explain, but instead his once apprentice simply shrugged, and spoke again.

'She gave you a forge.'

'Yes, I suppose she did,' Thorn agreed, wondering, hoping, if that meant what his heart thought it did as it leapt and bounded. 'A forge which I should show you now, see if you like it. I've been using it of late, but it would suit you well, if you wish, though I'll still come pester you now and then.'

'It sounds perfect,' Malek said, and the two rose. 'If it is near friends again, that will be enough for me.'

Too touched to speak, Thorn merely nodded, and patted the lad on the back, and led him onwards. And as they walked towards the forge, he thought how strange again life was, to bring answers, to bring friendship, to bring resolution and forgiveness, precisely at the time when it was needed most.

Odd as today has been, I find it restores my faith in order, design, and fate.

Taking a deep breath, reminding himself why he was doing this—*who* he was doing this for—Thorn stood up straight, trying to at once project confidence and appeasement, and knocked on the cottage door. It was a simple, small, but lovely place, surrounded by lovely fields and pastures, dotted with Reeves' fluffy white flocks, adding to the pretty picture.

He waited, not overly long, before finally the door

opened, Mr Quincy appearing on the other side, looking none too pleased at the visitor.

Well, now you know how that feels.

'What are you doing here?'

'There are some things which need to be discussed, and if you've any love for your daughter, you will let me in. Or we can all do this outside, if that is your preference.'

Mr Quincy looked about to refuse, but then carefully thought on what had been said, and nodded, stepping aside.

As he entered, Thorn vaguely noted how nicely Reeves had done up the cottage—simply, but tastefully, so that it felt homely, and lived-in, rather than a mere vacant space. He wondered too, as he stepped in the comfortably sized sitting room, with its plush chairs, and watercolours, flooded by afternoon sun despite lace curtains, who had lived here, or why it was kept thus; merely for visiting guests, yet-to-arrive tenants, or some other purpose entirely.

He shook off those thoughts, and nodded instead to the ladies waiting, perched on those chairs, looking rather red-eyed and forlorn, though attempting cold and distant disdain at his appearance.

'Mrs Quincy, Miss Quincy,' he greeted, pondering sitting, but thinking better of it, and leaning on the windowsill instead.

Mr Quincy thought about his position too, and fi-

nally settled between his wife and daughter, a hand on
both their shoulders in support.

'Say whatever it is you've come to, and be done with
it then,' Quincy ordered, and Thorn realised…many
things.

*How much love and protection there is in this room;
for one daughter, at least.*

*How lost they all are; caught in their own habits,
their own ways, as I was for so long.*

Yet they allowed me entry, so perhaps there is hope.

'I am not typically a man of many words, nor can
I claim to know much at all,' Thorn began, the mo-
mentousness of his task, his responsibility and potential inadequacy, even his audience being family of one
he loved dearly, hitting him more than it had before.
And luckily so, for if he had fully realised it before,
he might not have come at all. *What does that say of
me, I wonder?* 'I like to think, that somewhere inside
all of you, you know the truth of what I'm about to
say, and so will accept it, and find some way to facilitate change. You've never loved Hypatia well, any of
you.' Protestations rose to their lips, but Thorn raised
a warning hand. 'I believe you love your daughter, and
your sister, or at least, I hope so. And if you do, you
cannot deny the truth. You have not loved her well, as
a daughter, or a sister. Merely as your caretaker, your
assistant, your chaperone, your housekeeper… I do not
know what led to that, be it circumstance, or your own
upbringing. However, as a son who was loved by his

father, let me tell you how my heart broke when my wife told me she couldn't recognise me being proud of her, for she'd never seen such a thing in the eyes of another close to her.'

The Quincys hung their heads, and gulped, and Epi frowned, taking either longer to understand, or examining her own experience through that lens.

'Such wounds are not so easily repaired, deep as they are,' Thorn continued, after having afforded them a moment. 'And I do not know if they ever truly can be. I do know that she loves you, best she can, given your past. She doesn't want to lose you, but she needs time, to find herself, to learn what she wishes to, and be free of you, and your demands and needs. She is your daughter, and your sister, but now, she is herself too, in her own right. My wife, a woman I admire, and love, and a countess of this realm. When she is ready, I believe she will reach out to you. In the meantime, you should refrain from imposing yourselves on her, in any manner. And as for my last piece of advice, don't do to Iphigenia what you did to Hypatia. Don't sacrifice her at the altar of your ambitions, and self-involvement.'

Waiting, in case they had anything to say, Thorn watched them; watched guilt, indignation, regret, sadness, resignation, and incomprehension, appear in all of them, like a prism in light. Finally, believing nothing more would be said, he straightened, and made to leave.

'We don't…know what to do without her,' Mrs Quincy said, as quiet and frightened as a bird, and he turned back, offering as much sympathy as he could. 'London…that is, we are lost without her.'

'Perhaps you should try Bath, or Tunbridge Wells,' Thorn suggested gently. 'I've heard they're very popular, and I might also suggest the seaside. Some time, in new settings, with new people, might be just the ticket. You've money, and one daughter married to an earl, no matter how low of an earl I might be in Society's eyes. I believe, in time, you'll find a place to suit you all.'

'You don't deserve her any more than we do,' Mr Quincy said, not harshly, not cruelly, yet it struck truer for that very reason. 'And she certainly deserves better than this life.'

'I know,' Thorn said simply. 'Every moment I have with her is a gift I do not take lightly. As for the life she deserves… I seek only to facilitate the one she wants. Her freedom is, and will always be her own.'

'Not if you chain her with love, after such a lack as you say she felt in our house,' Epi chimed in, showing a rare amount of brilliance and understanding; or perhaps only one he hadn't expected, knowing her not at all.

The latter, I fear.

'Your carriage will be here in the morning,' Thorn said, swallowing the lump lodged in his throat. 'Dinner and breakfast will be brought to you, and if you require anything else, do advise whoever brings them to you. Mr Quincy, Mrs Quincy, Miss Quincy, good day, and safe travels to wherever you decide to go.'

With that, Thorn left, making his way back to Gadmin Hall, with even less of a spring in his step as he'd had previously.

He might've been more pleased with how the day had turned out; especially considering how it had taken a turn with the appearance of so many unexpected, and unwanted—but needed—guests. He might've felt good at having threads tied off, if not neatly, then simply. He might've felt more grateful to Fate, or God, or whatever powers, that he felt the weight lifting from having said what little he had to Helen, having Malek back in his life, and even knowing that the Quincys had *heard* all he'd said to them.

In many ways, he was pleased, grateful, *better*. However, Epi—Iphigenia's words—had mightily stuck in his craw. For he knew how dangerous his love could be to Hypatia, and all she'd found so far having left her family home for this one. Perhaps it was why he'd not been able to declare his love; not only because he feared she might not share it, or love him only for she knew no one else to love thusly, but because he didn't want to chain her to him. Stop her looking elsewhere, for someone, for something, for another life, more opportunities; anything she wished. The world was hers; she deserved it all and more, and making her feel any sense of duty towards him, or his feelings, would be risking her making the same choices she'd been taught to by the Quincys.

He needed her, so very much, to be himself, to

breathe, to get up in the morning, and be happy, but he'd always known, she didn't need him.

As. She. Shouldn't.

Telling her he loved her, it risked endangering her openness to all *else* life had to offer. It risked—

'Where have you been?' Hypatia asked, spotting him as he traversed the stable-yard, in which she was un-hooking one of the horses from the cart. 'I thought you'd be with Malek at the forge.'

'I was, earlier,' Thorn said, smiling away his thoughts softly, and focusing instead on his wife, and how beau-tiful she was, and lovely, and how he wouldn't ever do anything to chain her to any life. *Nor myself.* 'He liked it, and will stay, that is if you don't mind.'

'Of course not,' she smiled, eyes narrowing, as if she knew something was amiss.

'He's offered to do a reasonable amount of work for us, in exchange for the place. We'll speak of rent when he grows his business, and he knows I'll still pop in and make a nuisance of myself whenever possible. He'll be joining us for dinner, by the way.'

Hypatia nodded, and led the horse into the stable—which reminded him he had all these doors to repair at some point—gave him some food and water, and Thorn busied himself dragging the cart into its spot.

'So, where were you, that you avoid telling me?' Hypatia asked, emerging once again.

'I went to speak with your family,' he admitted, won-dering if she would think him too forward, too presumptuous, too anything, but obviously knowing she had the right to know what had been said. 'I…permitted myself to tell them some of what you did me. And advised them they should wait until you were ready to contact them again.'

Hypatia nodded, playing with her bottom lip between her teeth, her gaze moving to the woods, and pigs just visible beneath the semi-distant trees.

'Are you angry with me, Hypatia?'

'No,' she chuckled softly, looking back at him, her eyes holding a softness he'd never seen before, but then, perhaps that was a trick of the light. 'I just find it amusing, as I spoke to Helen, and mentioned some of what you told me. I thought you might be angry with me.'

'I'm not.'

'Sometimes I suppose we must slay each other's demons. Or so Helen said, in a more gracious and elegant manner.'

'I like your manner well enough,' Thorn told her, crossing the distance dividing them, meaning what he said far beyond what his words suggested, which he hoped she felt, or heard with her heart. 'You know, you're always free to leave,' he breathed. 'Tomorrow, in ten years, twenty. Whatever you want, you need, it is yours. With my blessing.'

'You're free too,' she told him, eyes narrowing, searching his for an explanation he couldn't give.

He wanted to tell her he wasn't, that she commanded him, that her happiness had become his chief concern, that he loved her, and that it terrified him more than he might have the strength for; that the possibility of loving her and being unworthy to do so, had perhaps been what had terrified him about her from the first. Instead, he leaned down, and told her what he could of that in the sweetest, most searching and relinquishing kiss he'd ever known.

Even if I wanted to, I could never be free of you, for you are part of me now, my love.

Though someday sooner than I wish, I fear I shall need to let you be free of me.

Before I no longer have the strength to do so.

Chapter Twenty-Three

Early October 1839

'I think I like this much better than market,' Hypatia said, aware that her eyes were likely bulging from their sockets, her mouth gaping as she attempted to take in everything before and around her, all while knowing it was a useless exercise, given the amount of *everything* on offer. 'No offence to our market, but this is rather something else entirely.'

'Well it is a fair, not a market,' Thorn commented wryly, and she made a face, shaking her head.

'A few months in the country and you become an expert, I see. I suppose you think yourself very clever.'

'As a matter of fact, I do.'

'Well come on then, show me around, My Lord Expert,' Hypatia ordered playfully, wrapping her arm around his.

'As my lady commands.'

Straightening, assuming a jestingly pompous and

self-important air, Thorn led them on into the fray; and what a fray it was.

Set on a grand swathe of land just south-east of an otherwise pleasant, but seemingly quiet and tranquil village—where they'd spent the night as it was too far to make the journey from home in a day—the fair had been held in these parts since the Conqueror had established his dominion on the isle, and grown, it appeared, with every passing year.

There was anything anyone could ever want, gathered right here, in tents, and enclosures and carts. Toys, jewellery, beautifully embroidered linens, ribbons, woollen blankets and gloves, baubles, tradesmen of every denomination showing off their skill and wares—from glasswork to smithing. There was entertainment—puppet shows and street games—and food galore. Pies and cakes and biscuits and gingerbread and meats and breads, spiced and cooked any way anyone could desire. There were exhibitions of tools, and the latest innovations in farming, and there was music, and a few thousand voices talking or touting wares.

There was produce too of course, the freshest vegetables, and sweetest fruits, and naturally, there was the reason they were here; the livestock sales, and displays. Cattle, chickens, sheep, pigs, goats, ducks, and all the others gathered, some in great numbers, others here as examples of their owners' mastery in rearing; horses trotted along with ribbons in their tails and manes, and cattle or goats lumbered and leapt with clanging bells upon them.

It was the most beautiful semi-organised chaos Hypatia had ever witnessed, and it filled her not only with excitement, but hope too, and a hunger to learn, to experience, to be part of this life, this innovation, this work, more than ever before. Thorn seemed just as invigorated, as they wandered and were pushed by crowds here and there, trying to visit and experience as much as they could, sample and learn about as much as they could, and it heartened her more than she could put into words.

The last couple months since that day by the seaside, and those visits from their past, had continued to be that potent blend of *hard*, and *good*. It had continued to be a blend of working the farm, growing it, and their relationships with neighbours, surrounding villages and markets, and working on Gadmin Hall itself, slowly, but surely. A blend of buying furniture, getting Belinda and Clyde into prize-winning form, and enjoying more delightful dinners with friends, who seemed to multiply with every passing day; be it Malek—who was settling in nicely, and already busy with orders that Thorn sometimes assisted him with—or other local landowners or tenants. It was working their first harvest, toiling in the fields, and protecting their crops from the increasing but so far not too destructive end-of-summer storms, and spending moonlit midnights in hers and Thorn's stream. It was not days ago attending Sandham's harvest festival, and dancing by fires to the tune of flutes and fiddles, and hosting their own end-of-harvest celebration with their many friends and neighbours. It was everything.

Thorn himself had been…himself. They spoke as profoundly as they had before, though not as often; still Hypatia felt she grew to learn a little more of him every day. Enough at least, to know for instance, that in the past couple months, he'd looked at her differently— though she'd not quite had the courage to ask what provoked that, and it didn't really matter, since it was soft, and sweet, and tender, and settled. It didn't matter that he felt more distant—or perhaps preoccupied was the word; he was present, vitally, with her, more passionate and stalwart than ever, and he would speak to her of whatever preoccupied him in time. Likely it was just the harvest, and all the rest to be done to prepare for winter in the coming weeks, which had and continued to preoccupy too, not only by the amount of work—and workers to keep happy—but also by the new skills to learn, and new season yet to greet them. As much as Hypatia relished the new challenges, the new knowledge, growing what they had already even more, she had to admit, everything in their life presented a risk just now, even if they were at a sort of pleasantly productive—including financially—state at last.

But then, such was life, really.

'It's nearly time, I think,' Thorn said, taking out the pocket watch she'd gifted him for his birthday a few weeks ago—which he'd only mentioned by accident—a necessity more than a trinket, or so she'd promised him; no matter that she'd had it engraved with poppies. 'We should make our way to wherever it is we are going,' he said with a light huff, his head craning above the crowd to get his bearings. 'I admit, it all looked rather differently last night, without all the people.'

'There, I think,' Hypatia pointed, spotting the church spire of the nearest village. She'd noticed it looking closer last evening when they'd come with Danny to drop off Belinda and Clyde for today's showing. 'I think it should be the general direction of *that* way.'

'How very precise, my dear. Perhaps you should explore navigation or map-making as your next occupations.'

'Perhaps I shall,' she said, as Thorn led the way, navigating the crush and din. Though she doubted that would ever be her life, they sounded interesting enough, so she wouldn't mind exploring them more. 'I cannot believe we've been here three hours already. I did not see the time pass.'

'Neither did I. Though I'm glad we came early, at the very least some good ideas for investment, particularly as regards some of those tools and contraptions for the farm. And we did get our gift-shopping done for everyone.'

'Very true, and very clever of us for being so prepared and organised,' Hypatia laughed gently. 'I must say, having seen this… I don't know that I can even begin to imagine the scale of the show in Oxford. Admittedly, I'm not sorry we missed our chance this year, as I don't think I would've been prepared for that.'

'Me neither.'

'Perhaps next year. If—*when*—we win here, it will be a very good start, and we shall have quite a while to enjoy our laurels and prepare to obtain new ones.'

'As you say,' Thorn smiled distractedly.

Something about the manner in which he said that, struck Hypatia as a bit odd, but then she dismissed it as distraction too, for they'd arrived at the wooden stage—decorated with banners and fanions—where the swine showing was about to commence.

Thorn once again examined it all from his vantage, and led them to the front of the gathered crowd, though slightly to the side, so there was a few more inches to breathe.

'And remember,' the announcer or presenter, or whatever he was meant to be called, boomed out from onstage. 'All these glorious and impressive animals are available for purchase at our auction following this presentation and prize, in the tent to my right!' he told the assembled crowd, showing the thing.

The crowd itself was a strange beast, Hypatia thought—a mix of farmers, locals, visitors of every class, people of the trade such as butchers, children, and so much more—half-caught between cheering as one would for a show, commenting quietly, or conducting business as it all went on before them.

'I'm nervous too,' Thorn whispered, leaning down to do so best he could by her ear, which was somewhat complex due to her rather large bonnet; *sans* grapes. He placed a kiss on her cheek too, and she calmed somewhat, at least outwardly, for inside she was still a jittering jar of flying ants. 'We did all we could, and whatever happens, we will be seen.'

'I know,' she breathed, steadying herself in his gaze, as she found she so often did now. Staying herself by marking all the familiar lines and details of him; as one might take comfort in reading a beloved book over and over again. 'It is likely foolish to hope that we might win…so many others have worked as hard as we, and we are new to this still, however, I cannot help myself.'

'Neither can I,' Thorn admitted, taking strength she hoped, from her too for a few moments, before they turned back to the stage.

The show itself was edifying and educational. Hypatia tried her hand at studying the beasts as those more informed in the crowd did—trying to note and distinguish aspects the presenter pointed out, neighbouring watchers or the judges all set on the stage now did—as it helped focus her mind away from their own entries.

From what she saw before Belinda and Clyde were brought out—all pigs being presented one after the other, though there were separate prizes for hogs and sows today—they would at the very least make a good show of it.

Finally, it was their turn, and Hypatia clutched

Thorn's arm tightly, as first Belinda—*'Admire the straightness of her lines, the beauty of those spots, the thickness and purity of her colour! Belinda weighs in at thirty-five stone one pound!'*—then Clyde—*'Another exceptional animal from Gadmin Hall, with a perfection of ear length, and again, that excellent coat, in marking, colour, and hair consistency, Clyde weighs in at forty-two stone and eight pound!'*—were led out and shown to an extremely enthusiastic crowd.

Thorn, like her, didn't dare breathe, or perhaps they were too caught up in the cheers and excited mutterings, not to mention the points and nods in their direction—*that's the Earl and Lady Gadmin there*; at least until another three or four pigs were brought up.

And this isn't even the most nerve-wracking part.

'We can hold our heads high,' Hypatia said once she'd regained some manner of breath and voice. 'As you say, at least we made a good show of it.'

Nodding, Thorn expelled a breath, and gave her as much of a smile as he could, patting her hands, still tightly holding his arm.

Time was lost to Hypatia as the showings finished, and the judges—local magistrates, mayors, and gentlemen with no proverbial *skin in the game*—debated their decisions, before handing their decisions off to the presenter, who shared it with the hands who would collect and bring back up the winning swine.

'All right, all right, settle down,' he called, and here it was, the most nerve-wracking part of this whole expedition. *Please*, she prayed to nothing and everything. *Please. One win.* 'Now, we'll be the gentlemen we are, and start off with the ladies!'

'Come on, Belinda,' Hypatia muttered.

'With a most excellent shape, and nigh-perfect features, our meritorious mention goes to Jilly of Thimble Farm!'

Cheers, and applause met that pronouncement; Jilly—a beautiful sow with a picture-perfect pinkish white coat—was brought back up, whilst her owner went up to shake the judges' hands, bow for the crowd, and lead Jilly off.

'Come on Belinda…'

'Our winner today, demonstrating true character, excellence of breeding, and the full potential in all characteristics, notably that sunnily sandy coat is Wyn, of Dashdown Estate!'

Hypatia's heart fell, though she tried to tell herself it was nothing, and they still had a chance. Thorn held her tighter to him despite the growing heat, whilst the same process was repeated again.

'All right, Clyde,' she whispered. 'It's all up to you now, we believe in you.'

'Moving on to the gents now! Our meritorious mention is a striking example from Berkshire,' the presenter called, and Hypatia would not lose hope until the final name was said. *Come on, Clyde…* 'Alfie, from Kithrow Manor!'

The cheers, the handshaking, the applause, and the lead-out.

'Come on, Clyde,' Thorn muttered, and Hypatia felt something change then inside her, though she had neither the time, nor the mind to study it.

Later. For now, COME ON, CLYDE!

'Our winner today, the undisputed favourite of our judges, and a real treat to see as we've not quite had such a specimen in years...'

'Come on, Clyde...'

'This beast of a boar, Clyde from Gadmin Hall! What a spectacular first entry from this farm!'

It wasn't until hundreds of eyes turned to them expectantly, and she saw him up there, gorgeous, wonderful Clyde, that Hypatia felt the impact, and the truth of their win.

Turning to Thorn disbelieving, she watched as the realisation washed over him too, though shock kept them still for instants, or minutes—she certainly didn't know—and then tears were falling, and he was holding her in a tight embrace, rocking her, as hands patted their backs, and encouraged them up.

'Go on,' Thorn whispered, urging her up, and she shook her head.

'Together.'

Hesitating for some reason she would ask him about later, he took a moment before nodding, and letting her drag him up.

It was a blur as they repeated the actions of the others—shaking hands, taking a bow, receiving a little ribbon to show their accomplishment—before leading Clyde, good, excellent boy that he was, back down and to the holding pens. Danny was waiting for them, and they embraced and shook his hand, congratulations flying around like shards of gold. Others came too—farmers, buyers, and so on—to chat, to congratulate, to share in the revelry, and Hypatia lost herself in that until it was time for Clyde to be taken away for the auction.

Knowing she likely wouldn't get the chance again, she knelt down, and hugged Clyde tightly.

'Thank you,' she whispered to him. 'You will not be forgotten, wherever your journey takes you from here.'

He snorted in her ear, and she laughed, tears streaming again as she released him, and watched him go.

'I'll go, if you don't wish to,' Thorn offered, slipping his hand into hers. 'Why don't you take Danny, get something to drink to celebrate. I'll bring news when it's done.'

'Yes, perhaps that's better,' she said, wondering when her heart had become too sore to watch what Belinda and Clyde's fates would be. 'We'll meet you by those Italian puppeteers.'

Thorn threw her a smile, and nodded, before disappearing towards the auction tent.

As she did, she had the queerest feeling that it was a presage of some sort, before reminding herself that she believed in no such things, and she was just over-whelmed, and so she and Danny went to find some delicious cider, and wait for Thorn by the puppeteers.

Chapter Twenty-Four

If Thorn hadn't believed in order, in design, in fate, in life making right, and prompting choices and changes in direction as he did, he might've been more surprised to find the letter he did, waiting for him when they returned from their victorious and intoxicating escapade to the fair. Only he did believe in such things, and so he wasn't surprised; he knew full well it was time, and that he'd held out as long as he'd been able to.

What a way to end one chapter, and begin another, he thought to himself in fact, when he'd finished reading it, and set it back down on the old, battered desk they'd found some weeks ago, and put to good use in many various ways since.

Clyde had fetched top price, beyond anything Thorn had dared hope for, and Belinda had also fared nicely. The connections they'd made at the fair, many thanks to Clyde's win, and both of their acceptable entries, as well as rumours from the various markets and buyers they'd sold to thus far, had promised—and in some cases already delivered—new clients and opportunities. Their bet—Hypatia's idea—had paid off with the success they'd both dreamt of, and it had been an exceptional few days away from home, to truly enjoy himself with Hypatia, and spoil her, and be near her, and see…

All he had. Including and not limited to the unfettered joy and pride he'd seen in her when Clyde had won, sharing that moment with her, seeing just how she spoke and dealt with all those staunch and sometimes stubborn buyers and farmers again, how perfectly extraordinary she was. It was a time, like that they'd spent at the seaside, that he would keep close, and remember forever.

However now, it is time to set her free in truth.

It was something, a time he'd felt approaching since her family's visit. Every day, as they toiled and laughed and shared pleasure and toiled and spoke and lived, he'd felt it nearing. Felt the truth of her sister's words; known that to continue on together, would stifle her. His love would stifle her, limit her, as her family's need of her had stifled her, trapped her. Perhaps it already had; perhaps in many ways she'd lost herself to her duty to their marriage, something she'd feared of love from the start. Since she'd come here, every moment had been devoted to the farm, to this endeavour, and though he knew she enjoyed it, and found much of herself in all she learned and did, found friends, and freedom, and joy, it stole much of her choice. His needs, the needs of the title, of his role…they would continue to do so; and that was without even factoring in his love. Whereas if he walked away, and let her find whatever she was meant to, she would…

Soar higher than I could ever imagine.

'Everyone has seen fit to point out to me that we should wait to properly celebrate,' Hypatia said, stirring him from his reveries of her, as he stared out the window, onto the grounds which were becoming ever more resplendent and grateful for their continued tending. 'Which of course makes complete sense, we've only just had our harvest dinner, but I feel is somewhat insulting to Clyde and Belinda's efforts. Or perhaps I'm just turning into an aristocrat after all, wanting to have parties for any reason.'

'I would say do as you like, we've money to spare, but even despite our recent success, and the purchase of that new coach, I'm afraid we're still pauperis lords and ladies.'

'Yes, yes. I've already chosen a date close to All Hallow's, once we've helped Reeves with his sheep, and much of our own winter preparations are set to be done, and plans are already underway for then. Any news I should know of?' Hypatia asked, and he heard her coming towards the desk.

For the briefest moment, he pondered letting her find the letter herself, so he wouldn't have to speak, or explain himself, and find words he'd not managed to in his months of preparation, yet he knew that wasn't fair, in the least, and not how he wanted to…

End this. That is the term.

'A letter from London,' he said, as unemotionally as he could, before turning to face her. *Damn it.* She looked so delightful, so reassuring and wondrous, standing there, a scarf on her head, her worst clothes on to prepare for a day with the pigs. *How I love you.* 'The solicitors have managed to secure me rooms of acceptable size, location, and price.'

'I didn't realise you'd asked them to do so,' she frowned slightly, taken off-guard. 'But then, it is clever, since it won't be long at all before we need return there.'

The slight darkening of her eyes, the memory perhaps of all that awaited there, or the anticipated loss of this life, told him he was doing the right thing.

I will not adulterate her life now that it is so full.

'We won't be going anywhere, Hypatia. I will be returning to London alone, likely first thing in the morning.'

'I don't understand,' she said, staring at him in that manner which broke his heart, and though he knew it was a risk, he rounded the desk to stand before her properly, taking her hands in his. 'Our plans, Reeves, the winter, you have time, we have time—'

'Everything will be fine and well without me here. If there is anything grave, or you need *anything*, send word, but otherwise, you don't need me here.' She opened her mouth to object, but he squeezed her hands gently, urging her to listen. 'We always knew this day would come, perhaps it's why we never spoke of it,

Hypatia. There is more to being the Earl of Gadmin than running this estate. I've responsibilities in London I can't eschew forever, much as I might like to. And to properly fulfil them, I need time, to learn how it all works, make myself known, understand where I stand on things… I won't just sit there as I did earlier this year, lost in a world I didn't understand. I can make a change now, make a difference, and to let the power I now hold go unused, would be a waste, and an insult to who I was before. Who I am now.'

'Then we go together. I'm your countess, I should be by your side—'

'You should stay here, Hypatia. You're happy here,' he breathed, willing her to disagree, which of course, she couldn't. 'With time, and work, perhaps we could find a way to be in the city together, but the truth is, you belong here. It is your home, and you are…yourself here. Magnificent. The best caretaker and manager of this place that anyone could ever be, though know, I don't leave you here to take care of all this for me. You have launched yourself into this farm, this life, with all you are, and set yourself, and any dreams you could find aside. It would be the same in London. So I leave you here, because you are happy, and I will not take that from you. I thought of hiring someone, to take over, but it would not have been fair, and said much I wouldn't have meant. But given time, alone, here, you will have the freedom, I hope, to see when you are ready for something more, and search for it. I want you to dream, and live those dreams. To go explore, to start something new. I'm leaving you here, because you were chained to a life you didn't want before, and I won't do that to you. It would kill that spirit I love so much. So I am telling you to stay, and be happy, and know that whatever you want, or need to do or become whatever you want, it will be yours. However, if we don't part now…together won't be your choice. It will be your duty, your responsibility, and you should only be responsible for what you choose to be. That's why I took care of Truffél, you know. So you would be free not to.'

'I won't be so happy without you,' she argued, incomprehension still filling her.

In time though, she'll see.

'Yes, you will. You don't need me, Hypatia. You never did, and that is good,' he reassured her, understanding that now, running his knuckles along her cheeks. 'I like to think that I helped you, gave you the means to escape a life you weren't happy in, to see what could be, but that is all. I love you, Hypatia,' he finally told her, and she blinked, frowning slightly more, not surprised, but mortally confused. 'And at first, when I realised, perhaps even before, I longed for you to need me as I do, to live, to breathe, but that isn't the right way of things. I shouldn't need you to be happy, and so I am glad that you don't. I didn't tell you before because my love for you, I never want it to limit you. I want you to grow, and experience all you might not if I remain with you. I understand, love was never part of our bargain, but I thank you, for allowing me to feel it again. Now consider this my gift to you. For you might miss me, and I will you, but in time, you will find another freedom you never had. And that day, you will understand why I am leaving, and I will rejoice for you.'

Tears gathered in Hypatia's eyes, as they did in his, and she shook her head, though she didn't argue; for he was right.

After a long moment silently battling with him, and herself most likely, she fell into him, hugging him tightly, and so he wrapped her in his arms, sure she could hear his heart breaking and rejoicing all at once for her future, and her tears soaked his shirt, while his fell into her hair, and they remained there a very, very long while.

And then they remained there a while longer than that.

This is all for the best, no matter how terribly it shatters my soul.

Chapter Twenty-Five

Goodbyes—at least ones of this magnitude—were foreign things to Hypatia; but then she supposed much, like love, was. There was a sense in her, that despite her thirty-some-odd years on this earth, despite all she'd learned and become, she was still so very inexperienced when it came to all that being alive, and being human, encompassed.

One thing her time on this earth had taught her, however, was that sometimes, one had to rely on the advice, and expertise of those who had experience in certain matters—be it sowing seeds, rearing pigs, or love.

So despite the fact that she was a mess inside, her heart aching beyond anything she'd known before; despite the fact that she didn't understand how someone could say they loved you in one breath, and then were leaving you in the next, the fact of the matter remained as it had from their very first meeting: she trusted Thorn. She'd trusted him from the first, and learned every day since to trust him more, until she trusted him with everything she was, and so if he said it was best that he left, she would believe him.

Yesterday, last night, had been so strange there weren't really words for it. It was as if she had become discorporate, and gone through the motions of living and breathing and doing by rote, rather than with any sort of awareness. She might've better prepared for this, *the goodbye*, had she been able to think on it at all, but she'd been too shocked, too discombobulated, to do anything but what she normally did. Even last night, sharing perhaps her last time with Thorn, she might've used *that* to say and express all she couldn't with words—that she would miss him, that she would mourn what they'd been, that she wanted him to stay, that she was angry with him—or even found some way to *make an occasion* of it. Instead, she'd just been with him, and tried to catalogue every detail again, and let every ounce of passion in her flesh express itself, and that was that.

And now it is too late.

'You'll write, as soon as you arrive,' she reminded Thorn, as he passed his last few things to Ian, to be stored in what little bags he brought with him, riding as he was.

'I promise,' he smiled gently, turning back to her, the pale pink, cerulean, and dusky lavender notes of dawn framing him as if in a watercolour, making him appear some great god of the dawn, or fae, or mythical hero, off to never return. *But he will, I will see him again, even if it doesn't feel thus just now.* 'And you'll send news, and let me know if anything is needed.'

Hypatia nodded, breathing mindfully, because if not she would stop, as he drew closer, until they were toe-to-toe, and she wanted to cry, and wanted to chain him here, but perhaps this was best for them all.

He says so, so I must trust him.

'Safe travels, my lord,' Henry said from behind her, and Thorn threw him a smile.

'Remember, ye're best off at the western bridges today,' Langton added.

'Thank you, I'll remember that.'

'Bye, lord!' Niamh cried.

'Goodbye, poppet.'

'You'll be missed, my lord,' Mary said softly, and he bowed his head.

'Until we meet again, my friend,' Malek chimed in.

'Well, there's nothing for it,' Thorn sighed after a long look at them all, and nod to Malek. 'I must be going if I'm to get there at a decent hour, and enjoy the road. You all look after yourselves, and I'll look forward to seeing you when I can.' Another smile, sad, though Thorn tried to make it seem otherwise, and his gaze turned back to her. 'Hypatia... Dash it.'

Sliding his arm around her waist as he had that first time, he pulled her in, and kissed her with as much passion and ceremony as the moment deserved, and she'd not known how to muster, while she clung to him, long as she could.

But all too soon, he broke the kiss, leaning his forehead on hers, his sad, dark grey eyes sparkless and heart-wrenching today.

'Goodbye, Thorn,' she breathed.

'Goodbye, Hypatia.'

With that, he turned away, jaw clenched, shoulders tight, and threw himself up on his horse. Only then did he, and the rest of them notice the gathered band of workers a few paces away on the path to the farm, and she saw him fight as much emotion as she did, before he waved, and was off, trotting down the drive.

A mournful silence fell over them all as they stood there, watching him go, until there was nothing more to watch. Still, Hypatia remained, as the others left, hands gently falling on her shoulder, or upper arm in comfort.

'We're all fools,' Henry said, startling her, having believed everyone long gone. 'When it comes to love, at least. It's a pity there's so much written about it.'

'Why so?' she dared to ask, ever so quietly, still staring at the empty drive, bathed in light hazy pastels.

'Gives us too many grand things to live up to. Like being noble, and selfless, and thinking what we feel can't surely be it. Rather than just being swept away by something incredible.'

Hypatia nodded absent-mindedly, and heard Henry's footsteps, along with the creak of the door.

The bloody broken door they'd fixed, and painted, so that it would be whole again.

Pink and lavender turned to orange and bright blue,

as the sun rose, and so did the haze before her. There was so much to do, and she should be doing it, yet she couldn't find the will to do it. This all felt too much. She'd known she would miss him, of course she would, especially given the abrupt nature of this departure, though she'd known one day he might, and of course she still felt too much, from *everything*, really—these past months, this leaving business, the future she'd dared to let herself imagine and was now not even in ruins, but in ashes, there, in the wake of Thorn's trail on the drive which still needed repairs—and…

She was startled again, this time when a rather large object collided with her side, and by object, she meant snout.

'That hurt, and will leave a mark, Truffél,' she chided, looking down at the offending party.

She didn't know where Lamb was, but she was glad she hadn't been assaulted by the two of them. Truffél looked up at her forlornly, then down the drive, as if even he knew what had passed.

'He's gone,' she told him. 'I don't know when and if he'll be back, or if he'll ever see you again. I hope he took the time to say goodbye, for if not that would be very poor form.'

Snort. Truffél looked back at her, then at the drive.

'He's gone, Truffél. Gone. Not coming back.'

Snort. Truffél repeated the exercise of looking up at her, then down the drive.

'What? I'm not going after him. I have to trust him. He says it's best.'

Snort.

'I don't quite understand it either, you know. But I don't understand a lot of things.' Tears pricked her eyes, and Truffél nudged her again. 'You're only a pig, you don't understand much either, but less than me, I think.'

Snort, look, nudge.

'I have to let him go too, so he can find happiness some other way. I can't be responsible for his. I can't carry that weight. Even he said so. I've never been in love, and I don't know how to…'

Snort.

'It's best to leave it thus, before one or both of us gets hurt even worse. He said he'd be limiting me, and I'd be limiting him, because I…love him too.'

That last snort Truffél sounded very much resembled a *finally!*

And in all fairness, she understood the sentiment, for she finally saw what she'd been unable to distinguish until now: love for Thorn had lived in her heart for a very long time. It had lived in her heart at the fair. When her parents had come; and the others. It had lived in her heart that morning in their hotel by the sea; before then too. How far back it had been part of her, she couldn't see, not precisely, except it didn't matter. What mattered was how it lifted, supported, enthralled, and comforted her. All while she hadn't recognised it, unable to even had she wished to, for she'd never known it, and feared it, and relied in many ways on what it should feel and look like, just as Henry said.

Hypatia let out a long sigh, and looked down the drive, as the all-knowing pig had.

'Fine. I will go after him. I've no idea what I'm going to say, or how I'm going to find him—it would be just my luck he took some roundabout way Ian told him of to London—but I will try.'

Turning, she launched herself at the door, and opened it, intending to start giving orders about preparing bags, and horses, and for the farm, and work to be done, but instead she nearly slid into Mary, who was waiting patiently, a bag in hand.

'Just whistle, my lady, and Ian will bring your horse round. We'll mind everything, just bring his lordship back, and we'll get you seen off to London all proper in a few days. Just in case, there's enough for a day or two in your bag, and coin for the tolls.'

'Thank you, Mary.'

'My pleasure.'

Turning on her heels, Hypatia hurried back outside, whistling, and waiting only moments before Ian popped out, a bright smile on his face as he handed her the horse.

'I sent him down Ditchrow Lane, my lady,' the old man grinned. 'If he kept pace as how he left, he'll be halfway down it, and will need turn back as there's a felled oak I forgot to tell him about, and no way to get into the fields and woods beside. Shame that. Old mind of mine isn't what it used to be,' he winked.

'You're the best man ever to live, Ian Farrow,' she grinned, kissing his cheek, before securing her bag, and jumping into the saddle.

And then, without a moment more to lose, she was off.

I am not done with you, Thorn Ackerman.

If not for the glint in Ian's eyes when he'd told him about this supposed short cut, Thorn might've thought the giant fallen oak cutting off the lane, to be a sign he should turn back *all the way*, to Gadmin Hall, and leave these foolish thoughts of London behind. He also pondered returning to Gadmin Hall to murder Ian for playing such an underhanded trick; however, he knew that he could not endure leaving again.

It should've helped, to know he was doing what was right. For the person he loved most in this world, and perhaps for him too. Wrapping himself in his love for Hypatia, his unrequited love for her, might've warmed cold nights, and woken him on dark mornings, but he had to learn how to be his own person too. How not to depend on her for happiness, and joy, and meaning. Some part of him whispered he might've done that very well wrapped up in his love for Hypatia, time, and life, giving him tools to do so, but he swatted those thoughts away, as he swatted away some flies and gnats, and pondered getting back on his horse, and getting on his way.

He'd decided to take a break on one of the oak's more solid branches, while his horse munched on some greenery nearby, so he could properly feel that goodbye. So he could feel, and cry, and mourn all he'd left behind for who-knew-how-long.

Certainly not I. A while, I think, unless she calls me for aid; enough time for her to spread those bright wings and soar beyond the clouds.

He should've stayed longer.

He should've allowed them both to accustom themselves to the idea, rather than leaving like a hasty idiot.

He should've…

He couldn't remember every sigh, every change in the colour of her eyes when he'd loved her last night.

He couldn't remember what colour the sun made her curls this morning, or how many times she'd bitten her lip as he'd packed his things.

One should know such things.

You know enough.

More time would've just made it more painful, for him, at the very least. For Niamh and Truffél too, perhaps. Malek, even.

When he'd seen them all gathered, and his tenants, his friends, he'd nearly—

'Thorn!' And now he was so far gone he was hearing Hypatia's voice. 'Thorn Ackerman!'

So perhaps not a dream.

Lifting his sad head, he looked up, to find Hypatia riding at nigh-on full tilt towards him, and his heart skipped one too many beats—in excitement, hope, and also alarm—as he rose to his feet quickly.

Skidding to a stop, she slid off her horse whilst he watched with wide eyes, trying to make sense of her expression, to know what he should expect from this meeting.

'Love doesn't feel like whisky,' she told him fiercely, without preamble, letting her horse's reins fall, and marching towards him until she was before him again, within reach, not that he dared. *Not yet, though I find myself hoping considering the word love just left her lips.* 'It feels like nothing at all, for there is no comparison. My love for you, it is settled, and invisible, and lives with me like the lightest cloak of protection and warmth ever created,' she told him, softer, catching her breath.

Thorn's eyes filled with tears, and he hoped, even as he knew, her loving him, it couldn't change anything, no matter how much he wanted it to.

I still have to go.

And perhaps she saw that, for she shook her head, and stood straighter.

'My love for you is vibrant, and steadying, and soothing. Ever-present, yet non-intrusive, and it supports my every thought, my every fibre, without ever demanding anything in return. I don't need you, Thorn,' she smiled, and her candour, the truth he heard but couldn't yet see, made him smile too, renewing his hope. 'I can live, and breathe, and walk, and speak, and eat, and dress, and go on without you. But if you leave, I won't be able to do any of it without pain, ever. Perhaps I could find happiness in time without you, perhaps I could find another version of freedom I've never experienced, but I don't want to. You were the first true risk I ever took, and if you are the only one I ever do, that will be enough for me. And this isn't a decision I take lightly. I need you, to live the life I wish to, to be the Hypatia I wish to. To dream as I wish to. And right now, I dream of *this* life. I dream of being a pig farmer, and seeing our house thrive, and learning more about pigs and crops and horses and roofs and drainage systems. They are *good* dreams. Exceptional dreams. And I dream of doing it all with you. Of coming to London with you, to be Countess of Gadmin. I will. I am your wife, and it is my choice. And we might be miserable, and we might struggle, but we will do so together. Someday, that may change, and I know if that day were ever to come, you would let me go. But in the meantime, you won't be rid of me so easily. Because I do need you, in ways I shouldn't, but that I allow myself to because life is better with you by my side. So I choose to need you, and that better be enough for you, because I'm not going back to live without you.'

'As you command, my lady,' he managed to choke out, tears streaming down his face, stopped only by the wrinkles in his cheeks from his broadest smile.

'Quite so. It's back to Gadmin Hall for us, so we can *properly* prepare for this new chapter, but not until after our celebratory party for Belinda and Clyde. I hope those rooms you secured are big enough for the two of us.'

'Afraid not,' he chuckled wetly, finally, *finally* daring to touch her, to ensure she was real. 'I'll have him find new ones, and advise of the changes.'

'Good.'

'Good.'

'Thorn?'

'Yes, Hypatia?'

'Time to kiss me now.'

'Very well, my lady.'

And so he did as he was commanded by his love, and his heart, and every fibre of his being, and he sealed this new deal, as he'd sealed the first with this woman.

It was the truest, most honest and messy kiss of their time thus far; full of love, and tears, and newness, and hope. Perhaps someday, he would tire of learning all the ways to love this woman, and be loved by her, but he doubted it. Just as he doubted that they would have anything short of an extraordinary, amusing, and joyful life.

Met on a Wednesday,
Married on a Friday,
Met again on a Wednesday,
Fell in love every Monday, Tuesday, Wednesday,
Thursday, Friday, Saturday and Sunday since,
Still tried to leave on a Tuesday,

But found my home, my purpose, my heart again,
So not another day shall pass in this life
Without being extraordinary.

Epilogue

This writer is pleased to not only report success as regards their porcine endeavours, but equally that this year's favourite earl and countess have descended upon London yet again. So whilst we may never know the true conclusion of their tale, one is rather intrigued and delighted to note that thus far any lucky enough to have met them qualified the two as sickeningly amorous and determined to make their mark on the town, and indeed the country. Whether Lord and Lady Gadmin shall be, as I hoped at the beginning of this great tale remains to be seen, though I am sufficed that it would be a rather good wager to make.

Jack the Cat, Londoner's Chronicle, November 1839

'Finally, I get to see this dress on you,' Thorn said, sliding up behind her as she finished pinning his iron rose to her belt. Glancing up at him in the mirror, she watched his hungry, once again sparkling eyes devour her whole, before sliding his arms around her, and resting his chin on her bare shoulder. 'I thought I'd never get the chance.'

'It would've been your own doing,' she pointed out wryly, and he chuckled, dropping a kiss where her neck met her shoulder.

'I'm never going to hear the end of that one, am I? We'll be eighty, sitting in our garden at Gadmin Hall, having a lovely spot of tea while Truffél's great-grandchildren run amok between our feet, and I'll be reminded of having tried to leave you.'

'Yes.'

'I suppose I'll deserve it, though I'll remind you, I was trying to do the right thing.'

'I might be persuaded to not bring it up in fifty years,' she sighed, tipping her head back just so she could lean against him, head, body, heart and soul. 'If you do something even more idiotic in the meantime, then I will hold that against you instead.'

'Very wise, and fair of you, my lady,' he grinned. 'I'll see what I can come up with.'

They stood there, rocking gently for a moment, their eyes connected through the glass; repeating *I love you*, as she could now see they did.

'Are you sure you're up for seeing your family?'

'Yes,' she reassured him, tangling her fingers in his as they held the sides of her waist. 'I think it's time. The first step at least, they seemed…much changed in their last letters. Being in public will help, assuage any awkwardness that may be present for any of us.'

'Good,' Thorn nodded.

'What about you? How are you feeling about your first Society soirée as a married man, and reputable pig farmer?'

'With my wife by my side, looking as tempting as you do, I am very much looking forward to it. And thanks to Henry's help, I shouldn't make too much of a fool of myself with the dancing. The only thing marring my mood is that damned Jack's last piece, though he seems to be done with us at last, and I am glad of it.'

'We cannot dispute that they helped us remain intriguing to many, and though neither of us like it, I think, considering the world as it is, it cannot hurt us in this next chapter.'

'Much as I am loath to admit it, I fear you are correct. I doubt that investigator would've offered such a rate for his services had it not been for the Cat's pieces.'

'And you thought going from blacksmith to earl-farmer was unusual.'

'Yes, sailor to investigator is rather unconventional.'

'He'll find Warren, won't he?'

'If not him, then the others we'll hire when we can, if we must.'

Nodding, Hypatia melted into him again, drawing as ever, more reassurance and strength, and pleasure from him, and Thorn returned to the important business of devouring her with his gaze, and fingers, and lips.

'Do remind me I must send Mrs Wilson a thank-you basket. The things that woman can do with green velvet…incandescently indecent. I should like all your gowns to be velvet.'

'They wouldn't fare well at the farm.'

'Fine… Then cut just as this one is.'

He showed his appreciation of the low-cut bodice again, torturing them both, for there wasn't time for such business; which he promptly realised with a sigh as the clock on the mantel of their little suite of rooms chimed the hour.

'They'll be all right,' she half-asked, half-stated, turning in his arms, winding her own about his neck. 'It's all well under control, especially with Danny and Fred taking over the management of it all. And we'll be back in December, perhaps even before, for a quick visit.'

'They'll be fine,' Thorn reassured her, kissing her forehead, and then her lips. 'So long as Henry doesn't feed Malek to the pigs in punishment for trying to befriend him, and Mary doesn't do the same to the new butler, and Niamh doesn't offer to help Langton too much, and Theo doesn't drive Danny and Fred to pandemonium with his management suggestions, they'll all be fine.'

'Very reassuring, Lord Gadmin.'

'I live to serve, Lady Gadmin.'

'Later,' she advised him, as his tone was unmistakably dangerous and lustful, placing a gentle kiss on his lips, and untangling them. 'Right now, we've lords and ladies to meet, and dances to dance, and music to hear, and food and wine to sample. We've all of London to sample.'

'As you command, Lady Gadmin.'

Thorn held out his hand, and Hypatia took it.

Together, as they'd vowed once to, but only truly begun to believe they always would after making said vow, they gathered their things, and made their way down to their awaiting conveyance; to Ian and his new apprentice.

And while they made their way through the streets of busy, bustling, and dizzying London, Hypatia thought how true it was, that love, in the end, could neither be written, nor described, nor prescribed nor defined.

It could only be known in its truest incarnation by being felt; and so, she did.

* * * * *

*If you enjoyed this story, make sure to read
Lotte R. James's other great historical romances*

A Governess to Redeem Him
A Liaison with Her Leading Lady
A Lady on the Edge of Ruin

*And why not check out her
Gentlemen of Mystery miniseries*

The Housekeeper of Thornhallow Hall
The Marquess of Yew Park House
The Gentleman of Holly Street

MILLS & BOON®

Coming next month

THE DUKE'S MEDDLESOME MATCHMAKER
Emily E K Murdoch

Book 1 in The Unconventional Oliver Sisters trilogy

'You are not my client,' said the proposal planner slowly.

Henry turned back to Miss Oliver. 'Absolutely not,' he said firmly.

She examined him for a moment, and heat grew in his chest at the attention. Not because it was her, naturally. He would have felt discomforted if it had been anyone.

'Well,' said Miss Oliver finally. 'Well. That changes things.'

'So you'll stay?' Henry said eagerly. He wouldn't be the one to ruin things for Charles. After all, it had been the one thing their father had asked of him, on his deathbed, Henry's years of medical training still not enough to keep the man he loved alive.

Look after your brother, whatever you do.

The proposal planner stepped down from the dog cart—which he had to assume was a good sign.

'My brother is a good man,' Henry snapped, trying to ignore the heat roaring through his body as she stepped closer. 'I want him to be happy.'

'Even if you think I am some sort of charlatan,' Miss Oliver said, halting before him and gazing up at him through long eyelashes.

Henry swallowed. Charlatan? Yes, that was one word for her. It wouldn't be particularly accurate. *Beauty*. That was more accurate. *Temptress*, for it was tempting to lean down and taste—

He stiffly stepped back, half wondering how he'd managed to get himself into such a situation. *Honestly, man. Pull yourself together!*

Miss Oliver was examining him closely. 'It appears most difficult to please you, Mr. Paisley.'

God in His heaven… 'All I am asking is that you fulfil your agreement with my brother,' was all he could manage. 'He is the only family I have left.'

Something flickered in Miss Oliver's gaze. 'I'll stay,' she said shortly, walking around for her trunk.

Henry almost tripped over his own feet to get out and retrieve it for her. It was the least he could do.

'Good,' he said, handing her the heavy thing. *What did she have in there?* 'I'm glad you're staying.'

'I'm not staying for you!' Miss Oliver bristled. 'I—I am already fatigued by avoiding your displeasure.'

They stood there for a heartbeat, glaring at each other, until Miss Oliver snorted, turned around and stamped over to the inn.

Henry watched her go. *Well!* That would be the last time he'd ever be tempted by Miss Oliver!

Continue reading

THE DUKE'S MEDDLESOME MATCHMAKER
Emily E K Murdoch

Available next month
millsandboon.co.uk

COMING SOON!

We really hope you enjoyed reading this book.
If you're looking for more romance
be sure to head to the shops when
new books are available on

Thursday 15th January

To see which titles are coming soon, please visit
millsandboon.co.uk/nextmonth

MILLS & BOON

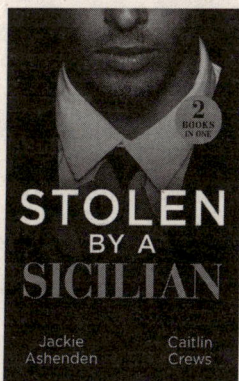

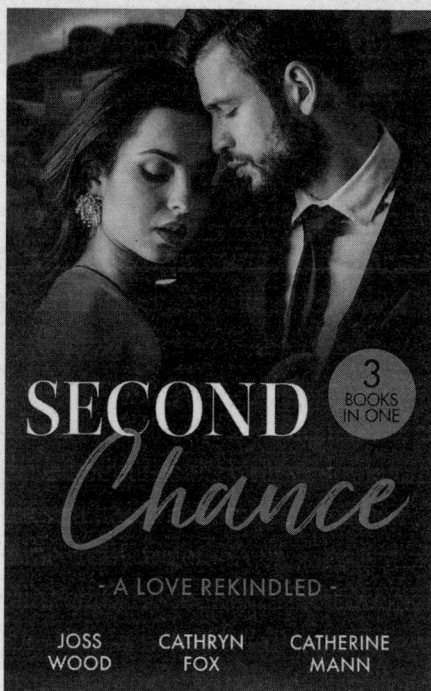